EXIT GHOST

In 1997, Philip Roth won the Pulitzer Prize for *American Pastoral*. In 1998 he received a National Medal of Arts at the White House and in 2002 the highest award of the American Academy of Arts and Letters, the Gold Medal in Fiction. He has twice won the National Book Award and the National Book Critics Circle Award. He has won the PEN/Faulkner Award three times. In 2005 *The Plot Against America* received the Society of American Historians' prize for 'the outstanding historical novel on an American theme for 2003–2004'. Recently Roth received PEN's two most prestigious prizes: in 2006 the PEN/Nabokov Award and in 2007 the PEN/Saul Bellow Award for achievement in American fiction. Roth is the only living American writer to have his work published in a comprehensive, definitive edition by the Library of America.

ALSO BY PHILIP ROTH

Zuckerman Books

The Ghost Writer
Zuckerman Unbound
The Anatomy Lesson
The Prague Orgy

The Counterlife

American Pastoral
I Married a Communist
The Human Stain

Exit Ghost

Roth Books

The Facts • *Deception*
Patrimony • *Operation Shylock*
The Plot Against America

Kepesh Books

The Breast
The Professor of Desire
The Dying Animal

Miscellany

Reading Myself and Others
Shop Talk

Other Books

Goodbye, Columbus • *Letting Go*
When She Was Good • *Portnoy's Complaint* • *Our Gang*
The Great American Novel • *My Life as a Man*
Sabbath's Theater • *Everyman* • *Indignation*

PHILIP ROTH

Exit Ghost

VINTAGE BOOKS
London

Published by Vintage 2008

2 4 6 8 10 9 7 5 3 1

First published in Great Britain in 2007 by Jonathan Cape

Vintage
Random House, 20 Vauxhall Bridge Road,
London SW1V 2SA

www.vintage-books.co.uk

Addresses for companies within The Random House Group Limited
can be found at: www.randomhouse.co.uk/offices.htm

The Random House Group Limited Reg. No. 954009

A CIP catalogue record for this book
is available from the British Library

ISBN 9780099516088

The Random House Group Limited supports The Forest
Stewardship Council (FSC), the leading international forest
certification organisation. All our titles that are printed on
Greenpeace approved FSC certified paper carry the FSC logo.
Our paper procurement policy can be found at:
www.rbooks.co.uk/environment

Printed and bound in Great Britain by
CPI Cox & Wyman, Reading, RG1 8EX

For B. T.

Before death takes you, O take back this.

—Dylan Thomas, "Find Meat on Bones"

EXIT GHOST

1   The Present Moment

I HADN'T BEEN in New York in eleven years. Other than for surgery in Boston to remove a cancerous prostate, I'd hardly been off my rural mountain road in the Berkshires in those eleven years and, what's more, had rarely looked at a newspaper or listened to the news since 9/11, three years back; with no sense of loss—merely, at the outset, a kind of drought within me—I had ceased to inhabit not just the great world but the present moment. The impulse to be in it and of it I had long since killed.

But now I'd driven the hundred and thirty miles south to Manhattan to see a urologist at Mount Sinai Hospital who specialized in performing a procedure to help the thousands of men like me left incontinent by prostate surgery. By going in through a catheter inserted in the urethra to inject a gelatinous form of collagen where the neck of the bladder meets the urethra, he was getting significant improvement in about fifty percent of his patients. These weren't great odds, especially as "significant improvement" meant only a partial alleviation of the symptoms—reducing "severe incontinence" to "moderate incontinence" or "moderate" to "light." Still, because his results were better than those that other urologists had achieved using roughly the same technique (there was nothing to be done about the other hazard of radical prostatectomy that I, like tens of thousands of others, had not been lucky enough to escape—nerve damage resulting in impotence), I went to New York for a consultation, long after I imagined myself as having adapted to the practical inconveniences of the condition.

In the years since the surgery, I even thought I'd surmounted the shaming side of wetting oneself, overcome the disorienting shock that had been particularly trying in the first year and a half, during the months when the surgeon had given me reason to think that the incontinence would gradually disappear over time, as it does in a small number of fortunate patients. But despite the dailiness of the routine necessary to keep myself clean and odor-free, I must never truly have become accustomed to wearing the special undergarments and changing the pads and dealing with the "accidents," any more than I had mastered the underlying humiliation, because there I was, at the age of seventy-one, back on the Upper East Side of Manhattan, not many blocks from where I'd once lived as a vigorous, healthy younger man—there I was in the reception area of the urology department of Mount Sinai Hospital, about to be assured that with the permanent adherence of the collagen to the neck of the bladder I had a chance of exerting somewhat more control over my urine flow than an infant. Waiting there envisioning the procedure, sitting and flipping through the piled-up copies of *People* and *New York* magazine, I thought, Entirely beside the point. Turn around and go home.

I'd been alone these past eleven years in a small house on a dirt road in the deep country, having decided to live apart like that some two years before the cancer was diagnosed. I see few people. Since the death, a year earlier, of my neighbor and friend Larry Hollis, two, three days can go by when I speak to no one but the housekeeper who comes to clean each week and her husband, who is my caretaker. I don't go to dinner parties, I don't go to movies, I don't watch television, I don't own a cell phone or a VCR or a DVD player or a computer. I continue to live in the Age of the Typewriter and have no idea what the World Wide Web is. I no longer bother to vote. I write for most of the day and often into the night. I read, mainly the books that I first discovered as a student, the masterpieces of fiction whose power over me is no less, and in some cases greater, than it was in my initial exciting encounters with them. Lately I've been rereading Joseph Conrad for the first time in fifty years, most recently *The Shadow-Line,* which I'd brought with me to New York to look through yet again, having read it all in one go only the other night. I listen to music, I hike in the woods, when it's warm I swim in my pond, whose temperature, even in summer, never gets much above seventy degrees. I swim there without a suit, out of sight of everyone, so that if in my wake I leave a thin, billowing cloud of urine that visibly discolors the surrounding pond waters, I'm largely unperturbed and feel nothing like the chagrin that would be sure to crush me should my bladder involuntarily begin emptying itself while I was swimming in a public pool. There are plastic underpants with strongly elasticized edges designed for incontinent swimmers that are advertised as watertight, but when, after much equivocation, I went ahead and ordered a pair from a pool-supply catalogue and tried them out in the pond, I found that though wearing these biggish white bloomers beneath a bathing suit diminished the problem, it was not sufficiently eradicated to subdue my self-consciousness. Rather than take the chance of embarrassing myself and offending others, I gave up on the idea of swimming regularly down at the college pool for the bulk of the year (with bloomers under my suit) and continued to confine myself to sporadically yellowing the waters of my own pond during the Berkshires' few months of warm weather, when, rain or shine, I do my laps for half an hour every day.

A couple of times a week I go down the mountain into Athena, eight miles away, to shop for groceries, to get my clothes cleaned, occasionally to eat a meal or buy a pair of socks or pick up a bottle of wine or use the Athena College library. Tanglewood isn't far away, and I drive over to a concert there some ten times during the summer. I don't give readings or lectures or teach at a college or appear on TV. When my books are published, I keep to myself. I write every day of the week—otherwise I'm silent. I am tempted by the thought of not publishing at all—isn't the work all I need, the work and the working? What does it matter any longer if I'm incontinent and impotent?

Larry and Marylynne Hollis had moved up from West Hartford to the Berkshires after he'd retired from a life-long position as an attorney with a Hartford insurance company. Larry was two years my junior, a meticulous, finicky man who seemed to believe that life was safe only if everything in it was punctiliously planned and whom, during the months when he first tried to draw me into his life, I did my best to avoid. I submitted eventually, not only because he was so dogged in his desire to alleviate my solitude but because I had never known anyone like him, an adult whose sad childhood biography had, by his own estimate, determined every choice he had made since his mother had died of cancer when he was ten, a mere four years after his father, who owned a Hartford linoleum store, had been bested no less miserably by the same disease. An only child, Larry was sent to live with relatives on the Naugatuck River southwest of Hartford, just outside bleak, industrial Waterbury, Connecticut, and there, in a boy's diary of "Things to Do," he laid out a future for himself that he followed to the letter for the rest of his life; from then on, everything undertaken was deliberately causal. He was content with no grade other than an A and even as an adolescent vigorously challenged any teacher who'd failed to accurately estimate his achievement. He attended summer sessions to accelerate his graduation from high school and get to college before he turned seventeen; he did the same during his summers at the University of Connecticut, where he had a full-tuition scholarship and worked in the library boiler room all year round to pay for his room and board so he could get out of college and change his name from Irwin Golub to Larry Hollis (as he'd planned to do when he was only ten) and join the air force, to become a fighter pilot known to the world as Lieutenant Hollis and qualify for the GI Bill; on leaving the service, he enrolled at Fordham and, in return for his three years in the air force, the government paid for his three years of law school. As an air force pilot stationed in Seattle he vigorously courted a pretty girl just out of high school who was named Collins and who met exactly his specifications for a wife, one of which was that she be of Irish extraction, with curly dark hair and with ice-blue eyes like his own. "I did not want to marry a Jewish girl. I did not want my children to be raised in the Jewish religion or have anything to do with being Jews." "Why?" I asked him. "Because that's not what I wanted for them" was his answer. That he wanted what he wanted and didn't want what he didn't want was the answer he gave to virtually every question I asked him about the utterly conventional structure he'd made of his life after all those early years of rushing and planning to build it. When he first knocked on my door to introduce himself—only a few days after he and Marylynne had moved into the house nearest to mine, some half mile down our dirt road—he immediately decided that he didn't want me to eat alone every night and that I had to take dinner at his house with him and his wife at least once a week. He didn't want me to be alone on Sundays—he couldn't bear the thought of anyone's being as alone as he'd been as an orphaned child, fishing in the Naugatuck on Sundays with his uncle, a dairy inspector for the state—and so he insisted that every Sunday morning we had a hiking date or, if the weather was bad, Ping-Pong matches, Ping-Pong being a pastime that I could barely tolerate but that I obliged him by playing rather than have a conversation with him about the writing of books. He asked me deadly questions about writing and was not content until I had answered them to his satisfaction. "Where do you get your ideas?" "How do you know if an idea is a good idea or a bad idea?" "How do you know when to use dialogue and when to use straight storytelling without dialogue?" "How do you know when a book is finished?" "How do you select a first sentence? How do you select a title? How do you select a last sentence?" "Which is your best book?" "Which is your worst book?" "Do you like your characters?" "Have you ever killed a character?" "I heard a writer on television say that the characters take over the book and write it themselves. Is that true?" He had wanted to be the father of one boy and one girl, and only after the fourth girl was born did Marylynne defy him and refuse to continue trying to produce the male heir that had been in his plans from the age of ten. He was a big, square-faced, sandy-haired man, and his eyes were crazy, ice-blue and crazy, unlike Marylynne's ice-blue eyes, which were beautiful, and the ice-blue eyes of the four pretty daughters, all of whom had gone to Wellesley because his closest friend in the air force had a sister at Wellesley and when Larry met her she exhibited just the sort of polish and decorum that he wanted to see in a daughter of his. When we would go to a restaurant (which we did every other Saturday night—that too he would have no other way) he could be counted on to be demanding with the waiter. Invariably there was a complaint about the bread. It wasn't fresh. It wasn't the kind he liked. There wasn't enough for everyone.

One evening after dinner he came by unexpectedly and gave me two orange kittens, one long-haired and one short-haired, just over eight weeks old. I had not asked for two kittens, nor had he apprised me of the gift beforehand. He said he'd been to his ophthalmologist for a checkup in the morning, seen a sign by the receptionist's desk saying she had kittens to give away. That afternoon he went to her house and picked out the two most beautiful of the six for me. His first thought on seeing the sign was of me.

He put the kittens down on the floor. "This isn't the life you should have," he said. "Whose is?" "Well, mine is, for one. I have everything I ever wanted. I won't have you experiencing the life of a person alone any longer. You do it to the goddamn utmost. It's too extreme, Nathan." "As are you." "The hell I am! I'm not the one who lives like this. All I'm pushing on you is a little normality. This is too separate an existence for any human being. At least you can have a couple of cats for company. I have all the stuff for them in the car."

He went back outside, and when he returned he emptied onto the floor a couple of large supermarket bags containing half a dozen little toys for them to bat around, a dozen cans of cat food, a large bag of cat litter and a plastic litter box, two plastic dishes for their food, and two plastic bowls for their water.

"There's all you'll need," he said. "They're beauties. Look at them. They'll give you a lot of pleasure."

He was exceedingly stern about all this, and there was nothing I could say except, "It's very thoughtful of you, Larry."

"What will you call them?"

"A and B."

"No. They need names. You live all day with the alphabet. You can call the short-haired one Shorty and the long-haired one Longy."

"That's what I'll do then."

In my one strong relationship I had fallen into the role that Larry prescribed. I was basically obedient to Larry's discipline, as was everyone in his life. Imagine, four daughters and not a single one of them saying, "But I'd rather go to Barnard, I'd rather go to Oberlin." Though I never had a sense of his being a frightening paternal tyrant when I was with him and the family, how strange it was, I thought, that as far as I knew not one of them had ever objected to her father's saying it's Wellesley for you and that's it. But their willingness to be will-less as Larry's obedient children was not quite as remarkable for me to contemplate as was my own. Larry's path to power was to have complete acquiescence from the beloved in his life—mine was to have no one in my life.

He'd brought the cats on a Thursday. I kept them through Sunday. During that time I did virtually no work on my book. Instead I spent my time throwing the cats their toys or stroking them, together or in turn in my lap, or just sitting and looking at them eating, or playing, or grooming themselves, or sleeping. I kept their litter box in a corner of the kitchen and at night put them in the living room and shut my bedroom door behind me. When I awoke in the morning the first thing I did was rush to the door to see them. There they would be, just beside the door, waiting for me to open it.

On Monday morning I phoned Larry and said, "Please come and take the cats."

"You hate them."

"To the contrary. If they stay, I'll never write another word. I can't have these cats in the house with me."

"Why not? What the hell is wrong with you?"

"They're too delightful."

"Good. Great. That's the idea."

"Come and take them, Larry. If you like, I'll return them to the ophthalmologist's receptionist myself. But I can't have them here any longer."

"What is this? An act of defiance? A display of bravado? I'm a disciplined man myself, but you put me to shame. I didn't bring two people to live with you, God forbid. I brought two cats. Tiny *kittens*."

"I accepted them graciously, did I not? I've given them a try, have I not? Please take them away."

"I won't."

"I never asked for them, you know."

"That doesn't prove anything to me. You ask for nothing."

"Give me the phone number of the ophthalmologist's receptionist."

"No."

"All right. I'll take care of it myself."

"You're crazy," he said.

"Larry, I can't be made into a new being by two kittens."

"But that's exactly what is happening. Exactly what you won't *allow* to happen. I cannot understand it—a man of your intelligence turning himself into this kind of person. It's beyond me."

"There are many inexplicable things in life. You shouldn't trouble yourself over my tiny opacity."

"All right. You win. I'll come, I'll get the cats. But I'm not finished with you, Zuckerman."

"I have no reason to believe that you are finished or that you can be finished. You're a little crazy too, you know."

"The hell I am!"

"Hollis, please, I'm too old to work myself over anymore. Come get the cats."

Just before the fourth daughter was to be married in New York City—to a young Irish-American attorney who, like Larry, had attended Fordham Law School—he was diagnosed with cancer. The same day the family went down to New York to assemble for the wedding, Larry's oncologist put him into the university hospital in Farmington, Connecticut. His first night in the hospital, after the nurse had taken his vital signs and given him a sleeping pill, he removed another hundred or so sleeping pills secreted in his shaving kit and, using the water in the glass by his bedside, swallowed them in the privacy of his darkened room. Early the next morning, Marylynne received the phone call from the hospital informing her that her husband had committed suicide. A few hours later, at her insistence—she hadn't been his wife all those years for nothing—the family went ahead with the wedding, and the wedding luncheon, and only then returned to the Berkshires to plan his funeral.

Later I learned that Larry had arranged with the doctor beforehand to be hospitalized that day rather than the Monday of the following week, which he could easily have done. In that way the family would be together in one place when they got the news that he was dead; moreover, by killing himself in the hospital, where there were professionals on hand to attend to his corpse, he had spared Marylynne and the children all that he could of the grotesqueries attendant upon suicide.

He was sixty-eight years old when he died and, with the exception of the plan recorded in his "Things to Do" diary to one day have a son named Larry Hollis Jr., he had, amazingly, achieved every last goal that he had imagined for himself when he was orphaned at ten. He had managed to wait long enough to see his youngest daughter married and into a new life and still wind up able to avoid what he most dreaded—his children witnessing the excruciating agonies of a dying parent that he had witnessed when his father and his mother each slowly succumbed to cancer. He had even left a message for me. He had even thought to look after me. In the mail the Monday after the Sunday when we all learned of his death, I received this letter: "Nathan, my boy, I don't like leaving you like this. In this whole wide world, you cannot be alone. You cannot be without contact with anything. You must promise me that you will not go on living as you were when I found you. Your loyal friend, Larry."

So was that why I remained in the urologist's waiting room —because one year earlier, almost to the day, Larry had sent me that note and then killed himself? I don't know, and it wouldn't have mattered if I did. I sat there because I sat there, flipping through magazines of the kind I hadn't seen for years—looking at photos of famous actors, famous models, famous dress designers, famous chefs and business tycoons, learning about where I could go to buy the most expensive, the cheapest, the hippest, the tightest, the softest, the funniest, the tastiest, the tackiest of just about anything produced for America's consumption, and waiting for my doctor's appointment.

I'd arrived the afternoon before. I'd reserved a room at the Hilton, and after unpacking my bag, I went out to Sixth Avenue to take in the city. But where was I to begin? Revisiting the streets where I'd once lived? The neighborhood places where I used to eat my lunch? The newsstand where I bought my paper and the bookstores where I used to browse? Should I retrace the long walks I used to take at the end of my workday? Or since I no longer see that many of them, should I seek out other members of my species? During the years I'd been gone there'd been phone calls and letters, but my house in the Berkshires is small and I hadn't encouraged visitors, and so, in time, personal contact became infrequent. Editors I'd worked with over the years had left their publishing houses or retired. Many of the writers I'd known had, like me, left town. Women I'd known had changed jobs or married or moved away. The first two people I thought to drop in on had died. I knew that they had died, that their distinctive faces and familiar voices were no more—and yet, out in front of the hotel, deciding how and where to reenter for an hour or two the life left behind, contemplating the simplest ways of putting a foot back in, I had a moment not unlike Rip Van Winkle's when, after having slept for twenty years, he came out of the mountains and walked back to his village believing he'd merely been gone overnight. Only when he unexpectedly felt the long grizzled beard that grew from his chin did he grasp how much time had passed and in turn learned that he was no longer a colonial subject of the British Crown but a citizen of the newly established United States. I couldn't have felt any more out of it myself had I turned up on the corner of Sixth Avenue and West 54th with Rip's rusty gun in my hand and his ancient clothes on my back and an army of the curious crowding around to look me over, this eviscerated stranger walking in their midst, a relic of bygone days amid the noises and buildings and workers and traffic.

I started toward the subway to take a train downtown to Ground Zero. Begin there, where the biggest thing of all occurred; but because I've withdrawn as witness and participant both, I never made it to the subway. That would have been wholly out of character for the character I'd become. Instead, after crossing the park, I found myself in the familiar rooms of the Metropolitan Museum, wiling away the afternoon like someone who had no catching up to do.

The next day when I left the doctor's office, I had an appointment to return the following morning for the collagen injection. There'd been a cancellation, and he could fit me in. The doctor would prefer it, his nurse told me, if, after the hospital procedure, I stayed overnight in my hotel rather than return immediately to the Berkshires—

complications rarely occurred in the aftermath of the procedure, but remaining nearby till the next morning was a worthwhile precaution. Barring any mishap, by then I could leave for home and resume my usual activities. The doctor himself expected a considerable improvement, not excluding the possibility of the injection's restoring close to complete bladder control. On occasion the collagen "traveled," he explained, and he'd have to go in a second or third time before getting it to adhere permanently to the neck of the bladder; then again, one injection could suffice.

Fine, I said, and instead of reaching a decision only after I'd had a chance to think everything over back home, I surprised myself by seizing at the opening in his schedule, and not even when I was out of the encouraging environment of his office and in the elevator to the main floor was I able to summon up an ounce of wariness to restrain my sense of rejuvenation. I closed my eyes in the elevator and saw myself swimming in the college pool at the end of the day, carefree and without fear of embarrassment.

It was ludicrous to feel so triumphant, and perhaps a measure less of the transformation promised than of the toll taken by the discipline of seclusion and by the decision to excise from life everything that stood between me and my task—the toll of which till then I'd remained oblivious (willed obliviousness being a primary component of the discipline). In the country there was nothing tempting my hope. I had made peace with my hope. But when I came to New York, in only hours New York did what it does to people—awakened the possibilities. Hope breaks out.

One floor below the urology department, the elevator stopped and a frail, elderly woman got on. The cane she carried, along with a faded red rainhat pulled low over her skull, gave her an eccentric, yokelish look, but when I heard her speaking quietly with the doctor who'd boarded the elevator with her—a man in his mid-forties who was lightly guiding her by the arm—when I heard the foreign tinge to her English, I took a second look, wondering whether she was someone I'd once known. The voice was as distinctive as the accent, especially as it wasn't a voice one would associate with her wraithlike looks but a young person's voice, incongruously girlish and innocent of hardship. I know that voice, I thought. I know the accent. I know the woman. On the main floor, I was crossing the hospital lobby just behind them, heading for the street, when I happened to overhear the elderly woman's name spoken by the doctor. That was why I followed her out the hospital door and to a luncheonette a few blocks south on Madison. I did indeed know her.

It was ten-thirty, and only four or five customers were still eating breakfast. She took a seat in a booth. I found an empty table for myself. She didn't seem to be aware of my having followed her or even of my presence a few feet away. Her name was Amy Bellette. I'd met her only once. I'd never forgotten her.

Amy Bellette was wearing no coat, just the red rainhat

and a pale cardigan sweater and what registered as a thin cotton summer dress until I realized that it was in fact a pale blue hospital gown whose clips had been replaced at the back with buttons and around whose waist she wore a ropelike belt. Either she's impoverished or she's crazy, I thought.

A waiter took her order, and after he walked away she opened her purse and took out a book and while reading it casually reached up and removed the hat and set it down beside her. The side of her head facing me was shaved bald, or had been not too long ago—fuzz was growing there—and a sinuous surgical scar cut a serpentine line across her skull, a raw, well-defined scar that curved from behind her ear up to the edge of her brow. All her hair of any length was on the other side of her head, graying hair knotted loosely in a braid and along which the fingers of her right hand were absent-mindedly moving—freely playing with the hair as the hand of any child reading a book might do. Her age? Seventy-five. She was twenty-seven when we met in 1956.

I ordered coffee, sipped it, lingered over it, finished it, and without looking her way, got up and left the lunch-eonette and the astonishing reappearance and pathetic reconstitution of Amy Bellette, one whose existence—so rich with promise and expectation when I first encountered her—had obviously gone very wrong.

The procedure the next morning took fifteen minutes. So simple! A wonder! Medical magic! I saw myself once again swimming laps in the college pool, clad in only an ordinary bathing suit and leaving no stream of urine in my wake. I saw myself going blithely about without carrying along a supply of the absorbent cotton pads that for nine years now I had worn day and night cradled in the crotch of my plastic briefs. A painless fifteen-minute procedure and life seemed limitless again. I was a man no longer powerless over something so elementary as managing to piss in a pot. To possess control over one's bladder—who among the whole and healthy ever considers the freedom that bestows or the anxious vulnerability its loss can impose on even the most confident among us? I who'd never thought along these lines before, who from the age of twelve was bent on singularity and welcomed whatever was unusual in me—I could now be like everyone else.

As though the ever-hovering shadow of humiliation isn't, in fact, what *binds* one to everyone else.

Well before noon I was back in my hotel. I had plenty to keep me busy while I waited out the day before returning home. The previous afternoon—after deciding to leave Amy Bellette undisturbed—I'd gone down to the Strand, the venerable used-book store south of Union Square, and for under a hundred dollars I'd been able to purchase original editions of the six volumes of E. I. Lonoff's short stories. The books happened also to be in my library at home, but I'd bought them anyway and carried them back to the hotel in order to skip chronologically through the various volumes during the hours I would have to remain in New York.

When you undertake an experiment like this after spending twenty or thirty years away from a writer's work, you can't be sure what you're going to turn up, about either the datedness of the once admired writer or the naiveté of the enthusiast you once were. But by midnight I was no less convinced than I was in the 1950s that the narrow range of Lonoff's prose and the restricted scope of his interests and the unyielding restraint he employed, rather than collapsing inward a story's implications and diminishing its impact, produced instead the enigmatic reverberations of a gong, reverberations that left one marveling at how so much gravity and so much levity could be joined, in so small a space, to a skepticism so far-reaching. It was precisely the limitation of means that made of each little story not something stultifying but a feat of magic, as if a folk tale or a fairy tale or a Mother Goose rhyme were inwardly illuminated by the mind of Pascal.

He was as good as I had thought. He was better. It was as though there were some color previously missing or withheld from our literary spectrum and Lonoff alone had it. Lonoff *was* that color, a twentieth-century American writer unlike any other, and he had been out of print for decades. I wondered if his achievement would have been so completely forgotten if he had finished his novel and lived to see it published. I wondered if he *had* been working on a novel at the end of his life. If not, how was one to understand the silence preceding his death, those five years that coincided with the breakup of his marriage to Hope and the new life undertaken alongside Amy Bellette? I could still remember the mordant, uncomplaining way he had described to me, a worshipful young acolyte eager to emulate him, the monotony of an existence that was composed of painstakingly writing his stories throughout the day, reading studiously, with a notebook at his side, in the evening, and, nearly mute from mental fatigue, sharing meals and a bed with a loyal, wretchedly lonely wife of thirty-five years. (For discipline is imposed not just on oneself but on those in one's orbit.) One might have imagined a regeneration of intensity—and, with it, of productivity—in an original writer of such imposing fortitude, still not quite into his sixties, who had arranged finally to escape this imprisoning regimen (or whose wife had forced him, by her angry, precipitate departure) and to take as his mate a charming, intelligent, adoring young woman half his age. One might have imagined that after tearing himself away from the rural landscape and the married life that together held him in check—that made the artistic enterprise for him so ruthlessly rock-bottom a sacrifice—E. I. Lonoff wouldn't have had to be quite so severely punished for his waywardness, needn't have had to be reduced to so annihilating a silence just for daring to believe that he might be permitted to rewrite fifty times over his paragraph a day while living in something other than a cage.

What *was* the story of those five years? Once something did happen to that sedate, reclusive writer who—assisted by the forlorn irony that pervaded his view of the world— had bravely resigned himself to nothing's ever happening to him, what then ensued? Amy Bellette would know—*she* was what had happened to him. If somewhere there was the manuscript of a Lonoff novel, finished or unfinished, she'd know about that, too. Unless the entire estate had passed on to Hope and the three children, the manuscript would be in her hands. And should the novel legally belong to the immediate family that had survived the author and not to her, Amy, who'd have been at his side while the book was being written, would have read every page of every draft and would know how well or how poorly the new venture had gone. Even if his death had cut short its completion, why hadn't finished sections of it been published in the literary quarterlies that used to regularly run his stories? Was it because the novel was no good that no one had seen to its publication? And if so, was that failure the consequence of his having left behind everything that he had counted on to chain him to his talent, of his having at long last gained the freedom and found the pleasure against which captivity had been designed to protect him? Or could he never subdue the shame of subverting his suffering at Hope's expense? But wasn't it Hope who had done the subverting *for* him—by doing the leaving? In so resolute and experienced a writer—one for whom realizing his distinctly laconic brand of vernacular fluency had been a perpetual ordeal to be surmounted only by the most diligent application of patience and will—why a five-year block? Why should so ordinary a renovation— the middle-age life change, commonly thought to be replenishing, of taking a new mate and setting up house in a new locale—cripple a man with the forbearance of a Lonoff?

If that's what had crippled him.

By the time I was ready for sleep, I knew how off the mark these questions might be in helping to understand what it was that stifled Lonoff in his final years. If, between the ages of fifty-six and sixty-one, he had failed at writing a novel, it was probably because (as he may always have suspected) the novelist's passion for amplification was just another form of excess that ran counter to his own special gift for condensation and reduction. A novelist's passion for amplification probably explained my having spent my day raising such questions in the first place.

What it didn't explain was my failing to introduce myself to Amy Bellette in that coffee shop and to find out from her, if not everything there was to know, whatever she was willing to tell.

The three children were grown and gone by the time I met Lonoff and Hope in 1956, and though the grinding discipline of his daily writing life was in no way altered by their dispersal—no more than by the disappearance of passion that dogs connubial life—Hope's response to her isolation in the remote Berkshire farmhouse was vividly on display in just the few hours I was there. Having valiantly tried to remain calm and sociable during dinner on the evening I arrived, she'd eventually broken down and, after hurling a wine glass at the wall, had run from the table in tears, leaving Lonoff to explain to me —or, as it happened, to feel unobliged to explain—what was going on. At breakfast the following morning, where Amy and I both were present and where the incendiary houseguest with her enchantingly serene, self-possessed demeanor—with the clarity of her mind, with her play-acting, with her mystery, with the sparklingness of her comedy—was being especially delightful, Hope's stoic façade had given way again, but this time when she left the table it was to pack a bag and to put on her coat and, despite the freezing weather and the snowy roads, to walk out the front door, announcing that she was leaving the post of great writer's neglected wife to none other than Lonoff's former student and (from all indications) his paramour. "This is officially your house!" she'd notified the young victor, and left for Boston. "You will now be the person he is not living with!"

I left only an hour later and never saw any of them again. It was by a fluke that I'd been there for the blowup at all. From a nearby writers' colony where I'd been stay-ing, I had sent Lonoff a packet of my first published short stories, along with an earnest introductory letter, and in this way managed to wangle the dinner invitation that had turned into an overnight stay only because bad weather had prevented me from departing till the next day. In the late forties, into the fifties, and until his death from leukemia in 1961, Lonoff was probably America's most esteemed short story writer—if not that to the country at large, then among many in the intellectual and academic elites—the author of six collections whose mingling of comedy and darkness had desentimentalized totally the standard hard-luck saga of the immigrant Jew; his fiction read like an unfolding of disjointed dreams, yet without sacrificing the factuality of time and place to surreal fakery or magic-realist gimmickry. The annual output of stories had never been great, and in his last five years, when he was supposedly working on a novel, his first, and the book that admirers claimed would win him international recognition and the Nobel Prize that should already have been his, he published no stories at all. Those were the years when he made his home with Amy in Cambridge and was affiliated loosely with Harvard. He had never married Amy; apparently, during those five years, he had never legally been free to marry anyone. And then he was dead.

The evening before I was to leave for home, I went to eat at a small Italian restaurant not far from the hotel. The ownership hadn't changed since I'd last eaten there back in the early nineties, and to my surprise I was greeted by name by the youngest of the family, Tony, who seated me at the corner table I'd always liked best because it was the quietest in the place.

You depart while others, unamazingly enough, stay behind to continue doing what they've always done—and, upon returning, you are surprised and momentarily thrilled to see that they are still there, and, too, reassured by there being somebody who is spending his whole life in the same little place and who has no desire to go.

"You moved away, Mr. Zuckerman," Tony said. "We don't ever see you."

"I moved up north. I live in the mountains now."

"It must be beautiful there. Nice and quiet to write."

"It is," I said. "How's the family?"

"Everybody's good. Celia, though, she passed. Remember my aunt? Who was at the register?"

"Sure I do. I'm sorry to hear Celia's gone. Celia wasn't that old."

"No, not at all. But last year she got sick, and she went like that. But you look good," he said. "You want something to drink? Chianti, right?"

Though Tony's hair had gone the same steel gray as his grandfather Pierluigi's—as revealed in the oil painting of the restaurant's immigrant founder, handsome as an actor in his chef's apron, that still hung just beside the coat-check room—and though Tony's frame had grown big and soft since I'd last seen him, in his early thirties, back when he was the only lean and bony member remaining in his well-fed restaurant clan, back some hundred thousand bowls of pasta ago, the menu itself hadn't changed, the specialties hadn't changed, the bread in the bread basket hadn't changed, and when the dessert cart was navigated past my table by the head waiter, I saw that the head waiter hadn't changed nor had the desserts. You would think that my relationship to all of this could not have shifted one iota, that once I had my drink in my hand and was chewing on a chunk of Italian bread of the kind that I'd eaten here dozens of times before I'd feel pleasantly at home, and yet I didn't. I felt like an impostor, pretending to be the man Tony had once known and suddenly craving to be him. But by living mostly in solitude for eleven years, I had got rid of him. I had gone off to flee a genuine menace; in the end, I stayed away to be rid of what no longer remained of interest and, as who doesn't dream of being, to be rid of the lingering consequences of a life's mistakes (for me, repeated marital failure, furtive adultery, the emotional boomerang of erotic attachment). Presumably by taking action rather than just dreaming of it, I had got rid of myself in the process.

I'd brought something to read, just as I used to do when I ate at Pierluigi's by myself. Living alone, I'd become habituated to reading with my meals, but on this night I set the paper down on the table and instead looked around at those eating their dinner in New York City on the evening of October 28, 2004. One of city life's notable satisfactions: strangers fostering the chimera of human accord by eating together in a good little restaurant. And I was one among them. Late in the day to find so commonplace an experience momentous, but I did.

Only with my coffee did I open the paper, the current issue of *The New York Review of Books*. I hadn't seen a copy since leaving New York. I hadn't wanted to see one, though I'd been a subscriber since the paper's inauguration in the early sixties and, in its first years, an occasional contributor. In passing a newsstand on the way to Pierluigi's I had caught a glimpse of the top of the front page, where above a set of David Levine caricatures of the presidential candidates there was printed an unfurled banner on which yellow lettering announced "Special Election Issue"—and beneath that, above a list of some dozen contributors, the words "The Election and America's Future"—and I had paid the newsdealer four dollars and fifty cents and carried the paper off with me to the restaurant. But now I was sorry I'd bought it, and even when curiosity got the best of me, instead of starting with the table of contents and the opening pages of the election symposium, I began my reimmersion by tiptoeing in at the back, reading the classified advertisements. "BEAUTIFUL photographer/art educator, loving mother . . ." "COMPLEX, THOUGHTFUL, DESIROUS and desirable woman, legally married . . ." "ENERGETIC, FUN-LOVING, FIT, established man of many interests . . ." "GREEN-EYED, funny, kooky, curvaceous . . ." I skipped to "Real Estate," and in the brief "Rentals" column—above the much longer "International Rentals" column, where the residences available were mainly in Paris and London—I came upon an ad so pointedly addressed to me that I felt myself being urged on, as though with a whip, by chance, sheer chance that seemed brimming with intention.

RELIABLE writing couple in early thirties wishes to swap homey, book-lined 3-room Upper West Side apartment for quiet rural retreat one hundred miles from New York. New England preferred. Immediate exchange, ideally for one year . . .

Without waiting—as precipitously as I had gone ahead with the collagen injection I'd intended to think about back home before committing myself to having it, as precipitously as I'd bought *The New York Review*—I went down the stairway alongside the kitchen to where I remembered a pay phone hung on the wall across from the men's room. I'd copied the phone number onto a piece of scrap paper on which I'd written the name "Amy Bellette." Quickly I dialed and told the man who answered that I was responding to his ad to exchange residences for a year. I owned a small house in rural western Massachusetts, located on a dirt road atop a mountain and across from a large marshy swamp that was a bird and wildlife refuge. New York was a hundred and twenty-eight miles away, my nearest neighbors were half a mile away, and it was eight miles down the mountain to a college town where you could find a supermarket, a bookstore, a wine shop, a good campus library, and a convivial bar with edible food. If that sounded like what he had in mind, I'd be interested in stopping by, I said, and seeing the apartment and discussing a swap. I was only blocks away from the Upper West Side; if it wasn't an inconvenience I could be there in minutes.

The man laughed. "You sound like you want to move in tonight."

"If you'll move out tonight," I told him, and I meant it.

Before returning to my table, I stopped off in the men's room and ducked into the single stall, where I lowered my trousers to learn whether the procedure had begun to work. To blot out what I saw I shut my eyes, and to blot out what I felt I cursed aloud. "A fucking dream!" by which I meant the dream of being suddenly like everyone else.

I set about removing the absorbent cotton pad from my plastic briefs and replacing it with a fresh one from a small packet I carried in my inside jacket pocket. I wrapped the dirty pad in toilet paper, threw it into a covered wastebasket beside the sink, washed and dried my hands, and, fighting off the gloom, went upstairs to pay my bill.

I walked to West 71st Street, startled, at Columbus Circle, to see that the bulky fortress of the Coliseum had metamorphosed into a pair of glass skyscrapers joined at the hip and lined at street level with swanky shops. I wandered into the arcade and out, and when I continued north on Broadway I felt not so much that I was in a foreign country as that some optical trick were being played on me, that things appeared as in the reflection of a funhouse mirror, everything simultaneously familiar and unrecognizable. Not without some hardship, as I've said, I'd conquered the solitary's way of life; I knew its tests and satisfactions and over time had shaped the scope of my needs to its limitations, long ago abandoning excitement, intimacy, adventure, and antagonisms in favor of quiet, steady, predictable contact with nature and reading and my work. Why invite the unanticipated, why court any more shocks or surprises than those that aging would be sure to deliver without my prompting? Yet I continued up Broadway—past the crowds at Lincoln Center that I did not wish to join, the theater complexes whose movies I had no inclination to see, the leather goods shops and the gourmet food shops whose merchandise I didn't care to buy—unwilling to oppose the power of the crazed hope of rejuvenation that was affecting all my actions, the crazed hope of the procedure's reversing the strongest side of my decline, and aware of the mistake I was making, a revenant, a man who'd cut himself off from sustained human contact and its possibilities yielding to the illusion of starting again. And not through my own distinctive mental capacities but through the body refashioned, life seeming limitless again. Of course this is the wrong thing to do, the insane thing to do, but if so, I thought, what is the right thing to do, the sane thing, and who am I to claim that I ever knew enough to do it? I did what I did—that's all one knows looking backward. I made the ordeal that was mine out of the inspiration and the ineptitude that were mine—the inspiration *was* the ineptitude—and more than likely I am now doing the same. And at this batty speed, no less, as though fearful that my insanity is going to evaporate at any minute and I'm going to stop being able to go on with all that I'm doing that I know very well I shouldn't be doing.

The elevator of the small six-story white-brick apartment building took me to the top floor, where I was greeted at the doorway of apartment 6B by a chubby young man with a soft, agreeable manner who immediately said, "You're the writer." "I am. And you?" "*A* writer," he said with a smile. He led me inside and introduced me to his wife. "Yet a third writer," he said. She was a tall, slender young woman who, unlike her husband, no longer had a playful, childlike aspect in evidence anywhere, at least not tonight. Her long, narrow face was curtained by straight, fine black hair that fell to her shoulders and a little below, the cut seemingly designed to conceal some disfiguring blemish, though by no means one that was physical—she had an impeccable, creamily soft surface, whatever else she might be hiding. That she was boundlessly loved by her husband and the source of his sustenance was apparent in the undisguised tenderness with which his every gaze and gesture enveloped her, even when what she said was not necessarily to his liking. It was clear that she was considered by them the more brilliant of the two and that his personality was swaddled in hers. Her name was Jamie Logan, his Billy Davidoff, and as they walked me through the apartment, he seemed to take pleasure in deferentially calling me Mr. Zuckerman.

It was an attractive apartment of three spacious rooms, furnished with pricey European-designed modern furniture and Oriental throw rugs and a beautiful Persian rug in the living room. There was a large workspace in the bedroom overlooking a tall plane tree in the rear yard and another workspace in the living room, which looked across to a church. Books were piled everywhere, and hanging on the walls where there weren't book-laden shelves were framed photographs of statuary in Italian cities taken by Billy. Who was funding the modest opulence of these two thirty-year-olds? My guess was that the money was his, that they had met at Amherst or Williams or Brown, a tame, wealthy, kindhearted Jewish boy and an intense poor girl, Irish, maybe half Italian, who from grade school on had never stopped excelling, self-propelled, perhaps even something of a climber . . .

I had it wrong. The money was hers and it came from Texas. Her father was a Houston oilman with origins as American as American origins could be. Billy's Jewish family owned a luggage and umbrella shop in Philadelphia. The two had met in the graduate writing program at Columbia. Neither had as yet published a book, though five years earlier she'd had a short story in *The New Yorker* that had prompted inquiries about a novel from agents and publishers. I wouldn't have guessed right off that hers was the more developed creative disposition.

After I was shown around, we sat in the quiet living room, where the windows were double-glazed. The small Lutheran church across the street, a charming little building with narrow windows and pointed arches and a rough stone façade, though probably built in the early 1900s, seemed designed to transport its Upper West Side congregants back five or six centuries to a rural village in northern Europe. Immediately outside the window the fanlike leaves of a thriving ginkgo tree were just beginning to lose their summertime green. A recording of Strauss's *Four Last Songs* had been playing softly in the background when I'd come into the apartment, and when Billy went to turn off the CD player, I wondered if the *Four Last Songs* were what he or Jamie happened to have been listening to before I came or if my arrival had prompted one or the other of them to play such dramatically elegiac, ravishingly emotional music written by a very old man at the close of his life.

"His favorite instrument is the female voice," I said.

"Or two," said Billy. "His favorite combination was two women singing together. The end of *Rosenkavalier*. The end of *Arabella*. In *The Egyptian Helen*."

"You know Strauss," I said to him.

"Well, my favorite instrument is the female voice too."

His intention in saying that was to flatter his wife, but I pretended otherwise. "Do you write music as well?" I asked him.

"No, no," said Billy. "I have a hard enough time with fiction."

"Well, my house in the woods," I told them, "is no more peaceful than this."

"We're leaving for only a year," Billy said.

"May I ask why?"

"Jamie's idea," he answered, sounding not as tamed as I'd imagined him.

Reluctant to appear to interrogate her, I merely looked her way. Her sensual presence was strong—perhaps she kept herself on the thin side so it wouldn't be stronger. Or maybe so it would, since her breasts weren't those of an undernourished woman. She wore jeans and a low-cut, lacy silk blouse that resembled a little lingerie top—that *was* a little lingerie top, I realized upon looking again— and wrapping her torso was a longish cardigan with a thick edge of wide ribbing and a tie of the same ribbing pulled loosely around her narrow waist. It was a garment at the other end of the spectrum of female apparel from the hospital gown Amy Bellette had converted into a dress, its color paler and softer than tan and woven of a thick, soft cashmere. The sweater could easily have cost a thousand bucks, and she looked languid wearing it, languid and in enticing repose, as though she were wearing a kimono. She spoke rapidly and quietly, however, as highly complicated people will do, under pressure particularly.

"Why are you coming to New York?" was Jamie's response to my gaze.

"I have a friend who's ill here," I said.

I still had no clear idea what I was doing in their apartment, what it was I wanted. To make things different for myself? Exactly how? To see a Victorian replica of a medieval church out the window while I worked rather than my mammoth maples and uneven stone walls? To see cars moving when I looked down to the street below rather than the deer and the crows and the wild turkeys that populated my woods?

"She has a brain tumor," I explained, merely out of a need to talk. To talk to her.

"Well, we're leaving," Jamie told me, "because I don't wish to be snuffed out in the name of Allah."

"Isn't that unlikely," I asked, "on West Seventy-first?"

"This city is at the heart of their pathology. Bin Laden dreams only of evil, and he calls that evil 'New York.'"

"I wouldn't know," I said. "I don't see any papers. I haven't for years. I picked up a *New York Review* for the ads. I have no idea what's going on."

"You do know about the election," Billy said.

"Practically nothing," I said. "People don't talk openly about politics in the hick town where I live, certainly never to an outsider like me. I don't turn on the TV much. No, I don't know a thing."

"You haven't followed the war?"

"No."

"You haven't followed Bush's lies?"

"No."

"That's hard to believe," Billy said, "when I think of your books."

"I've served my tour as exasperated liberal and indignant citizen," I said, seemingly talking to him while once again talking for her, and out of a motive hidden even from myself when I began, out of a yearning whose might I would have hoped had all but withered away. Whatever the force prying me back open at seventy-one—whatever the force that had sent me down to New York to the urologist in the first place—was quickly regathering its strength in the presence of Jamie Logan wearing her wide-necked thousand-buck cardigan sweater hanging loose over a low-cut camisole. "I don't wish to register an opinion, I don't want to express myself on 'the issues'—I don't even want to know what they are. It no longer suits me to know, and what doesn't suit me, I expunge. That's why I live where I do. That's why you want to live where I do."

"Why Jamie wants to," Billy said.

"It's so. I'm scared all the time," she said. "A new vantage point might help." Here she broke off, but not because she had thought better of admitting her fears to someone interested in swapping his safely remote rural residence for a potentially imperiled New York apartment, but because Billy was looking at her as though she were deliberately attempting to provoke him in front of me. If his relationship to her was worshipful, it wasn't exclusively worshipful. This was a marriage, after all, and he could be tried by his lovely wife as well.

"Are others leaving," I asked her, "because they're frightened of a terrorist attack?"

"Others have certainly been talking about it," Billy allowed.

"Some have left," Jamie put in.

"People you know?" I asked.

"No," Billy said decisively. "We'll be the first."

With a smile not overly generous, with what I, transfixed by her (subjugated as quickly as I imagined Billy to have been, though for reasons having to do with finding myself at the other edge of experience from him, at the rim that borders oblivion), took to be the air of a temptress—a tauntingly aloof temptress—Jamie added, "I like to be first."

"Well, if you want my place," I said, "it's yours. Here, I'll draw a diagram of the house."

When I got back to the hotel, I phoned Rob Massey, the local carpenter who's worked for ten years as my caretaker, and his wife, Belinda, who during that time has been cleaning my place once a week and who does the grocery shopping when I don't want to drive the eight miles into Athena. I read out a list to them of what I wanted packed and brought to New York and told them about the young married couple who would be moving up to my place the following week and living there for the next year.

"I hope this doesn't have to do with your health," Rob said. It was Rob who'd driven me to Boston and then home from the hospital when I'd had my prostate surgery nine years earlier, and Belinda who'd cooked for me and, with great sickroom sensitivity and gentleness, assisted me during the uncomfortable weeks of recovery. I hadn't been hospitalized since or ill with anything other than a cold, but they were a kindly, childless middle-aged couple—a wiry, shrewd, agreeable husband and a buxom, gregarious, hyperefficient wife—and since the operation they had treated my slightest needs as if they were of uppermost importance. I couldn't have done better if I'd had children of my own to watch me grow old, and might have done a lot worse. Neither had read a word I'd written, though whenever they spotted my name or my photo in a paper or a magazine, Belinda never failed to clip the article and bring it to me. I'd thank her, admit I hadn't seen it, and, later, to ensure that I didn't inadvertently offend this warm, bighearted woman who believed I kept the clippings in what she referred to as my "scrapbook," I'd tear it into the tiniest, unrecognizable pieces before throwing it into the garbage, unread. That stuff too I'd expunged long ago.

For my seventieth birthday Belinda had cooked a dinner of venison steaks and red cabbage for the three of us to eat at my place. The meat—hunted down by Rob in the woods back of my house—was wonderful, and so was the cheery generosity and warm affection of my two friends. They toasted me with champagne and gave me a maroon lamb's wool sweater they'd bought for me down in Athena; then they asked me to make a speech about what it was like to be seventy. After donning their sweater, I rose from my chair at the head of the table and said to them, "It'll be a short speech. Think of the year 4000." They smiled, as though I were about to crack a joke, and so I added, "No, no. Think seriously about 4000. Imagine it. In all its dimensions, in all its aspects. The year 4000. Take your time." After a minute of sober silence, I quietly said to them, "That's what it's like to be seventy," and sat back down.

Rob Massey was the fantasy caretaker, the caretaker everybody wants, Belinda the fantasy cleaning woman, the cleaning woman everyone wants, and though I no longer had Larry Hollis watching over me, I still had the two of them, and all the time I devoted to my writing, even the writing itself, was in part the result of their looking so well after everything else. And now I was letting them go.

"My health's fine. I've just got some work to do down here, and so I exchanged houses with them. I'll stay in touch with you, and if there's anything I should know, call me collect."

Good-naturedly, Rob said to me, "Nathan, nobody's called anybody collect for twenty years."

"Is that so? Well, you know what I mean. I'm going to tell them to keep Belinda on once a week and to turn to you two if anything goes wrong. I'll pay you directly, unless Jamie Logan or Billy Davidoff asks you to do something especially for them, and that you can work out together." It gave me a surprising pang to say Jamie's name and to think that I was not only losing her along with Rob and Belinda but arranging for the loss of her to befall me. It was as if I were losing the thing I loved best in the world.

I told them that after I'd moved into the West 71st Street apartment we'd make arrangements for them to drive my stuff down to the city and for one of them then to drive my car back and, while I was away, for them to keep the car in their garage and be sure to run it from time to time. I had finished a book two months earlier and hadn't yet begun another one, so there were no manuscripts or notebooks to transport. Had there been a new book under way I probably wouldn't have contemplated the move at all; if I had, I certainly wouldn't have left the manuscript to anyone's care other than my own. What's more, had I to return for any reason to my house in the woods, I knew I would never head back to New York again, though not for Jamie's reasons, not because of the fear of terrorist danger, but because everything essential I had where I was, the unbroken stretches of tranquil time that my writing now required, the books I needed to satisfy my interests, and an environment in which I could best maintain my equilibrium and keep myself fit to work for as long as I could. All the city would add was everything I'd determined I no longer had use for: Here and Now.

Here and Now.

Then and Now.

The Beginning and the End of Now.

These were the lines that I jotted onto the scrap of paper where I'd previously written Amy's name and the phone number of my new New York apartment. Titles for something. Perhaps this. Or should I just come right out with it—call it *A Man in Diapers*. A book about knowing where to go for your agony and then going there for it.

The next morning I received a phone call from the urologist's office asking if everything was all right and if I'd noticed any change in my condition—a fever, pain, anything out of the ordinary. I said I felt fine but reported that, as best I could tell, the incontinence hadn't lessened. The doctor's calm, comforting nurse advised me to continue to be patient and to wait to see if there was an improvement, which was not an unlikely possibility, even in some cases weeks after the procedure, and she reminded me that it required a second and sometimes a third procedure to achieve the desired effect and that one could safely undergo the procedure once a month for three months. "By giving you a narrower opening, the chances are good that we will have reduced or controlled the dripping. Please don't fail to contact us and let the doctor know exactly what's going on. Whatever happens, we'd like you to call us here within a week. Do that for us, Mr. Zuckerman, please."

The urge was overwhelming now to cut loose from the shallow, soft-headed fantasy of regeneration, get my car from the garage around the corner, and speed north for home, where I could quickly put my thoughts back where they belonged, under the transforming exigencies of prose fiction, which allow for no sweet dreams. What you do not have, you live without—you're seventy-one, and that's the deal. The vainglorious days of self-assertion are over. Thinking otherwise is ridiculous. There was no need to learn anything more about Amy Bellette or Jamie Logan, nor was there any need to learn anything about myself. That too was ridiculous. The drama of self-discovery was long over. I had not lived as a child all these years, and I knew more than was useful on the subject as it was. Until well into my sixties, I'd not looked away, drifted off, turned my back, I'd tried my best to show no fear, but whatever work might remain could be completed without knowing or hearing more about Al Qaeda, terrorism, the war in Iraq, or the possible reelection of Bush. It was not advisable to collide with all this indignant, highly emotional crisis-brooding—I'd been more than susceptible to my own obsessive brand during the Vietnam years—and if I moved back to the city it wouldn't be long before I was blanketed by it and by the not necessarily enlightening loquaciousness that accompanied such brooding and that, at the end of a nightlong spell submerged in its emptiness, could leave you seething like a lunatic, shattered and stupid, and that surely had contributed to Jamie Logan's decision to take flight.

Or was the history of the past few years sufficient in itself to lead her to expect a second gruesome Al Qaeda attack that would carry her off along with Billy and thousands more? I had no way of judging if she'd concluded correctly or was half demented by the situation (as perhaps the rational, patient young husband believed), or if her foresight was to be substantiated by bin Laden, or if by staying I'd be inflicting on myself a blow more devastating than the disorientation visited on Rip Van Winkle. As a onetime creature of intense responsiveness who'd over the preceding decade tautened himself into a lowkeyed solitary, I'd got out of the habit of giving in to every impulse that crossed my nerve endings, and yet, in just my few days back, I had arrived at what might turn out to be the most thoughtless snap decision I'd ever made.

The hotel phone rang. A man who introduced himself as a friend of Jamie Logan's and Billy Davidoff's. Knew Jamie from Harvard, where she was two years ahead of him. A freelance journalist. Richard Kliman. Wrote on literary and cultural subjects. Articles in the *Times* Sunday magazine, *Vanity Fair, New York,* and *Esquire.* Was I free today? Could he take me to lunch?

"What do you want?" I asked.

"I'm writing about an old acquaintance of yours."

I was no longer skilled in indulging journalists, if I ever had been, nor was I heartened at being so easily located, touching as it did on the immediate circumstances that had first exiled me from New York.

Without explanation, I hung up. Kliman called back within seconds. "We were cut off," he said.

"I cut us off."

"Mr. Zuckerman, I'm writing a biography of E. I. Lonoff. I asked Jamie for your number because I know you met Lonoff and corresponded with him back in the 1950s. I know that as a young writer you were his great admirer. I'm now just a few years older than you were then. I'm not the prodigy you were—this is my first book, and it's not fiction. But I'm trying to do no more or less than you did. I know what I'm not, but I also know what I am. I'm trying to give it everything I have. If you'd like to call and ask Jamie to confirm my credentials—"

No, I'd like to call and ask Jamie why she had informed Mr. Kliman of my whereabouts.

"The last thing Lonoff wanted was a biographer," I said. "He had no ambition to be talked about. Or read about. He wanted anonymity, a harmless enough preference achieved automatically by most and surely a desire easy enough to respect. Look, he's been dead for over forty years. Nobody reads him. Nobody remembers him. Next to nothing is known about him. Any biographical treatment would be largely imaginary—in other words, a travesty."

"But *you* read him," Kliman responded. "You even mentioned his work to us when you came to have lunch at the Signet Society with a bunch of students back in my sophomore year. You told us which stories of his to read. I was there. Jamie was a member and she invited me to come along. Do you remember the Signet Society, the arts club where you had lunch at a big communal table, and afterward we went into the living room—remember that? The evening before, you'd read from your work in Memorial Hall, and one of the students invited you, and you agreed to come for lunch before you left the next day."

"No, I don't remember," I said, though I did—the reading because it was the last I'd given before my prostatectomy and the last ever, and I even remembered the lunch, when Kliman spoke of it, because of the dark-haired girl who'd sat looking at me from across the table. That must have been Jamie Logan at twenty. She'd pretended on West 71st Street that we'd never met, but we had, and I'd noticed her then. What struck me as unusual? Was it merely that she was the prettiest of them all? That could have done it, of course—that and the self-assured reserve suggested by a serene silence that might as easily have indicated that she was just too shy at the time to speak up, though not so shy that she couldn't stare and invite being stared back at in turn.

"You're still interested in him," Kliman was saying. "I know because only the other day you bought the cloth-bound Scribner's edition of the stories. At the Strand. A friend of mine works at the Strand. She told me. She was thrilled to see you there."

"A tactically stupid remark to make to a recluse, Kliman."

"I'm not a tactician. I'm an enthusiast."

"How old are you?"

"Twenty-eight," he said.

"What's your game?" I asked.

"What motivates me? I'd say the spirit of inquiry. I'm driven by my curiosity, Mr. Zuckerman. That's not necessarily something that makes me popular. It already hasn't made me popular with you. But to answer the question, that's the drive that's strongest."

Was he naively obnoxious or obnoxiously naive or just young or just cunning? "Stronger than the drive to kick off a career?" I asked. "To make a splash?"

"Yes, sir. Lonoff is an enigma to me. I'm trying to puzzle him out. I want to do him justice. I thought you could help. It's important to speak to people who knew him.

Some still live, fortunately. I need people who knew him to corroborate my idea of him or, if they see fit to, to challenge it. Lonoff was in hiding, not just as a man but as a writer. The hiding was the catalyst for his genius. The wound and the bow. Lonoff kept a great secret from his early years. It's only coincidental that he lived in Hawthorne country, but it's been argued that Nathaniel Hawthorne lived with a great secret too, and one not that dissimilar. You know what I'm talking about."

"I have no idea."

"Hawthorne's son wrote that Melville had been convinced in his later years that all his life Hawthorne had 'concealed some great secret.' Well, I'm more than convinced that was true of E. I. Lonoff. It helps to explain many things. His work among them."

"Why does his work need explaining?"

"As you said, nobody reads him."

"Nobody reads anyone when you think about it. On the other hand, as I needn't bother to tell you, there's a huge popular appetite for secrets. As for the biographical 'explanation,' generally it makes matters worse by adding components that aren't there and would make no aesthetic difference if they were."

"I know what you're telling me," he said, clearly prepared to shake off what I was telling him, "but I can't be that cynical and do the job decently. The disappearance of Lonoff's fiction is a cultural scandal. One of many, but one I can try to address."

"So," I said, "you've taken it upon yourself to undo the

scandal by revealing the great secret from his early years that explains everything. I assume the great secret is sexual."

Dryly he said, "That's very astute of you, sir."

I would have hung up again, but I was the curious one now, curious to see how dogged and smug he intended to be. Without its ever turning outright belligerent, the unfaltering forward march of the voice made clear he was prepared to do battle. It was, unexpectedly, a passing rendition of me at about that stage, as though Kliman were mimicking (or, as now seemed more to the point, deliberately mocking) my mode of forging ahead when *I* started out. There it was: the tactless severity of vital male youth, not a single doubt about his coherence, blind with self-confidence and the virtue of knowing what matters most. The ruthless sense of necessity. The annihilating impulse in the face of an obstacle. Those grand grandstand days when you shrink from nothing and you're only right. Everything is a target; you're on the attack; and you, and you alone, are right.

The invulnerable boy who thinks he's a man and is seething to play a big role. Well, let him play it. He'll find out.

"I wish you weren't entirely antagonistic," he said, though it didn't sound now as if he cared. "I wish you'd give me the chance to explain to you the significance of his story as I see it and how it explains what happened to his writing when he left Hope and went off with Amy Bellette."

His saying "when he left Hope" galled me. I understood him—the uncompromising tenacity, the bluntness, the indomitable virus of superiority (he was going to be kind enough to explain things to me)—but that didn't mean I had to trust him. Other than hearsay and gossip, what could he know about "when he left Hope"?

"That needs no explaining either," I said.

"A thoroughly documented critical biography could go a long way toward resurrecting Lonoff and restoring his rightful place in twentieth-century literature. But his children won't talk to me, his wife is the oldest person in America with Alzheimer's and *can't* talk to me, and Amy Bellette no longer bothers to answer my letters. I've also sent you letters you haven't answered."

"I don't remember any."

"They were sent in care of your publisher, the proper method, I thought, of contacting someone known to be as private as you. The envelopes came back with a sticker attached: 'Return to sender. Unsolicited mail no longer accepted.'"

"That's a service any publisher will provide. I learned about it first from Lonoff. When I was your age."

"On that sticker that you use, that's Lonoff's language —his formulation?"

It *was* Lonoff's language—I couldn't have improved on it—but I didn't answer.

"I've found out a lot about Miss Bellette. I want to verify it. I need a credible source. You're certainly that. Are you in touch with her?"

"No."

"She lives in Manhattan. She works as a translator. She

has brain cancer. If the cancer gets worse before I get to speak with her again, everything she knows will be lost. She could tell me more than anyone."

"To what end tell you more?"

"Look, old men hate young men. That goes without saying."

So offhand, the cryptic flash of wisdom he suddenly displays. Is this generational dispute something he read about or something someone told him about or something that he knows from his own prior experience, or did the awareness of it arrive out of the blue? "I'm just trying to be responsible," Kliman added, and now it was the word "responsible" that galled me.

"Isn't Amy Bellette why you're in New York?" he asked. "That's what you told Billy and Jamie, that you were here to attend to a friend with cancer."

"This time when you're cut off," I said, "don't call back."

Billy phoned fifteen minutes later to apologize for any indiscretion he or Jamie had committed. He hadn't known that our meeting was to be treated as confidential, and he was sorry for the discomfort they may have caused. Kliman, who had just phoned them to report how badly things had gone with me, was a college boyfriend of Jamie's she was friendly with still, and she had meant no harm in telling him who it was that had answered their ad. Billy said that—wrongly, as he now understood it—neither he nor Jamie had foreseen my objections to talking to the biographer of E. I. Lonoff, a writer I was known by all of them to admire. He assured me that they wouldn't again make the mistake of speaking about the arrangement we'd reached, though I had to realize that once I moved into their place, it wouldn't be long before their network of friends and acquaintances knew who was there, and, likewise, once they'd moved into my place . . .

He was polite and thorough, he made sense, and so I said, "No harm done." Of course Kliman had been a boyfriend of Jamie's. Another reason I couldn't bear him. *The* reason.

"Richard can be insistent," Billy said. "But," he repeated, "we do want to apologize for telling him where you're staying. That was thoughtless."

"No harm done," I repeated, and once again told myself to get in the car and drive home. New York was full of people motivated by "the spirit of inquiry," and not all of them ethically up to the job. If I were to take over the 71st Street apartment—and the telephone there—I would unavoidably find myself in the sort of circumstances that were superfluous to me and that, as I had just demonstrated, I no longer had the wherewithal to finesse. Not that my curiosity hadn't been aroused by what Kliman was insinuating about Lonoff. Not that I wasn't surprised by the unlikeliness of my coming upon Lonoff's Amy for the first time in close to fifty years, and by my following her from the hospital to that luncheonette, and by Kliman's then calling to tell me about Amy's brain cancer and to try to tantalize me with his insider's knowledge of Lonoff's Hawthorne-like "secret." For one who had cultivated seclusion and bound himself to repetitiveness and thrown in his lot with monotony, who had banished everything deemed by him nonessential (purportedly in the service of his work, more likely at the mercy of a failing), it was like being overwhelmed by some rare astronomical event, as though an eclipse of the sun had taken place in the way eclipses had occurred throughout the prescientific eons: without resident earthlings anticipating their imminence.

Precipitously stepping into a new future, I had retreated unwittingly into the past—a retrograde trajectory not that uncommon, but uncanny anyhow.

"We want to invite you to spend election night with us," Billy said. "It'll just be Jamie and me. We're going to be at home to watch the results. We can have dinner here. Stay afterward for as long as you like. Why don't you come?"

"Tuesday night?"

He laughed. "Still the first Tuesday after the first Monday in November."

"I will be there," I said, "I accept," thinking not of the election but of Billy's wife and Kliman's former girlfriend and of the pleasure I could no longer provide a woman, even should the opportunity present itself. Old men hate young men? Young men fill them with envy and hatred? Why shouldn't they? The preposterous was seeping in fast from every quarter, and my heart pounded away with lunatic eagerness, as if the medical procedure to remedy incontinence had something to do with reversing impotence, which of course it did not—as though, however sexually disabled, however sexually unpracticed I was after eleven years away, the drive excited by meeting Jamie had madly reasserted itself as the animating force. As though in the presence of this young woman there was hope.

Through a single, brief meeting with Billy and Jamie I was not merely dropping back into a world of ambitious literary youth that was of no interest to me but opening myself to the irritants, stimulants, temptations, and dangers of the present moment. In my case, the specific danger threatening me back when I decided to leave the city for good—the danger of fatal attack—didn't emanate from the menace of Islamic terrorism but from death threats that I'd begun to receive and that the FBI determined to be issuing from a single source. Each was written on a picture postcard bearing a postmark from somewhere in northern New Jersey, the region where I'd been raised. The same location never appeared on a postmark twice, though the figure pictured on the front of the card was invariably the current pope, John Paul II, either blessing the crowd at St. Peter's or kneeling at prayer or sitting resplendent in brocaded white robes. The first postcard read:

> Dear Jew Bastard, We are part of a new international organization to counter the growth of the racist, filth-laden philosophy ZIONISM. As yet another Jew parasitizing "goy" countries and their inhabitants, you have been marked down to be targeted. Because of the location of your Jew York apartment, it has fallen to this "department" to do the "targeting." This notice marks the beginning.

The second card bearing John Paul's picture carried the same salutation and message, the text's only alteration in the conclusion: "NOTICE NUMBER TWO, JEW!"

Now, I had received communications as vile and ominous in the past, but never more than a couple a year, and most years none at all. Also, on the streets of New York, strangers would intermittently gravitate toward me and initiate a difficult encounter because of something in my fiction that enticed them or that infuriated them or that enticed them because it infuriated them or that infuriated them because it enticed them. I'd been through more than one such unsettling intrusion because of the conception of their author that the books had inspired in minds easily swayed into fantasy by fiction. But this was being *targeted*: not only did these postcards arrive weekly for months on end, but during this same period a reviewer living in the Midwest who'd once written a laudatory review of a book of mine in *The New York Times Book Review* also received a threatening postcard picturing the pope, his addressed to him at the college where he taught, in care of the "Department of Sycophancy and English." No salutation. Just this, written in a tiny hand:

Only a cheap little asskissing two-bit fucking "English professor" would have stooped to calling this Jew bastard's latest pile of dogshit "his richest and most rewarding." What a tragedy that scum like you get away with wrenching young minds out of shape. AK-47 fire. That remedy would restore American higher education to what it once was. Or help to.

It was my New York lawyer who put me in touch with the FBI. As a result, I was visited at my apartment on East 91st Street by an agent named M. J. Sweeney, a small, sprightly southerner in her early forties, who took all of the cards (which she sent on to Washington, along with the one received by the reviewer, for examination and analysis) and who advised me of the precautions I should observe, as though she were instructing me in the basic rules of a sport or game I was unfamiliar with. I wasn't to leave a building without first scrutinizing the street in both directions and across the way for anyone suspicious-looking. On the street, if approached by people I didn't know, I was to keep my eyes on their hands instead of their faces to be sure they didn't reach for a weapon. There were more suggestions like these, and I immediately set out to follow them, but not with much conviction that they would furnish serious protection against someone dedicated to gunning me down. The words "AK-47 fire," which had appeared first in the reviewer's postcard, now began to turn up in the messages addressed to me. Some weeks, "AK-47 fire," written with a black felt-tip marker in characters two inches high, constituted the entire message.

M.J. and I spoke each time a new postcard arrived, and I would photocopy both sides before putting the original in an envelope and mailing it off to her. When I called one day to tell her that my latest book had been nominated for a prize and I was expected to attend the award ceremony in a midtown Manhattan hotel, she asked, "What

kind of security do they have?" "I would think very little."
"It's open to the public?" "It's not *not* open to the public,"
I said; "I can't imagine anybody determined to get in having trouble. I'd guess there'll be around a thousand people." "Well, watch yourself," she said. "You sound as if you
don't think I ought to show up." "I can't speak for the
FBI," M.J. said. "The FBI cannot advise you on this."
"Should I happen to win, if I have to go up on the stage
to accept the prize, I'd make an easy target, would I not?"
"If I were speaking as a friend," she replied, "I'd say you
would." "If you were speaking as a friend, what would
you suggest I do?" "Does it mean a lot to you to be there?"
"It means nothing." "Well, if it were me to whom it meant
nothing," M.J. said, "and I'd just got twenty-some death
threats in the mail, I wouldn't go anywhere near the place."

The next morning I rented a car and drove to western
Massachusetts, and within forty-eight hours I'd bought my
cabin, two large rooms with a big stone fireplace in one
and a wood stove in the other and between them a small
kitchen with a window looking out back onto a grove of
twisted old apple trees to a good-sized oval swimming
pond and a big storm-damaged willow tree. The twelve
acres were situated across from a picturesque swamp where
waterfowl were plentiful and a couple hundred feet back
from a dirt road that you followed for close to three miles
before you reached the blacktop that wound five more
miles down the mountain to Athena. Athena was where
E. I. Lonoff was teaching when I met him in 1956, along
with his wife and Amy Bellette. The Lonoff house, built

in 1790 and passed down over the years through his wife's family, was a ten-minute drive from the house I'd just bought. It was because this locale had been Lonoff's place of refuge that I had instinctively chosen it as my own—because of that and because I was twenty-three years old when I'd met him, and never forgotten it.

I'd learned to use a rifle in the army, and so I bought a .22 at a local gun shop and spent a few afternoons firing alone in the woods until I got the hang of it again. I kept the rifle in a closet next to my bed and a box of ammunition beside it on the closet floor. I arranged to have a security system installed that connected to the local state troopers' barracks, and to have outdoor spotlights fixed at the corners of my roof so that the grounds wouldn't be pitch-black if I got home after dark. Then I called M.J. and told her what I'd done. "Maybe I'm worse off out here in the woods, but so far I'm feeling less exposed and anxious than I felt in the city. I'm keeping my apartment for the time being, but I'm going to live up here for now, till there are no more death threats coming my way." "Does anybody know where you are?" "So far only you. I've arranged for my mail to be forwarded elsewhere." "Well," M.J. said, "it wouldn't have been my first recommendation, but you must do whatever makes you feel safe." "I'll be in and out of the city, but I'll be living here." "Good luck," she said, then went on to tell me she'd now have to transfer my file to the Boston office. After she said goodbye and hung up, I agonized all night long over what I had done, convinced that all the while I'd been receiving the death threats, it had been M. J. Sweeney who had been the barrier between me and my correspondent's AK-47.

When the death threats eventually stopped coming by mail I didn't forsake the cabin. By then it had turned into a home, and there I lived those eleven years writing books, staying fit, getting cancer, taking the radical cure, and, off by myself, without my quite knowing it or my keeping track, advancing in age by the day. The habit of solitude, of solitude without anguish, had taken hold of me, and with it the pleasures of being unanswerable and being free—paradoxically, free above all of oneself. For days on end of only work, I would feel sweetened by luxurious contentment. Loneliness, raving loneliness, was sporadic and amenable to strategy: should it sweep over me during the day, I'd leave my desk and go for a five-mile walk in the woods or along the river, and when it insinuated itself at night, I'd temporarily put aside the book I was reading and listen to something requiring the whole of my attention—something, say, like a Bartók quartet. Thus did I restore stability and make the loneliness bearable. All in all, being without any need to play a role was preferable to the friction and agitation and conflict and pointlessness and disgust that, as a person ages, can render less than desirable the manifold relations that make for a rich, full life. I stayed away because over the years I conquered a way of life that I (and not just I) would have thought impossible, and there's pride taken in that. I may have left New York because I was fearful, but by paring and paring and paring away, I found in my solitude a species of freedom that was to my liking much of the time.

I shed the tyranny of my intensity—or, perhaps, by living apart for over a decade, merely reveled in its sternest mode.

It was on the last day of June 2004 that the name "AK-47" returned to alarm me. I know it was on June 30 because that's the day that the female snapping turtles in my part of New England make their annual trek out from their watery habitat to find an open sandy spot to dig a nest for their eggs. These are strong, slow-moving creatures, large turtles with sawtooth armored shells a foot or more in diameter and long, heavily scaled tails. They appear in abundance at the south end of Athena, troops of them crossing the two-lane macadam road that leads into town. Drivers will patiently wait for minutes on end so as not to hit them as they emerge from the deep woods whose marshes and ponds they inhabit, and it is the annual custom of many local residents like me not merely to stop but to pull over and step out onto the shoulder of the road to watch the parade of these rarely seen amphibians, lumbering forward inch by inch on the powerful, foreshortened, scaly legs that end in prehistoric-looking reptilian claws.

Every year you hear pretty much the same joking and laughter and wonderment from the onlookers, and from the pedagogical parents who've brought their children around to see the show you learn yet again how much the turtles weigh, and how long their necks are, and how strong their bite is, and how many eggs they lay, and how long they live. Then you get back in the car and drive into town to do your errands, as I did on that sunny day just four months before I traveled down to New York to inquire about the collagen treatment.

After having parked diagonally alongside the town green, I ran into several of the local merchants I know who'd come out of their shops to momentarily bask in the sunshine. I stood and talked for a while—about very little, all of us assuming the amiable attitude of men who think only the best of everything, a haberdasher, a liquor store owner, and a writer all exuding the contentment of Americans living safely beyond the reach of the nerve-racking world.

It was after I'd crossed the street and was on my way to the hardware store that I suddenly heard "AK-47" muttered into my ear by the person who had just passed me, heading in the other direction. I swung around and from the mass of his back and the pigeon-toed gait recognized him right off. He was the painter whom I'd hired the summer before to paint the outside of my house, and whom, because he failed to turn up for work just about every other day—and when he put in an appearance did so for no more than two or three hours—I'd had to fire less than halfway into the job. He then sent me a bill so exorbitant that rather than argue with him—and because, on the phone or in person, we'd had noisy arguments nearly every day about either his hours or his absences—I turned the bill over to my local lawyer to deal with. The house-painter's name was Buddy Barnes and rather too late I learned that he was one of Athena's leading alcoholics. I'd never much liked the bumper sticker on his car that read CHARLTON HESTON IS MY PRESIDENT, but I paid little attention to it because, though the legendary movie star had been renowned as the celebrity president of the recklessly irresponsible National Rifle Association, he was well on his way to dementia by the time I got around to hiring Buddy, and the bumper sticker struck me as foolish and innocuous more than anything else.

I was stunned, of course, by what I'd heard on the street, so stunned that rather than give myself a moment to contemplate how best to respond or to determine whether I should respond at all, I raced across to the green, where he had just climbed into his pickup truck. I called his name and banged a fist on his fender until he rolled his window down. "What did you just say to me?" I asked him. Buddy had an almost angelic pink-complexioned look for a gruff-mannered man in his forties, angelic despite the blond hairs growing thinly under his nose and on his chin. "I got nothing to say to you," he replied in his customary high-pitched howl. "What did you say to me, Barnes?" "Je-*sus*," he replied, rolling his eyes. "Answer me. Answer me, Barnes. Why did you say that to me?" "You're hearing things, nutcase," he said. Then, throwing the truck into reverse, he backed out, and with a teenage tire-screech, he was gone.

In the end, I decided that the incident had nothing like the dramatic meaning I had first lighted on. Yes, "AK-47" was what he said, and yes, I was so sure that as soon as I got home, I placed a call to the New York office of the FBI to speak to M. J. Sweeney, only to be told that she had left the agency two years earlier. I reminded myself that those postcards had been sent to me months before I had moved up here and before anybody like Buddy Barnes knew of my existence. It was impossible for Barnes to have sent them, especially as they were postmarked from cities and towns in north Jersey, over a hundred miles south of Athena, Massachusetts. His intending to harass me with the very word that I'd been harassed with through the mails some eleven years earlier was nothing but the weirdest of coincidences.

Nonetheless, for the first time since I'd bought the .22 and practiced firing it in the woods, I opened the box of ammunition and instead of keeping the weapon as I had all these years, standing unloaded at the back of my bedroom closet, I slept with it loaded, on the floor by the side of my bed. And I did this until I left for New York, even after I wondered whether Buddy had said nothing at all to me, even after I concluded that on that beautiful early summer morning, when I'd enjoyed the sight of the female snapping turtles laboriously crossing the road to fulfill their reproductive function, I'd had the most lifelike of auditory hallucinations, one whose cause was inexplicable, at least to me.

The incontinence was wholly unaffected by the collagen treatment, and when I reported this on the morning of the election, the doctor's office recommended that I schedule an appointment for a second procedure the following month. If there was an improvement in the interim, I could always cancel it; if not, the procedure would be repeated. "And if it's not effective?" "Then we repeat it. The third time, we don't go in through the urethra," the nurse explained, "but through the scars from the prostate operation. Just a puncture. Local anesthetic. No pain." "And if a third procedure doesn't work?" I asked. "Oh, that's a long way off, Mr. Zuckerman. Let's just take one step at a time. Don't lose heart. This is not going to come to nothing."

As if incontinence weren't indignity enough, one had then to be addressed like a churlish eight-year-old balking at taking his cod liver oil. But that's how it goes when an elderly patient refuses to resign himself to the inevitable travails and totter politely toward the grave: doctors and nurses have a child on their hands who must be soothed into soldiering on in behalf of his own lost cause. That, at any rate, was my thinking when I hung up the phone, drained of pride and feeling all the limitations of my strength, the man at the point where he fails whether he resists or acquiesces.

What surprised me most my first few days walking around the city? The most obvious thing—the cell phones. We had no reception as yet up on my mountain, and down in Athena, where they do have it, I'd rarely see people striding the streets talking uninhibitedly into their phones. I remembered a New York when the only people walking up Broadway seemingly talking to themselves were crazy. What had happened in these ten years for there suddenly to be so much to say—so much so pressing that it couldn't wait to be said? Everywhere I walked, somebody was approaching me talking on a phone and someone was behind me talking on a phone. Inside the cars, the drivers were on the phone. When I took a taxi, the cabbie was on the phone. For one who frequently went without talking to anyone for days at a time, I had to wonder what that had previously held them up had collapsed in people to make incessant talking into a telephone preferable to walking about under no one's surveillance, momentarily solitary, assimilating the streets through one's animal senses and thinking the myriad thoughts that the activities of a city inspire. For me it made the streets appear comic and the people ridiculous. And yet it seemed like a real tragedy, too. To eradicate the experience of separation must inevitably have a dramatic effect. What will the consequence be? You know you can reach the other person anytime, and if you can't, you get impatient—impatient and angry like a little stupid god. I understood that background silence had long been abolished from restaurants, elevators, and ballparks, but that the immense loneliness of human beings should produce this boundless longing to be heard, and the accompanying disregard for being overheard—well, having lived largely in the era of the telephone booth, whose substantial folding doors could be tightly pulled shut, I was impressed by the conspicuousness of it all and found myself entertaining the idea for a story in which Manhattan has turned into a sinister collectivity where everyone is spying on everyone else, everyone being tracked by the person at the other end of his or her phone, even though, incessantly dialing one another from wherever they like in the great out of doors, the telephoners believe themselves to be experiencing the maximum freedom. I knew that merely by thinking up such a scenario I was at one with all the cranks who imagined, from the beginnings of industrialization, that the machine was the enemy of life. Still, I could not help it: I did not see how anyone could believe he was continuing to live a human existence by walking about talking into a phone for half his waking life. No, those gadgets did not promise to be a boon to promoting reflection among the general public.

And I noticed the young women. I couldn't fail to. The days were still warm in New York and women were clad in ways I couldn't ignore, however much I wanted not to be aroused by the very desires actively quelled through living in seclusion across the road from a nature preserve. I knew from my trips down to Athena how much of themselves college girls now exposed with neither shame nor fear, but the phenomenon didn't stun me until I got to the city, where the numbers were vastly multiplied and the age range expanded and I enviously understood that women dressing as they did meant that they weren't there only to be looked at and that the provocative parade was merely the initial unveiling. Or perhaps it meant that to someone like me. Maybe I had got it all wrong and this was just how they dressed now, how T-shirts were cut now, how clothes were designed now for women, and though walking around in tight shirts and low-cut shorts and enticing bras and with their bellies bare looks like it means that they're all available, they're not—and not only not to me.

But it was noticing Jamie Logan that bewildered me most. I hadn't sat so close to such an irresistible young woman in years, perhaps not since I last sat opposite Jamie herself in the dining room of a Harvard arts club. Nor had I understood how disconcerted I had been by her until we'd all agreed on the exchange of residences and I left to go back to the hotel and found myself thinking how pleasant it would be if no swap took place—if Billy Davidoff stayed where he wanted to stay, which was right there, across from the little Lutheran church on West 71st Street, while Jamie escaped her dread of terrorism by coming back to the tranquil Berkshires with me. She had a huge pull on me, a huge gravitational pull on the ghost of my desire. This woman was in me before she even appeared.

The urologist who had diagnosed the cancer when I was sixty-two had commiserated with me afterward by saying, "I know it's no comfort, but you're not alone—this disease has reached epidemic proportions in America. Your struggle is shared by many others. In your case, it's just too bad that I couldn't have made the diagnosis ten years from now," suggesting that the impotence brought on by the removal of the prostate might by then seem a less painful loss. And so I set out to minimize the loss by struggling to pretend that desire had naturally abated, until I came in contact for barely an hour with a beautiful, privileged, intelligent, self-possessed, languid-looking thirty-year-old made enticingly vulnerable by her fears and I experienced the bitter helplessness of a taunted old man dying to be whole again.

2   Under the Spell

O N THE WALK from my hotel up to West 71st Street I stopped at a liquor store to buy a couple of bottles of wine for my hosts and then proceeded quickly on my way to watch the election results of a campaign that, for the first time since I was made aware of electoral politics—when Roosevelt defeated Willkie in 1940—I knew barely anything about.

I had been an avid voter all my life, one who'd never pulled a Republican lever for any office on any ballot. I had campaigned for Stevenson as a college student and had my juvenile expectations dismantled when Eisenhower trounced him, first in '52 and then again in '56; and I could not believe what I saw when a creature so rooted in his ruthless pathology, so transparently fraudulent and malicious as Nixon, defeated Humphrey in '68, and when, in the eighties, a self-assured knucklehead whose unsurpassable hollowness and hackneyed sentiments and absolute blindness to every historical complexity became the object of national worship and, esteemed as a "great communicator" no less, won each of his two terms in a landslide. And was there ever an election like Gore versus Bush, resolved in the treacherous ways that it was, so perfectly calculated to quash the last shameful vestige of a law-abiding citizen's naiveté? I'd hardly held myself aloof from the antagonisms of partisan politics, but now, having lived enthralled by America for nearly three-quarters of a century, I had decided no longer to be overtaken every four years by the emotions of a child—the emotions of a child and the pain of an adult. At least not so long as I holed up in my cabin, where I could manage to remain in America without America's ever again being absorbed in me. Aside from writing books and studying once again, for a final go-round, the first great writers I read, all the rest that once mattered most no longer mattered at all, and I dispelled a good half, if not more, of a lifetime's allegiances and pursuits. After 9/11 I pulled the plug on the contradictions. Otherwise, I told myself, you'll become the exemplary letter-to-the-editor madman, the village grouch, manifesting the syndrome in all its seething ridiculousness: ranting and raving while you read the paper, and at night, on the phone with friends, roaring indignantly about the pernicious profitability for which a wounded nation's authentic patriotism was about to be exploited by an imbecilic king, and in a republic, a king in a free country with all the slogans of freedom with which American children are raised. The despising without remission that constitutes being a conscientious citizen in the reign of George W. Bush was not for one who had developed a strong interest in surviving as reasonably serene—and so I began to annihilate the abiding wish *to find out.* I canceled magazine subscriptions, stopped reading the *Times,* even stopped picking up the occasional copy of the *Boston Globe* when I went down to the general store. The only paper I saw regularly was the *Berkshire Eagle,* a local weekly. I used the TV to watch baseball, the radio to listen to music, and that was it.

Surprisingly, it took only weeks to break the matter-of-fact habit that informed much of my nonprofessional thinking and to feel completely at home knowing nothing of what was going on. I had banished my country, been myself banished from erotic contact with women, and was lost through battle fatigue to the world of love. I had issued an admonition. I was out from under my life and times. Or maybe just down to the nub. My cabin could as well have been adrift on the high seas as set twelve hundred feet up on a rural road in Massachusetts that was less than a three-hour drive east to the city of Boston and about the same distance south to New York.

The television set was on when I arrived, and Billy assured me the election was in the bag—he was in touch with a friend at Democratic national headquarters, and their exit polls showed Kerry winning all the states he needed. Billy graciously accepted the wine and told me that Jamie had gone out to buy food and should be back at any minute. Once again he was expansively agreeable and exuded a jovial softness, as though he weren't yet and probably never would be expert at wielding authority. Is he a throwback, I wondered, or do they still exist like this, middle-class Jewish boys who continue to be branded with the family empathy that, despite the unmatchable satisfaction of its cradling sentiments, can leave one unprepared for the nastiness of less kindly souls? In the Manhattan literary milieu particularly, I would have expected something other than the brown eyes weighty with tenderness and the full angelic cheeks that lent him the air, if not still of a protected small boy, then of the generous young man wholly unable to inflict a wound or laugh with scorn or shirk the smallest responsibility. I speculated that Jamie might be a lot more than could be managed by the sweet selflessness of one whose every word and gesture was permeated with his decency. The trusting innocence, the mildness, the sympathetic understanding—what a setup for the rogue with an eye to stealing the wife whose infidelity would be unimaginable to him.

The phone rang just as Billy was preparing to open one of the bottles of wine, and he handed it across to me to uncork while he snatched up the phone and said, "What now?" After a moment he looked up to tell me, "New Hampshire's sewed up. D.C.?" Billy then asked the friend who was phoning. To me again he said, "In D.C. they're going eight to one for Kerry. That's the key—the blacks are turning out en masse. Okay, great," Billy said into the phone, and upon hanging up told me happily, "So we live in a liberal democracy after all," and, to toast the mounting thrill, he poured each of us a big glass of wine. "These guys would have devastated the country," he said, "had they won a second term. We've had bad presidents and we've survived, but this one's the bottom. Serious cognitive deficiencies. Dogmatic. A tremendously limited ignoramus about to wreck a very great thing. There's a description in *Macbeth* that's perfect for him. We read aloud together, Jamie and I. We're doing the tragedies. It's in the scene in act three with Hecate and the witches. 'A wayward son,' Hecate says, 'spiteful and wrathful.' George Bush in six words. It's all so awful. If you're for your kids and God, you're a Republican—meanwhile, the people who are being screwed the most are his base. It's amazing they pulled it off for even one term. It's terrifying to think what they would have done with a second term. These are terrible, evil guys. But their arrogance and their lies finally caught up with them."

My mind still full of my own thoughts, I allowed a couple of minutes more for him to continue to watch the first election results trickle in before I asked, "How did you meet Jamie?"

"Miraculously."

"You were students together."

He smiled most appealingly, when, given my thoughts,

he would have done better pulling the dagger that had done in Duncan. "That makes it no less miraculous," he said.

I saw there was no need to stop myself from hurtling forward for fear of being found out. Clearly Billy couldn't begin to imagine that someone of my years might be asking about his young wife because his young wife was now all I could think about. There was my age to mislead him, and my eminence too. How could he possibly believe the worst about a writer he'd begun reading in high school? It was like meeting Henry Wadsworth Longfellow. How could the author of "The Song of Hiawatha" take a licentious interest in Jamie?

To be on the safe side, I asked first about him.

"Tell me about your family," I said.

"Oh, I'm the only reading person in the family, but that doesn't matter; they're good people. In Philly now for four generations. My great-grandfather started the family business. He was from Odessa. His name was Sam. His customers called him Uncle Sam the Umbrella Man. He made and repaired umbrellas. My grandfather expanded into luggage. In the teens and the twenties, train travel boomed and suddenly everybody needed a piece of luggage. And people were traveling by ship, transatlantic ships. It was the era of the wardrobe trunk—you know, the big, heavy trunks people took on long journeys that opened up vertically and had hangers and drawers in them."

"I know them well," I said. "And the others, the smaller black ones that opened up horizontally like a pirate's chest.

I had a trunk like that to go off to college with. Nearly everyone did. It was constructed of wood and the corners were sheathed in metal and the fancy ones were girdled with bands of embossed metal and the lock was brass and made to withstand an earthquake. You used to ship your trunk by Railway Express. You'd take it down to the train station and leave it with the clerk at the Railway Express desk. The guy at Newark's Penn Station in those days still wore the green eyeshade and kept his pencil tucked behind his ear. He'd weigh the trunk and you'd pay per pound and off your socks and underwear would go."

"Yes, every city of any size had a luggage store, and the department stores all had luggage departments. It's airline stewardesses," Billy told me, "who revolutionized how Americans felt about luggage in the fifties—people saw that it could be light and chic. That's about when my father went into the business and modernized the store and changed the name to Davidoff's Fashionable Luggage. Until then, the place was still known by the original name, Samuel Davidoff and Sons. About this time along came the luggage on wheels—and that, vastly abridged, is the story of the luggage business. The full version runs to a thousand pages."

"You're writing about the family business, are you?"

He nodded and he shrugged and he sighed. "*And* the family. I'm trying to, anyway. I more or less grew up in the store. I've heard a thousand stories from my grandfather. Every time I go to see him I fill another notebook. I've got stories enough to last a lifetime. But it's all a matter of how, isn't it? I mean, how you tell them."

"And Jamie. How did she grow up?"

And so he told me, lavishly expatiating on her accomplishments: about Kinkaid, the exclusive private school in Houston from which she'd graduated valedictorian; about her stellar academic career at Harvard, where she graduated summa cum laude; about River Oaks, the wealthy Houston neighborhood where her family lived; about the Houston Country Club, where she played tennis and swam and had come out as a debutante against her will; about the conventional mother she tried so hard to accommodate and the difficult father she could never please; about the favorite haunts she took Billy to visit when they first went together to Houston for Christmas; about the places where she played as a child that he wanted her to show him and the menacing beauty of the ugly Houston bayous at dawn and Jamie's defiantly swimming in the murky water with a wild older sister, who, he informed me, pronounced the word "buy-ohs," like the old Houstonians.

I had simply asked him to tell me about her; what I'd gotten was a speech appropriate to the dedication of some grand edifice. There was nothing strange about such a staunchly tender performance—men who fall madly in love can make Xanadu of Buffalo if that's where their beloved was raised—and yet the ardor for Jamie and Jamie's Texas girlhood was so undisguised that it was as though he were telling me about somebody he had dreamed up in jail. Or about the Jamie that *I* had dreamed up in jail. It was as it should be in a masterpiece of male devotion: his veneration for his wife was his strongest tie to life.

He was elegiac when recounting to me the route they jog together when they visit her folks.

"River Oaks, where they live—it's an anomaly in Houston. Old neighborhood with old houses, though there are some nice ones that have been torn down for McMansions. Jamie's is one of the few neighborhoods in Houston where there's still some feeling for the past. Beautiful houses, big oaks, magnolias, a few pines. Huge manicured gardens. Teams of gardeners. Mexican. Thursdays and Fridays the streets are lined with the pickup trucks of gardening companies and with armies of workers out clipping and manicuring and mowing and planting for the weekend, for the parties and gatherings that are going to go on. We jog through the older part of River Oaks, where the original oil families have had their big spreads for two and three generations. We jog past the older houses and run along kind of a busy street, and then we get to the bayou that runs from River Oaks down through a park where you can jog for miles and miles until you get to downtown. Or we run along the bayou and back. Just after dawn it's cool and it's wonderful. The quiet, discreet part of River Oaks, where people aren't consuming conspicuously and parking multiple Mercedeses in front of their McMansions, is a beautiful community. There's a rose garden we especially like, a community project, kept up and cared for by the residents. I love the mornings running past that rose garden with Jamie. Some of the old estates back up onto the bayou, and to get to where we can see the bayou and run by it, we have to get out of River Oaks. And so there's the rest of Houston. River Oaks is an insular, prosperous haven of uniformity, old-money families and new-money families at the top of the Houston caste system, and a lot of the rest of the city is hot and humid and flat and ugly— tattoo parlors next to office buildings, running-shoe stores in rickety houses, everything just jumbled together. The most beautiful thing in the city to me is the old cemetery with the old live-oak trees where some of Jamie's family are buried, right down by the bayous, almost downtown."

"Is Jamie's an old- or a new-money family?" I asked Billy.

"Old. The old money is oil money, and the new money is professional money."

"How old is the old money?"

"Well, not that old, because Houston's relatively young. But since the oil tycoons like Jamie's grandfather, whenever that would have been."

"And how did the old Houston money feel about your being a Jew?" I asked.

"Her parents weren't thrilled. The mother just cried. It was the father who took the cake. When Jamie came home to tell them we were engaged, he put his head in his hands, and that's what he did from then on, every time my name was mentioned. She'd e-mail him from back east and he deliberately wouldn't answer her for three, four weeks at a time. She'd check her e-mail hourly and he would not have answered her. An authentically coarse tyrant, this guy. A travesty of a father. Selfish. Thoughtless. Big temper. Utterly irrational. Domineering. Venomous. No good boorish bastard through and through. Imagine: trying, by not answering her, to break his own daughter down, consciously and deliberately exploiting a daughter's decency to make her feel herself in the wrong. Wants to *crush* her. And, of course, to crush me too. I had never laid eyes on him, nor he on me, yet he wanted to harm me nonetheless. And who had ever purposefully set out to harm me before? To my knowledge, Mr. Zuckerman, no one. But this brute feels himself wholly entitled to do harm to a man his daughter happens to love! Now, Jamie is a good daughter, a very good daughter—she'd given her all trying to love this person who was persistently on the wrong side of the argument, tried as hard as she could however much she'd hated his bullying of her mother and his politics and his arrogant right-wing friends. After one three-week silence, he finally sends her a one-sentence e-mail: 'I love you, sweetheart, but I cannot accept that boy.' But Jamie Logan's got guts, dignity and guts, and even though the old man held the purse strings, even though he began to hint, not very subtly, that if she went through with marrying a Jew he would cut her off, she wouldn't break. She stuck it out, and eventually the bigoted son of a bitch had to either swallow his animus and accept me or lose his beloved summa-cum-laude child. A lesser girl of twenty-five, one lacking Jamie's courage, lacking Jamie's independence, would have capitulated. But Jamie is a lesser nothing. Jamie is neither spoiled nor a fraud nor without a sense of honor and would never dream of submitting to what she could not stand. Jamie is the best. She said to me, 'I love you and I want you and I will not be a slave to his dough.' She as good as told him to take the money and shove it, and so in the end *she* crushed *him*. Oh, Mr. Zuckerman, it was a thing of beauty watching Jamie hold out. Though you would have thought that the father would have been used to it by the time she got around to me. 'It' being Jamie and Jews. Their country club lets in Jews now. That wouldn't have been the case in her grand-parents' time, or even as recently as fifteen years ago, with her parents' generation. It's all pretty new. Like letting Jews and blacks into Kinkaid. That's relatively new. The Jewish girls were Jamie's study buddies. You can imagine how much the great hothead loved that. But they were talented and smart, and they didn't try to hide their book-ishness to be popular. The brother of one of Jamie's Jew-ish girlfriends—Nelson Speilman, who attended St. John's, the other prestigious prep school in Houston—was her boy-friend for two years, until he went off to Princeton the year before she graduated from Kinkaid. Jamie was one of the dedicated studious ones in a very protected place where to be socially acceptable was everything. It's a school where the football team votes for the homecoming queen, and the girls can't be seen with a public school boy, only with Kinkaid or St. John's boys. The Kinkaid boys drive Broncos and hunt and watch sports, and all of them want to go to UT, and there's a lot of drinking and a lot of parental looking-the-other-way at the drinking."

"You know a lot about her school. You know a lot about her city."

"I'm fascinated," he said with a laugh. "I am. I'm a slave to Jamie's background."

"And that never happened with any girl you'd taken out before her?"

"Never."

"Well," I said, "that's probably as good a reason to marry as any."

"Oh," he said jokingly, "there are a few more."

"I can imagine," I said.

"She makes me proud of her all the time. Do you know what she did four years back when her older sister, Jessie, the wild one, was in the last stages of Lou Gehrig's disease? She picked up and got on a plane to Houston and stayed there at Jessie's bedside and nursed her till she died. Stayed there night and day for five horrible, misery-ridden months while I was here in New York. It's a nightmarish disease. It's usually not till their mid-fifties that people come down with it, but Jessie was thirty when suddenly her hands and feet began to weaken, and the diagnosis was made. Over time, all the motor neurons go, but because the brain alone is spared, the person is fully cognizant that she's a living corpse. In the end, all Jessie could move were her eyelids. That's how she communicated with Jamie—by blinking. For five months Jamie didn't leave her side. At night she slept on a cot in Jessie's room. Early on, their mother had gone to pieces and was utterly useless, and their father, from start to finish, was himself to a T— would have nothing to do with the daughter who'd inconvenienced him by coming down with a fatal disease. Wouldn't tend to her, after a while wouldn't even go into her room to say a fatherly word to soothe her, let alone touch her or give her a kiss. Went on making money as though everything at home was just fine, while his younger daughter, twenty-six, was helping his older daughter, thirty-four, to die. But the night before it happened, the night before Jessica succumbed, he was in the kitchen with Jamie, where the maid was preparing them something to eat, and all at once he broke down. In the kitchen, he finally broke down and began to sob his heart out like a child. He clung to Jamie and you know what he said to her? 'If only it were me instead of her.' And you know what Jamie said back to him? 'If only it were.' That's the girl I fell for. That's the girl I married. That's Jamie."

When Jamie came through the door carrying her bags of food, she said, "On the street somebody told me Ohio doesn't look good."

"I just spoke to Nick," Billy said. "Kerry's going to win Ohio."

She turned to me. "I don't know what I'd do if Bush gets back in. It'll be the end of the road for a whole way of political life. All their intolerance focuses on a liberal society. It'll mean that the values of liberalism will continue to be reversed. It'll be terrible. I don't think I could live with it."

As she was hurriedly speaking, Billy had taken the groceries from her and gone into the kitchen to sort things out.

"It's a flexible instrument that we've inherited," I told her. "It's amazing how much punishment we can take."

My effort to be consoling seemed to strike her as condescension, and she all but snapped at me for the imagined affront. "Have you ever lived through an election like this one? With the magnitude of this one?"

"Some. This is one I haven't followed."

"Haven't you?"

"I told you the other night—I don't follow such things."

"So you don't care who wins." She gave me a hard look of disapproval for the willed quality of my obliviousness.

"I didn't say that."

"These are terrible, evil people," she told me, echoing her husband. "I know these people. I grew up with these people. It wouldn't just be a shame if they won—it could prove to be a tragedy. The turn to the right in this country is a movement to replace political institutions with morality—*their* morality. Sex and God. Xenophobia. A culture of total intolerance . . ."

She was too agitated by the menacing world she lived in to stop herself—and, for whatever reason, to be entirely civil to me—and so I listened to her while making no further foolish attempt to embark on the knightly quest for the Holy Grail of her attention. The slender, full-breasted frame and the curtain of black hair pleased me no less than on the evening I'd come to look at the apartment. She'd returned from shopping wearing a wine-colored, closely fitted corduroy blazer, which she'd taken off after Billy had relieved her of the groceries—taken off along with her low-heeled dark brown boots. Beneath the blazer she wore a ribbed black cashmere turtleneck that was also close-fitting, as were the dark denim jeans that flared just a bit at the bottom, probably to accommodate the boots. To walk around the apartment she'd put on a pair of flat shoes that looked like ballet slippers. Though the calculation was subtle, she didn't look as if she were necessarily pursuing guileless ends by the way she dressed or as if she lacked confidence in her power to arouse the admiration of men. Did she care one way or another whether I was as wowed as the others? If not, why had she gotten herself up so appealingly just to go for the groceries and watch the election results? Though maybe any unknown guest would have prompted her to choose to wear something attractive. Regardless, the lure of the apparel was matched by the voice, the rapid speech, warm and musical even when she was upset, and with a lot of Texas in it, or her part of Texas, a relaxing of vowels, a softening, particularly in the soft "I," and then her connecting the words a little lazily, one word running into the next. It wasn't the kind of twang that's harsh on the ear—not the Wild West Texas accent that George W. Bush took on but the well-bred Texas accent belonging more to the South that his Yankee father picked up. There's a gentility to it, certainly as spoken by Jamie Logan. Maybe it's just the accent of the cream of River Oaks and the Kinkaid School.

I was as glad as Billy that she was home. It didn't matter if the clothes had nothing to do with my presence. In its deliberateness, there was something intensely exciting about her not giving me a tumble. There is no situation that infatuation is unable to feed on. Looking at her provided a visual jolt—I allowed her into my eyes the way a sword swallower swallows a sword.

As though to an ailing child, Billy said, "You're not going to be devastated. You're going to be dancing in the street."

"No," she replied, "no, this country is a haven of ignorance. I know—I come from the fountainhead. Bush talks right to the ignorant core. This is a very backward country, and the people are so easily bamboozled, and he's exactly like a snake-oil salesman . . ." She must have been angrily brooding aloud for months now, and so, for the moment, she seemed to give out, and I wondered if she was someone who didn't ever know how to say anything unseriously, or if the election overrode everything and for now I could have no idea what Jamie was like without an ordeal and whether her response to the great world was ever anything but painfully intense.

We arranged ourselves around the coffee table with the plates, the cutlery, and the linen napkins Billy had set out, taking what we wanted from the platters of food and, while we steadily emptied my two bottles of wine, watching the screen where the available results were being tabulated state by state. By a little after ten the phone calls from Nick at Democratic headquarters were becoming less optimistic, and by a quarter to eleven they were dour. "The exit polls," Billy told us after hanging up, "aren't proving to be accurate. Things don't look good in Ohio, and he's not going to win Iowa *or* New Mexico. Florida is lost."

Most of this we knew from watching television, but Jamie had no faith in the television tabulations, and so the call from Nick caused her to cry, a little drunkenly, "This is now the night before it all got even worse! I don't know what to think!" while I thought, At some point capitulation will kick in, but till then it'll be a big job to exorcise the illusions. Till then she'll be thrashing around in pain or hiding away like a wounded animal. Hiding away in my house. In these clothes. In no clothes. In my bed, beside Billy, unclothed.

"I don't know what to think!" she cried again. "There's nothing to stop them now, except Al Qaeda."

"Sweetheart," Billy said softly, "we don't yet know what will happen. Let's wait it out."

"Oh, the world is so dim," Jamie exclaimed with tears in her eyes. "Last time it seemed like a fluke. There was Florida. There was Nader. But this I don't understand! I can't believe it! It's incredible! I'm going to go out and get an abortion. I don't care if I'm pregnant or not. Get an abortion while you can!"

She was looking at me when she made this bitter joke, now without antipathy—looking at me the way somebody being helped from a burning building or freed from a car crash looks at you, as though as an observer you might have something to say that could account for the catastrophe that's altered everything. All the things I thought to tell her would likely strike her as cant. I thought to repeat, It's amazing how much punishment we can take. I thought to say, If in America you think like you do, nine times out of ten you fail. I thought to say, It's bad, but not like waking up the morning after Pearl Harbor was bombed. It's bad, but not like waking up the morning after Kennedy was shot. It's bad, but not like waking up the morning after Martin Luther King was shot. It's bad, but not like waking up the morning after the Kent State students were shot. I thought to say, We have all been through it. But I said nothing. She didn't want words anyway. She wanted murder. She wanted to wake up the morning after George Bush had been shot.

It was Billy who said, "Something will be their undoing, honey. Terror will be their undoing."

"Oh, what's the sense of living with it?" Jamie asked, and so deep was her dismay, and so close to the surface her vulnerability, that she broke into sobs.

Each of their cell phones started ringing then—the cruelly disappointed friends calling, many of them in tears as well. The first time, as Jamie said, it seemed like a fluke, but this was their idealism's second staggering electoral shock and the dawning of the hard realization that they could not will this country back into being the Roosevelt stronghold it had been some forty years before they were born. For all their sharpness and articulateness and savoir-faire, and despite Jamie's knowledge of rich Republican America and the brand of ignorance bred in Texas, they'd had no idea who the great mass of Americans were, nor had they seen so clearly before that it was not those educated like themselves who would determine the country's fate but the scores of millions unlike them and unknown to them who had given Bush a second chance, in Billy's words, "to wreck a very great thing."

I sat there, in what was soon to be the home where I would awaken every morning, and listened to the two of them, who'd soon be waking up each day in my house, a place where, if you liked, you could erase the rage about how much worse it all was than you thought and the sorrow over how far down your country had sunk and, if you were young and hopeful and engaged by your world and still enraptured by your expectations, learn instead to relinquish caring about America in 2004—to live and not be on the rack because of how stupid and corrupt it all is—by looking for fulfillment to your books, your music, your mate, and your garden. Watching these two, I got the sense easily enough of why anyone their age with their commitments would want to flee the pain-inducing lover their country had become.

"Terrorism?" Jamie cried into her phone. "But all the states that were touched by terrorism, the places where it happened and the places where people came from who were killed—all of them voted for Kerry! New York, New Jersey, D.C., Maryland, Pennsylvania—none of them wanted Bush! Look at the map east of the Mississippi. It's the Union versus the Confederacy. The same split. Bush carried the old Confederacy!"

"Do you want to know the sick next war?" Billy was telling someone. "They need a victory. They need a clean victory and without a messy occupation. Well, it's sitting ninety miles off the Florida coast. They'll connect Castro to Al Qaeda and go to war against Cuba. The provisional government is already in Miami. The property maps have already been drawn up. Wait and see. In their war against the infidel, Cuba will be next. Who is there to stop them? They don't even need Al Qaeda. They're intent on more violence, and Cuba's criminal enough on its own. The constellation that elected him will love it. Drive the last of the Communists into the sea."

I hung around long enough to be able to overhear them talk to their folks. By then they were feeling so drained that all they could do was wish they had parents with whom they could emotionally give way and be succored in return. Both were dutiful children, so when the time came they dutifully phoned, but Jamie's parents, as I knew from Billy's rendering of Jamie's Houston, were members of the same country club as the elder George Bush—and so on the phone Jamie vainly tried to remember that she was a married woman living more than a thousand miles away from where she was indoctrinated in privilege by archconservative Texans, led by the father, whom she mainly despised for his unconscionable disregard for her dying sister and whom she had flatly and obstinately defied by daring him to disinherit her by boldly marrying a Jew.

She had by now become something a good deal more than somebody beautiful I was staring at. In her voice you could hear just how battered she was, not least by the fact that her parents were the very sort of people her liberal conscience couldn't abide, and yet she still happened to be their daughter and still needed, apparently, to lay her troubles at their feet. You could hear both the great bond and the great struggle against. You could hear all it had cost her to forge a new being and all the good it had done.

Billy's parents in Philadelphia were by no means alien or adversarial or distasteful, but clearly very dear to him; yet when he hung up the phone, he shook his head and had to empty his half-full wine glass before he spoke. His gentle face could not hide the disappointment or the humiliation that he felt, and the tender heart attuned always to the feelings of others would not allow for an airing of the disgust that might have gone a ways toward easing the pain. At the moment a tender heart had no useful function, and Billy was at sea. "My father voted for Bush," he said, as surprised as if he'd discovered that his father had robbed a bank. "My mother told me. When I asked her why, she said, 'Israel.' She had him all lined up to vote for Kerry, and when he comes out of the booth he tells her, 'I did it for Israel.' 'I could have killed him,' my mother said. 'He still believes they'll find the weapons of mass destruction.'"

When I returned to the hotel, I wrote this little scene:

HE

You didn't tell me that we met before.

SHE

I didn't think it was worth mentioning. I didn't think you'd remember.

HE

I thought perhaps *you* didn't remember.

SHE

No, I remember.

HE

You remember where we met?

SHE

The Signet.

HE

Right. Do you remember that day at all?

SHE

I remember it quite well. I was a member of the Signet but I didn't go to lunch there much. And a friend of mine called to tell me that she had invited you to lunch the next day, and she wasn't sure if you would show up but you'd said that you would and that I ought to come. So I did. I brought Richard, and luckily I got to sit at your table instead of the table in the other room. And I sat down and you came in and sat at our table, and I watched you during lunch.

HE

You didn't speak, but you did stare.

SHE

(*Laughing apologetically*) I'm sorry if I was forward.

HE

I stared back at you. And not merely in self-defense. Do you remember that?

SHE

I thought perhaps I was imagining that. I couldn't believe I could get a response. I couldn't believe you'd take any notice of me. I had you down for inaccessible. You remember sitting opposite me, truly?

HE

It's only ten years ago.

SHE

Ten years is a long time to remember somebody you don't speak to. What impression did I make on you?

HE

I couldn't tell if you were shy or just had great serene reserve.

SHE

Both.

HE

Did you go to the reading the night before?

SHE

Yes. I remember sitting in the living room on the leather sofas after lunch. About half of us stayed. I thought what an awkward thing this must be for this man. All of us crowding around him, waiting for him to say something that we can all go home and write in our journals.

HE

Did you go home and write in your journal?

SHE

I'll have to go and check in my journal. I can do that, you know. I could if you wanted me to. I keep them all. What did you think of that day?

HE

I don't remember what I thought. It was not unusual to be asked to do such a thing. Usually it's a class you're asked to attend. You do it, and then you go home. But why didn't you mention it the other day, when we met?

SHE

Why bring up that I gawked at you once over lunch? I don't know, I wasn't keeping it a secret. We're exchanging houses. I didn't see any reason to talk about when I sat in an audience and stared at you in college. Why did *you* agree to go and have lunch with a bunch of undergraduates?

HE

I must have thought it might be interesting. The night before I'd just read for an hour and taken some questions. I hadn't met anyone other than the people who'd invited me. I don't remember anything about it except you.

SHE

(*Laughing*) Are you flirting with me?

HE

Yes.

SHE

That seems so unlikely it's almost hard to believe.

HE

It shouldn't be. It's not unlikely at all.

On rereading the scene in bed before I went to sleep, I thought: If ever there was something that didn't need doing, it's this. Now you are taken up with her totally.

It was dreadful in New York the next day, a lot of enraged people walking around looking glum and disbelieving. It was quiet, the traffic so thin you could barely hear it in Central Park, where I had gone to meet Kliman on a bench not far from the Metropolitan. There had been a message from him on my voice mail at the hotel when I got back around midnight from West 71st Street. It would have been easy enough to ignore it and I intended to, until, under the spell of this impetuous reimmersion—and stimulated by the prospect of a meeting with Amy Bellette, whose whereabouts I could probably extract from him—I phoned Kliman the next morning at the number he'd left, despite my having twice hung up on him the day before.

"Caligula wins," he said upon answering the phone. He was expecting someone else, and after a second's pause I said, "So it seems, but this is Zuckerman." "It's a dark day, Mr. Zuckerman. I've been eating crow all morning. I couldn't believe it would happen. People voted for moral values? What values are those? Lying to get us into a war? The idiocy! The idiocy! The Supreme Court. Rehnquist will be dead by tomorrow. Bush'll make Clarence Thomas chief justice. He'll have two, three, maybe even four appointments—horrendous!"

"You left a message last night about our meeting."

"Did I?" he asked. "I haven't slept. Nobody I know has slept. A friend of mine who works at the Forty-second Street library phoned to tell me that there are people crying on the library steps."

I was familiar with the theatrical emotions that the horrors of politics inspire. From the 1965 transformation into a Vietnam hawk of the peace candidate Lyndon Johnson until the 1974 resignation of all-but-impeached Richard Nixon, they were a staple in the repertoire of virtually everyone I knew. You're heartbroken and upset and a little hysterical, or you're gleeful and vindicated for the first time in ten years, and your only balm is to make theater of it. But I was merely onlooker and outsider now. I did not intrude on the public drama; the public drama did not intrude on me.

"Religion!" Kliman cried. "Why don't they put their trust in crystal gazing as a means of apprehending the truth? Suppose evolution should turn out to be a crock, suppose Darwin *was* nuts. Could he begin to be as nuts as Genesis on the origins of man? These are people who don't believe in knowledge. They don't believe in knowledge in exactly the same way I don't believe in faith. I feel like going outside," Kliman told me, "and delivering a long speech."

"Wouldn't help," I told him.

"You've been around. What does?"

"The senile solution: forget it."

"You're not senile," Kliman said.

"But I've forgotten it."

"All of it?" he asked, providing a glimpse of a possible relationship he might try to work up and exploit: the young man asking the older man for his sage advice.

"Everything," I replied truthfully enough—and as though I'd fallen for his ploy.

Kliman was jogging around the oval of the big green lawn and waved at me when I approached the Central Park bench where we were to meet. I waited for him, thinking that once I had made the original mistake—of coming to New York for the collagen procedure—thinking things through had given way to meandering erratically into a renewal I'd had no idea I had the slightest longing for. To disrupt the basic unity of one's life and change the patterns of predictability at seventy-one? What could be more fraught with the likelihood of disorientation, frustration, even of collapse?

Kliman said, "I had to get those shits out of my head. I thought a run would do it. Didn't work."

He wasn't a genial, chubby Billy but well over two hundred pounds, easily six-three, a large, agile, imposing young man with a lot of dark hair and pale gray eyes that were the wonder that pale gray eyes are in the human animal. A beautiful fullback built to pile-drive. My first (untrustworthy) impression was of someone also constrained by a generalized bafflement—at only twenty-eight bowed by the unwillingness of the world to submit without objection to his strength and beauty and the pressing personal needs they served. That's what was in his face: the angry recognition of an unexpected, wholly ridiculous resistance. He had to have been a very different sort of lover for Jamie from the young man she married. Where Billy had the soft, skillful tact of an obliging brother, Kliman had retained much of the schoolyard menace. That's what I perceived when he phoned me at the hotel, and so it was: self-control was not his watchword. Soon enough, it turned out not to be mine.

In running shorts, running shoes, and a damp sweatshirt, he sat dejectedly beside me, his elbows on his knees and his head in his hands. Dripping with sweat—this is how he comes to meet someone who is a key component of his first big professional endeavor, someone he desperately wants to win over. Well, he's genuine, I thought, whatever else he may be, and, if an opportunist, not quite the slick, self-interested opportunist I had imagined from our first conversation.

He wasn't finished expressing himself about the election. "That a right-wing administration motivated by insatiable greed and sustained by murderous lies and led by a privileged dope should answer America's infantile idea of morality—how do we live with something so grotesque? How do you manage to insulate yourself from stupidity so bottomless?"

They were some six to eight years out of college, I thought, and so Kerry's loss to Bush was taking a prominent place in the cluster of extreme historical shocks that would mentally shape their American kinship, as Vietnam had publicly defined their parents' generation and as the Depression and the Second World War had organized the expectations of my parents and their friends. There had been the barely concealed chicanery that had given Bush the presidency in 2000; there had been the terrorist attacks of 2001 and the indelible memory of the doll-like people leaping from the high windows of the burning towers; and now there was this, a second triumph by the "ignoramus" they loathed as much for his undeveloped mental faculties as for his devious nuclear fairy tales, to

97

enlarge the common experience that would set them apart from their younger brothers and sisters as well as from people like me. To them Bush Junior's was never an administration but a regime that had seized power by judicial means. They were meant to be reclaiming their franchise in 2004, and horribly they didn't, leaving them with the feeling, along about eleven last night, not only of having lost but in some way or other of having been defrauded again.

"You wanted to tell me Lonoff's unpardonable secret," I said.

"I never said 'unpardonable.'"

"You were suggesting that much."

"Do you know about his childhood?" he asked me. "Do you know anything about his growing up? Can I trust you not to repeat what I'm about to tell you?"

I leaned back on the bench and erupted with my first laugh since returning to New York. "You want to shout from the rooftops whatever it is that constitutes this utterly private man's carefully kept and plainly humiliating 'great secret,' and you ask me to be discreet enough not to repeat it? You're about to write a book to destroy the dignity that he rigidly protected and that meant everything to him and was legitimately his, and you ask if *I* can be trusted?"

"But this is the same as the phone call. You're being awfully hard on someone you don't even know."

I thought, But I do know you. You're young and you're

handsome and nothing gives you more assurance than being devious too. You have a taste for deviousness. It's another of your entitlements to do harm should you want to. And, strictly speaking, it's not harm that you do—merely the fulfilling of a right you would be a fool to relinquish. I know you: you wish to gain the approval of the adults you clandestinely set about to defile. There's a cunning pleasure in that, and safety too.

There was some foot traffic around the big oval lawn, women pushing baby carriages, elderly folks on the arms of black caretakers, and a couple of joggers in the distance whom I at first took for Billy and Jamie.

I could have been a fifteen-year-old boy on that bench, my mind given over completely to the new girl who'd been seated next to me on the first day of school.

"Lonoff declined membership in the National Institute of Arts and Letters," Kliman was telling me. "Lonoff wouldn't contribute a biography to *Contemporary Authors*. Lonoff never in his life gave an interview or made a public appearance. He did everything to remain as invisible as he could out there in the boondocks where he lived. Why?"

"Because he preferred the contemplative life to any other. Lonoff wrote. Lonoff taught. In the evenings Lonoff read. He had a wife and three children, beautiful, unspoiled rural surroundings, and a pleasant eighteenth-century farmhouse full of fireplaces. He made a modest income that sufficed. Order. Security. Stability. What more did he need?"

"To hide. Why else did he wear that bridle all his life? He stood perpetual vigil over himself—it's in his life, it pervades his work. He sustained his constraints because he lived in fear of exposure."

"And you are to do him the favor of exposing him," I said.

There was a moment of unhappiness while he searched for a reason not to punch me in the mouth for having failed to be bowled over by his eloquence. I remembered such moments easily enough, having known them myself as a literary young man just about his age and fresh to New York, where I'd been treated by writers and critics then in their forties and fifties as though I didn't and couldn't know anything about anything, except a little something perhaps about sex, knowledge they considered essentially fatuous, though of course they were themselves endlessly at the mercy of their desires. But as for society, politics, history, culture, as for "ideas"—"You don't even understand when I say you don't understand," one of them liked to tell me while waving his finger in my face. These were my notables, the intellectually exceptional American sons of immigrant Jewish housepainters and butchers and garment workers who were then in their prime, running *Partisan Review* and writing for *Commentary* and *The New Leader* and *Dissent,* irascible rivals sharply contentious with one another, bearing the emotional burden of having been raised by semiliterate Yiddish-speaking parents whose immigrant limitations and meager culture evoked ire and tenderness in equally crippling portions. If I dared to speak, these elders would scornfully shut me up, sure that I knew nothing because of my age and my "advantages"—advantages wholly imagined by them, their intellectual curiosity curiously never extending to anyone younger, unless the younger one was much younger and pretty and a woman. In their later years, marital hardships having left them badly bruised (and financially busted), the diseases of age and difficult children having taken their toll, a few of them softened toward me and became friends and didn't necessarily dismiss everything I had to say all the time.

"You see—I'm reluctant even to tell you," Kliman said at last. "You jump on me when I ask if I can tell you something in confidence, but why do you think I bother to ask?"

"Kliman, why don't you forget about whatever it is you think you've found out? Nobody knows who Lonoff is anymore. What's the point?"

"*That.* He should be in the Library of America. Singer is, with three volumes of stories. Why not E. I. Lonoff?"

"So you're going to redeem Lonoff's reputation as a writer by ruining it as a man. Replace the genius of the genius with the secret of the genius. Rehabilitation by disgrace."

When, after another angry pause, he resumed speaking, it was in the voice you use with a child who's failed to understand for the umpteenth time. "It won't be ruined," he explained to me, "if the book is written the way I intend to write it."

"Doesn't matter how you write it. The scandal will do

the job by itself. You won't restore him to his place—you'll deprive him of his place. And what is it that happened anyway? Someone remember something 'inappropriate' Lonoff did fifty years ago? Defiling revelations about another contemptible white male?"

"Why do you insist on trivializing what I want to do? Why do you rush to cheapen what you know nothing about?"

"Because the dirt-seeking snooping calling itself research is just about the lowest of literary rackets."

"And the savage snooping calling itself fiction?"

"You characterizing me now?"

"I'm characterizing literature. It nurtures curiosity too. It says the public life is not the real life. It says there is something beyond the image you set out to give—call it the truth of the self. I'm not doing anything other than what you do. What any thinking person does. Curiosity is nurtured by *life*."

We had come to our feet at the same time. There is no doubt that I should have walked quickly away from those pale gray eyes, eerily lit up now by our antipathy. For one thing, I could tell that the pad cradled in my plastic underwear to absorb and contain my urine was heavily soaked and that it was time to hurry back to the hotel to wash and change myself. There is no doubt that I should have said no more. Why else had I lived apart from people for eleven years if not to say not one word more than was in my books? Why else had I given up reading the papers and listening to the news and watching television if not to hear nothing further about all that I couldn't stand and was powerless to alter? I lived, by choice, where I could no longer be drawn down into the disappointments. Yet I couldn't stop myself. I was back, I was on a tear, and nothing could have inspired me more than the risk I was taking, because not only was Kliman forty-three years younger than me, a hulking, muscular figure wearing just his running attire, but he was enraged by the very resistance that he could not abide.

"I'm going to do everything I can to sabotage you," I told him. "I'm going to do everything I can to see that no book by you about Lonoff ever appears anywhere. No book, no article, nothing. Not a word, Kliman. I don't know the great secret that you turned up, but it's never going to see the light of day. I can prevent your being published, and, whatever the expense, whatever the effort, I will."

Back in the drama, back in the moment, back into the turmoil of events! When I heard my voice rising, I did not rein it in. There is the pain of being in the world, but there is also the robustness. When was the last time I had felt the excitement of taking someone on? Let the intensity out! Let the belligerence out! A resuscitating breath of the old contention luring me into the old role, both Kliman and Jamie having the effect of rousing the virility in me again, the virility of mind and spirit and desire and intention and wanting to be with people again and have a fight again and have a woman again and feeling the pleasure of one's power again. It's all called back—the virile man called back to life! Only there is no virility. There is only the brevity of expectations. And that being so, I thought, in taking on the young and courting all the dangers of someone of this age intermingling too closely with people of that age, I can only end up bloodied, a big fat target of a scar for unknowing youth, savage with health and armed to the teeth with time. "I'm warning you, Kliman—leave Lonoff alone."

People walking round the oval looked our way as they passed. Some slowed to a stop, fearful that an elderly man and a young man were about to commence swinging at each other, most likely out of some dispute over the election, and that a slaughter was in store.

"You stink," he shouted at me, "you smell bad! Crawl back into your hole and die!" Shambling athletically, loose and limber, he sprinted off, calling back over the swell of his shoulder, "You're dying, old man, you'll soon be dead! You smell of decay! You smell like death!"

But what could a specimen like Kliman know about the smell of death? All I smelled of was urine.

I had come to New York only because of what the procedure had promised. I had come in search of an improvement. However, in succumbing to the wish to recover something lost—a wish I'd tried to put down long ago—I had opened myself up to believing I could somehow perform again as the man I once was. A solution was obvious: in just the time it took to return to the hotel—and to undress, shower, and put on fresh clothes—I decided to abandon the idea of exchanging residences and leave immediately for home.

Jamie answered when I phoned. I said I had to talk to her and Billy, and she replied, "But Billy's not here. He left about two hours ago to go look at your house. He should be at your caretaker's soon to pick up a key. He was going to call me when he arrived."

But I had no knowledge of having arranged for Billy to see the house or for Rob to give him the key so he could let himself in. When had these arrangements been made? Couldn't have been the night before. Had to have been the night we met. Yet I had no memory of making them.

Alone in my hotel room, without even Jamie's face before me, I felt myself flushing furiously, though, in fact, in recent years I had been having a problem remembering any number of small things. To address the difficulty, I had begun to keep, along with my daily calendar, a lined school composition book—the kind with the black-and-white marbled covers that has the multiplication tables inside the back—in which to list each day's chores and, in more abbreviated form, to note my phone calls, their content, and the letters I wrote and received. Without the chore book, I could (as I'd just proven) easily forget whom I had spoken to about what as recently as yesterday, or what someone was supposed to be doing for me the following day. I had started accumulating chore books some three years before, when I first realized that a perfectly reliable memory was beginning to fray, back when drawing a blank was no more than a minor nuisance and before I came to understand that the process of my forgetting things was ongoing and that if my memory continued to deteriorate at the pace at which it had advanced in these first few years, my ability to write could be gravely impaired. If one morning I should pick up the page I'd written the day before and find myself unable to remember having written it, what would I do? If I lost touch with my pages, if I could neither write a book nor read one, what would become of me? Without my work, what would be left of me?

I did not let on to Jamie that I didn't know what she was talking about and that I had begun to live in a world full of holes, my mind—from the minute I hit New York as an alien species, as a stranger to the world everyone else was inhabiting—swinging to and fro from obsession to forgetfulness. It's as though a switch has been pulled, I thought, as though they're starting to shut the circuits down one by one. "Any questions," I said, "have him call me. Rob knows more about the place than I do, and Billy will make out fine."

I wondered if I hadn't just repeated to her what I had said to them on the occasion of arranging for Billy's inspection of the house.

It was not the time to explain that I'd changed my mind. That would have to wait until Billy got home. Maybe by then he'd have found my little house unsuitable and everything could be resolved without difficulty.

"I would have thought you would have gone with him. Especially as you're not in great shape."

"I'm in the middle of a story," she said, but I didn't believe that writing was her reason for staying. Kliman was her reason for staying. She's the one who wants to move up to Massachusetts; isn't she the one who would check out the house? She's stayed to see Kliman.

"And how do you like your America now," she asked me, "on the first day of the second coming?"

"The pain will recede," I said.

"But Bush won't. Cheney won't. Rumsfeld won't. Wolfowitz won't. That Rice woman won't. The war won't recede. Nor will their arrogance. This useless, stupid war! And soon they'll work up another useless, stupid war. And another and another until everyone on earth will want to blow us up."

"Well, chances are slight of your being blown up at my place," I said, having phoned a moment earlier intending to rescind the agreement that would have furnished her the haven of my place. But I didn't want the phone call to end. She needn't say anything inviting or provocative. She had merely to speak into my ear to furnish a pleasure I hadn't known for years.

"I met your friend," I said.

"You thoroughly befuddled my friend."

"How would you know? I only just left him."

"He phoned from the park."

"As a child at the beach, I once watched while an ambitious swimmer drowned far out at sea," I told her. "Nobody had known he was in trouble until it was too late. With a cell phone, he could have dialed for help, just like Kliman, the instant the tide began to pull him away from shore."

"What do you have against him? Why do you belittle him? What do you even know of him?" Jamie asked. "He's in awe of you, Mr. Zuckerman."

"I honestly felt the fervor running in another direction."

"It was an important encounter for him," she said. "There's nothing in his life these days but Lonoff. He wants to resurrect a writer he considers great and whose work is lost."

"To resurrect him *how* is the question."

"Richard is a serious man."

"Why do you act as his advocate?"

"I 'act as his advocate' because I know him."

I preferred not to think too graphically about why she was arguing the cause of the serious man who had been a boyfriend at college and with whom (I could imagine all too easily) the link had remained sexual even after her marriage to devoted Billy . . . who was not there, by the way; who at this moment was a hundred miles north of New York while his wife was alone in their apartment across from the church, suffering Bush's reelection.

There could be nothing better to round out the folly of my coming back for the reasons I did—and then thinking that I should remain for an entire year—than my trying to get to see Jamie before Billy returned.

"So you know about the scandal," I said.

"What scandal?"

"The Lonoff scandal. Kliman hasn't told you?"

"Of course not."

"But of course he has—you especially, boasting of what he alone knows and of the great uses to be made of his discovery."

This time she didn't bother with the denial.

"You know the whole story," I said.

"If you didn't want the whole story from Richard, why should you want it from me?"

"May I come by?"

"When?"

"Now."

She left me dazed by quietly saying, "If you wish."

I began to pack my things to leave New York. I tried to fill my mind with all that I had to do at home in the coming weeks, to think of the relief to be found in my daily routines and in giving up on any further medical procedures. Never again would I create a circumstance where piercing regret, in its thirst for recompense, would be permitted to determine my next step. Then I set out for West 71st Street, yielded immediately to the ruthlessness of a desperate infatuation guaranteed to be anything but harmless to a man bearing between his legs a spigot of wrinkled flesh where once he'd had the fully functioning sexual organ, complete with bladder sphincter control, of a robust adult male. The once rigid instrument of procreation was now like the end of a pipe you see sticking out of a field somewhere, a meaningless piece of pipe that spurts and gushes intermittently, spitting forth water to no end, until a day arrives when somebody remembers to give the valve the extra turn that shuts the damn sluice down.

She'd been reading the *New York Times* for every bit of news about the election. The pages of the paper were strewn across the orange-gold intricacies of the softly worn Persian carpet, and her face bore traces of real misery.

"It's too bad Billy couldn't be here today," I said. "It's not good to be alone with so much disappointment."

She shrugged helplessly. "We thought there'd be jubilation."

While I was on my way, she'd prepared coffee for us and we sat across from each other in a pair of black leather Eames chairs by the window, sipping from our cups in silence. Expressing our uncertainty in silence. Accepting the unpredictability of what was to come in silence. Hiding our confusion in silence. I hadn't noticed on my previous visits that there were two orange cats in residence until one pounced weightlessly onto her lap and lay there being stroked by Jamie while I, observing, continued to say nothing. The other appeared from nowhere to straddle her bare feet, creating the pleasant illusion (in me) that it was her feet and not himself that he had set to purring. One was longhaired and one was shorthaired, and the sight of them astonished me. They were what the two kittens Larry Hollis had given me would have grown up to look like had I kept them for more than three days.

Though she was wearing a faded blue sweatshirt and loose-fitting gray workout pants, I was no less transfixed by her beauty. And we were alone, and so, far from feeling like some personage able to inspire awe, I felt myself stripped of my status by her hold over me, all the more so since she herself appeared so depleted by Kerry's defeat and the fearsome uncertainties it aroused.

In keeping with my wildly fluctuating behavior in New York, I now wondered what the writing of Lonoff's biography could possibly have to do with me. After my visit to his house in 1956, I'd never again been in his presence, and the one letter I sent him after that visit he had not answered, thus stifling any dream I may have had of his serving as master to my apprenticeship. As regards either a biography or a biographer, I had no responsibility to E. I. Lonoff or his heirs. It was seeing Amy Bellette after so many years—especially seeing her infirm and disfigured, evicted from the dwelling of her own body—and after that going out to buy his books and rereading them at the hotel, that had set in motion the response that Kliman would elicit with his allusions to a sinister Lonoff "secret." Surely if I had been at home and received a letter out of the blue from some Kliman or other, more or less inveigling me for the same reasons, I wouldn't have bothered to reply, let alone have threatened to all but destroy him should he dare to pursue this project further. Left merely to his own devices, Kliman wasn't likely to succeed in his grandiose plans; probably the greatest encouragement he'd had so far wasn't from a literary agent or a publishing house but from my strenuous opposition. And now here I was with Jamie, ending our silence by asking, "Whom am I dealing with? Will you tell me? Who is this boy?"

Suspiciously she said, "What do you want to know?"

"How does he come to imagine himself adequate to this job? Have you known him for long?"

"Since he was eighteen. Since his freshman year. I've known him ten years."

"Where is he from?"

"He's from Los Angeles. His father is a lawyer. An entertainment lawyer, a notoriously aggressive one. His mother is entirely different from his father. She's a professor of, I think, Egyptology, at UCLA. She meditates for a couple of hours every morning. She claims to be able to make a green ball of light levitate in front of her at the end of her meditations on a good day."

"How did you meet her?"

"Through him, of course. Whenever they'd come to town they'd take his friends out to dinner. Just as when my parents came to town, he was among my friends, and he would go out to dinner with us."

"So he grew up in a professional household."

"Well, he grew up with a headstrong, aggressive father and an intellectual and quiet mother. He's smart. He's very smart. He's very sharp. Yes, he's got his own aggressiveness, which clearly has put you off. But he's no dummy.

There's no reason why he shouldn't be able to write a book —other than why anybody shouldn't be able to write a book."

"Why is that?"

"Because it's hard."

She was studiously saying no more than she was saying, trying to impress me with her unimpressibility and determined not to submit but merely to answer. She was strongly disinclined to appear to be a pushover because of the differences in status and age. Despite her obvious complacency about her effect on men, she hadn't seemed to realize as yet that she had already triumphed and the pushover was me.

"What was he like to you?" I asked.

"When?"

"When you were friends."

"We had a wonderful time together. We had fathers comparably bullheaded to contend with, so we had plenty of survival stories to swap. That's how we got so devoted so quickly—they provided us with delightful tales of horror and mirth. Richard's robust and energetic and always up for trying new things, and he's fearless. He holds nothing back. He's adventurous and he's fearless and he's free."

"Aren't you a little over the top?"

"I'm accurately answering your questions."

"Fearless of what, may I ask?"

"Of contempt. Of disapproval. He doesn't have the limitations that other people have about being in the group of people they feel comfortable with. There's nothing hesitant about him. He's a succession of decisive deeds."

"And he gets along with the notoriously aggressive father?"

"Oh, I think they fight. They're both fighting men, so they fight. I don't think it's taken so seriously, as if I were to fight with my mother. They'll fight like dogs on the phone and the next night they're back on the phone as though nothing had ever happened. That's the way it is with them."

"Tell me more."

"What more do you want to know?"

"Whatever you're not telling me." Of course I wanted to know only about her. "Did you ever visit him in Los Angeles?"

"Yes."

"And?"

"He lives in a big house in Beverly Hills. It's, in my book, extremely ugly. It's large, it's ostentatious. Not at all cozy. His mother collects, I guess you'd call it ancient art—sculpture, little objects. And there are display cases, niches in the wall that are too large—the way everything there is too large—for what they hold. It's a place without any warmth. Too many columns. Too much marble. A huge pool in the back yard. Extremely landscaped. Very manicured. That's not his world. He went to college in the Northeast. He's come to New York. He's chosen to live in New York and work in the literary world and not become super-rich and live in a marble palace in L.A. and hound people for a living. He's got the skills to be a professional hound—he learned them from his father—but that's not what he wants."

"The parents are still married?"

"Shockingly, yes. I don't know what they have in common. She meditates and then goes off to work all day. He's at work all the time. They share the house together, I guess. I never saw them talk about anything with each other."

"Is he in touch with them?"

"I suppose so. He doesn't talk about them."

"He wouldn't call his parents on election night."

"I suppose not. Though I'm sure his parents would be much more pleasant to talk to on election night than mine. They're good L.A. liberals."

"And his friends in New York?"

Here she sighed, the first irritated sign of impatience. Till then she'd been completely unrattled and calculatingly aloof. "He's gotten occupied with a group of men he met at the gym. They're young professionals, probably between twenty-five and forty. They all play basketball together and he hangs out with them a lot. Lawyers. Media people. Some of our mutual friends from college work at magazines and in publishing. He's got a good friend who started a video game company."

"I think he should go in with that friend. I think he should be in video games. Let him be fearless there. Because he thinks this is a game. He thinks 'Lonoff' is the *name* of a game."

"You're wrong," she said, and betrayed herself with a quick smile for having so flatly let me know that. "He comes across to you like his father, this bullying man, but he's much more his mother. He's an intellectual. He's thoughtful. Yes, he's got extraordinary energy. Dynamic and exciting and strong and obstinate and sometimes scary, too. But he's not a thoughtless opportunist out for himself."

"I would have said that's just what he was."

"What kind of opportunist goes after a literary biography of a writer who by now is virtually unknown? If he were an opportunist, he'd follow in his father's footsteps. He wouldn't write a biography of a writer nobody under fifty has heard of."

"You're selling him. You're idealizing him."

"Not at all. I know him a lot better than you do and I'm trying to correct you. You need a corrective."

"He's not serious. There's no sobriety in him. It's all audacity, defiance, and highjinks. There's no gravity."

"Perhaps he doesn't have the restraint other people have or the finesse, but he's not without sobriety."

"And integrity. Is he at all corrupted by integrity? I don't think scheming is foreign to Kliman. Is integrity lurking anywhere?"

"You're not describing him, Mr. Zuckerman—you're burlesquing him. It's true that he doesn't always get why he shouldn't behave the way he does. But he has his principles. Look, Richard's not alone—he lives in a careerist world, a world where if you're not careerist you feel like a failure. A world that's all about reputation. You're an older person coming back, and you don't know what it is to be young now. You're from the 1950s and he's from now. You're Nathan Zuckerman. It's probably been a long time since you had contact with people who aren't established in their professional lives. You don't know what it is not to be safe in a reputation in a world where reputation is everything. But if you're not a Zen master in this careerist world, if you're a part of it and struggling to be recognized, are you, ipso facto, the evil enemy? Admittedly, Richard is not perhaps the most profound person I know, but there's no reason why, in the world of his experience, he would anticipate that his headlong pursuit of what he's pursuing should be offensive to anyone."

"I would say, on the subject of his profundity, that he's not half as profound as your husband. And that your husband is not a tenth as careerist as Kliman, and doesn't feel like a failure because of it."

"He doesn't feel like a success either. But basically that's true."

"Lucky girl."

"Very lucky. I love my husband very much."

All the faultless display of self-assurance had done in under ten minutes was to deepen my desire and make her far and away the biggest problem of my life. The velocity of the attraction allows for no resignation and contains no resignation—there is only room for the greed of desire.

"Surely you would agree that Kliman, at the least, is a very disagreeable person."

"I wouldn't agree," she replied.

"And the secret? The pursuit of the secret? Lonoff's great secret?"

Without altering her rhythmic stroking of the cat, she replied, "Incest."

"And how does Kliman know this?"

"He has documentation. He's been in touch with some people. Beyond that, I don't know."

"But I was with Lonoff. I met Lonoff. I've read all of Lonoff more than once. This is impossible to believe."

With just a whisper of superiority, she said, "It's always impossible to believe."

"It's nonsense," I insisted. "Incest with whom?"

"A half-sister," Jamie said.

"Like Lord Byron and Augusta."

"Not at all like them," she answered—and sharply this time—and proceeded to exhibit her (or Kliman's) erudition on the subject. "Byron and his half-sister barely knew each other as children. They were only lovers when they were adults and she was the mother of three children. The sole similarity is that Lonoff's half-sister was also older. She was from the father's first marriage. The girl's mother died when she was small, the father quickly remarried, and Lonoff was born. She was then three years old. They grew up together. They were raised as brother and sister."

"Three years old. That means she was born in 1898. She must be gone a long time now."

"She had children. The youngest son is still alive. He

must be eighty or more. In Israel. She left America to live in Palestine after they were discovered. The parents took her there to escape the disgrace. Lonoff stayed behind and set off on his own. He was seventeen by then."

The story I knew of Lonoff's origins was similar only up to a point. The parents had emigrated from Russia's Jewish Pale to Boston but in time found American society repellently materialistic, and when Lonoff was seventeen, they moved on to pre-Mandate Palestine. It was true that Lonoff had remained behind, but not because he was abandoned as a deviant wrongdoer of a son; he was a fully grown American boy and preferred to become an American-speaking American man rather than a Hebrew-speaking Palestinian Jew. I'd never heard anything about a sister or any other sibling, but then, since he was devoted to preventing his fiction from being speciously misinterpreted as a gloss on his life, Lonoff had never revealed more than the most rudimentary facts of his biography to anyone, except perhaps to his wife, Hope, or to Amy.

"When did this affair begin?" I asked.

"He was fourteen."

"Who told Kliman about it—the son in Israel?"

"Richard would have told you who told him, if you'd let him," she said. "He'd have told you all of this himself. He would have known the answers to every one of your questions."

"And told how many besides me? How many besides you?"

"I don't see what crime he's committing by telling who-ever he wants to tell. You wanted me to tell you. That's why you called and came here. Have I now committed a crime? I'm sorry that the thought of an incestuous Lonoff tortures you. It's hard for me to believe that the man who wrote your books would rather he be sanctified."

"It's a long way from reckless accusation to sanctifica-tion. Kliman can't possibly prove anything about intimate events that he claims happened close to one hundred years ago."

"Richard's not reckless. I told you: he is adventurous. He's drawn to daring ventures. What's wrong with that?"

Daring ventures. I had gorged on them.

I said, "Has Kliman spoken to the son in Israel, to Lon-off's nephew?"

"Several times."

"And he corroborates the story. He's given him a record of the copulations. Is there a log that young Lonoff kept?"

"The son denies everything, of course. The last time he and Richard spoke, he threatened to come to the U.S. and initiate a lawsuit should Richard make public any such characterization of his mother."

"And Kliman maintains that he's lying for the obvious reasons, or that he just doesn't know—what mother would confide such a secret to her son? Look, too little can be known for him to conclude anything about incest. There's the not-so that reveals the so—that's fiction; and then there's the not-so that just isn't so—that's Kliman."

Jamie promptly stood, sliding the one cat off her lap

and dislodging the other from her feet. "I don't see that this conversation is going in a helpful direction. I shouldn't have intervened. I shouldn't have invited you here to try to do Richard's bidding for him. I have sat obediently and answered your questions. I didn't raise a single objection while you took your deposition. I answered you honestly and have been nothing but respectful, if not downright slavish. I'm sorry if anything I've said or how I've said it has rubbed you the wrong way. But without intending to, that's what I've done."

I stood too—only inches away from her—and said, "It's I who's rubbed you the wrong way. Beginning with the deposition." It was the moment to tell her that the deal was off. But I could only keep her realistically in my thoughts if the deal was on and we went ahead to exchange my house for their apartment. Then she would be living amid my things and I amid hers. Could there have been a more ridiculous motive for maintaining the impetuous arrangement I wanted so badly to break? I was hardly unaware of the flimsiness of the reasons I kept turning up to materially alter my life, and yet all that was happening seemed to be happening despite my awareness and without regard for my condition.

The phone rang. It was Billy. She listened for a long time before telling him that I happened to be right there. He must then have asked her why I was, because she replied, "He wanted to look at the apartment again. I'm showing him around."

Yes, Kliman *was* the lover. She was so used to lying to

Billy—to cover her tracks with Kliman—that she'd lied to him now about me. As earlier she'd lied to me on the phone about Kliman. Either that or I was so blinded by her appeal that my mind was riveted to the one thing as it hadn't been for years. Hadn't she lied to her young husband simply because it was easier than going into the truth while I was present and they were miles apart?

There was nothing Jamie could do or say to which I did not register a disproportionate response, including her casual chitchat with Billy on the phone. I was continuously unstable. There was no repose. I might have been gazing upon young womanhood for the very first time. Or the last. All-enveloping either way.

I left without daring to touch her. Without daring to touch her face, though it was well within my reach throughout what she had characterized as my deposing her. Without daring to touch the long hair that was within my reach. Without daring to place my hand on her waist. Without daring to say that we'd met once before. Without daring to say whatever words a man mutilated as I was says to a desirable woman forty years his junior that will not leave him covered in shame because he is overcome by temptation for a delight he cannot enjoy and a pleasure that is dead. I was in deep enough with nothing having happened between us but our abrasive little talk about Kliman, Lonoff, and the allegation of incest.

I was learning at seventy-one what it is to be deranged. Proving that self-discovery wasn't over after all. Proving that the drama that is associated usually with the young as they fully begin to enter life—with adolescents, with young men like the steadfast new captain in *The Shadow-Line*—can also startle and lay siege to the aged (including the aged resolutely armed against *all* drama), even as circumstance readies them for departure.

Maybe the most potent discoveries are reserved for last.

SITUATION: *The young husband is away, the sweet, obliging husband who adores her. It's November 2004. She's scared and distraught over the election, over Al Qaeda, over an affair with a college boyfriend who's around and still in love with her, and over "daring ventures" of a kind she married to renounce. She is wearing the soft cashmere sweater, wheat or camel in color, something paler and softer than tan. Wide cuffs hang off her wrists, and loose sleeves connect to the body of the sweater quite low. The cut is reminiscent of a kimono, or better yet, a late-nineteenth-century men's smoking jacket. A thick edge of wide ribbing runs around the neck and all the way to the sweater's bottom edge, creating a collar effect, although there is no actual collar: the sweater lies flat against her. Low on the waist, a tie made of the same broad ribbing is cinched in a careless half-bow. The sweater hangs open from the neck almost to the waist, giving a long, narrow glimpse of her mostly concealed body. Because the sweater is so loosely draped, her body is mostly hidden. But he can tell she is slim—only a thin woman can carry off such roomy clothing successfully. The sweater reminds him of an extremely short bathrobe, and so, although he can see little of her, he has the impression he is in her bedroom and will soon see more. The woman wearing this sweater must be well-off (to afford such an expensive item) and also she must place high value on her physical pleasure (since she has chosen to spend her money on clothing used almost exclusively for lolling about the house).*

To be performed with appropriate pauses, as each will sometimes stop to think before answering the other's question.

MUSIC: *Strauss's* Four Last Songs. *For the profundity that is achieved not by complexity but by clarity and simplicity. For the purity of the sentiment about death and parting and loss. For the long melodic line spinning out and the female voice soaring and soaring. For the repose and composure and gracefulness and the intense beauty of the soaring. For the ways one is drawn into the tremendous arc of heartbreak. The composer drops all masks and, at the age of eighty-two, stands before you naked. And you dissolve.*

SHE

I understand why you're coming back to New York, but why did you go away in the first place?

HE

Because I began to get a series of death threats in the mail. Postcards with death threats on one side and a picture of the pope on the other. I went to the FBI, and the FBI told me what to do.

SHE

Did they ever find the person?

HE

No, they never did. But I stayed where I was.

SHE

So—screwballs send death threats to writers. We weren't alerted in the MFA program.

HE

Well, I'm not the first, even in recent years, who's received death threats. The case of Salman Rushdie is most famous.

SHE

That's true. Of course.

HE

I don't compare my situation to his. But leaving Salman Rushdie aside, I can't imagine that what happened to me has happened to me alone. You have to ask yourself if the threat is prompted by what the writer writes or if there are people who just become inflamed by certain names and who obey urges that are alien to the rest of us. They may only have to see a photograph in a newspaper to become inflamed. Imagine what can happen should they go ahead and open one of your books. They experience your words as malevolent, as a spell cast over them that they cannot bear. Even civilized people have been known to throw a book they hate across the room. For those less restrained, it's only a small step to loading the pistol. Or they may genuinely loathe what you are, as they perceive what you are—as we know from the motives of the Twin Towers terrorists. Rage is plentiful out there.

SHE

Yes, the rage is out there, and it's unrivaled and insane.

HE

And it's frightened you silly.

SHE

It has. I'm in a state. Just being nervous and afraid all the time—and the shame associated with being like that. At home I've become silent and narcissistic and obsessed with my own safety, and my writing is awful.

HE

Were you always frightened of the rage?

SHE

No, it's a recent thing. All the trust has gone out of me. You don't merely have your enemies now. The people who are meant to protect you, they've become your enemy. The people who are meant to take care of you, they've become your enemy. It's not Al Qaeda that scares me—it's my own government.

HE

Al Qaeda doesn't scare you? You're not afraid of the terrorists?

SHE

Yes. But the deeper fear is roused by the people who are supposed to be on my side. There will always be enemies out in the world, but . . . in your turning to the FBI, if at a certain point you had started to feel not that it was the FBI who was protecting you from the person who was sending the death threats but that it was the FBI who was endangering you, that would have given a whole new depth to the terror, and that's why I feel as I do now.

HE

And you think you won't have these fears up where I live?

SHE

I think living there will quell my more reasonable anxieties by taking away the aspect of physical danger, and I think that will calm me down somewhat. I don't think it will get rid of my own rage—my rage at my government —but I can't do anything right now, I feel so on edge. Since I can't even begin to know what to do, I *have* to go away. May I ask you something? (*Politely laughing beforehand at her presumptuousness*)

HE

Of course.

SHE

Do you think you would have gone away anyway if you hadn't gotten the death threats? Do you think at a certain point you would have left anyway?

HE

I don't honestly know. I was alone. I was free. My work is portable. I had reached an age where I was no longer looking for certain kinds of involvement.

SHE

How old were you when you left?

HE

Sixty. Seems quite old to you.

SHE

Yes. Yes, it does.

HE

How old are your parents?

SHE

My mother is sixty-five and my father is sixty-eight.

HE

I was just a bit younger than your mother when I left.

SHE

That's a different thing from what we're doing now. Billy is not too pleased about the whole thing. Or about what it's revealed about me.

HE

Well, he can write there too.

SHE

I think it will be good for both of us, and I think he'll see that in time. He's more adaptable to begin with.

HE

Is there anything that you wish you weren't leaving behind? What will you miss?

SHE

I'll miss some friends. But it's good to be without them for a while.

HE

Do you have a lover?

SHE

Why do you say that?

HE

Because of the way you say you'll miss some friends.

SHE

No. Yes.

HE

You do. How long have you been married?

SHE

Five years. We were young.

HE

Does Billy know you have a lover?

SHE

No, no he doesn't.

HE

Does he know your lover?

SHE

He does.

HE

What does your lover think about your going away? Does he even know you're going away? Is he angry about it?

SHE

He doesn't know yet.

HE

You haven't told him?

SHE

No.

HE

Are you telling the truth?

SHE

Yes.

HE

Why are you telling the truth?

SHE

Something about you seems trustworthy. I've read you. You're not easily scandalized. I imagine from what I've read of your work that you're a curious person rather than one who makes superficial judgments. I guess there's a pleasure in having a curious person's curiosity fixed on you.

HE

Are you trying to make me jealous?

SHE

(*Laughing*) No. Are you jealous?

HE

I am.

SHE

(*A bit startled*) Really. Of my lover?

HE

Yes.

SHE

How could that be?

HE

Does it seem so impossible to you?

SHE

It seems very strange to me.

HE

Truly?

SHE

Truly.

HE

You don't know how attractive you are.

SHE

Why did you come here today?

HE

To be alone with you.

SHE

I see.

HE

Yes, to be alone with you.

SHE

Why do you want to be alone with me?

HE

Shall I be truthful?

SHE

I've been truthful with you.

HE

Because it excites me to be alone with you.

SHE

Good. I suppose it excites me to be alone with you too. Perhaps for different reasons. We could probably both use a little excitement.

HE

Doesn't your lover supply the excitement?

SHE

He's been around my life a long time. Being my lover is a relatively recent development. There's nothing new.

HE

He was your lover in college.

SHE

But then he wasn't for many years. It's going backwards with him. The absorption is long over. It's retrograde now.

HE

So your lover is not exciting. And your marriage is not exciting. Did you expect marriage to be exciting?

SHE

(*Laughing*) Yes.

HE

You did really?

SHE

Yes.

HE

Didn't they teach you anything at Harvard?

SHE

(*Laughs softly again*) We were very in love when we got married, and the prospect of the future, of merely having a future, seemed glorious. To get married seemed like the greatest adventure possible. The newest thing we could possibly do. The great next step. (*Silence*) Are you glad you went away? Are you glad you did what you did?

HE

I would have answered differently several weeks ago. I would have answered differently several hours ago.

SHE

What's changed that answer?

HE

Meeting a young woman like you.

SHE

What interests you so much about me?

Your youth and your beauty. The speed with which we've entered into communication. The erotic environment you create out of words.

SHE

New York is full of beautiful young women.

HE

I've been without the companionship of a woman and all that goes with it for years now. This is a startling turn of events and not necessarily in my interest. Someone wrote —I don't remember who—"Great love later in life comes at cross-purposes to everything."

SHE

Great love? Can you explain yourself, please?

HE

It's a sickness. It's a fever. It's a kind of hypnosis. I can only explain it by saying that I want to be alone in a room with you. I want to be under your spell.

SHE

Well, I'm glad. I'm glad you're getting what you want. It's a good thing.

HE

It's heartbreaking.

SHE

Why?

HE

Why do you think? You're a writer. You want to be a writer. Why would a man of seventy-one find this heart-breaking?

SHE

(*Delicately*) Because you have all this feeling again and you can't take it to its next step.

HE

That's correct.

SHE

But there's pleasure in this, isn't there?

HE

Of the heartbreaking variety.

SHE

(*She's learned something*) Hmmm. (*After a long pause, with mock theatricality*) Oh, what is to be done?

HE

Do you have any suggestions?

SHE

No. I have no idea what's to be done. I'm going away because I can't think what to do about anything.

HE

You seem close to tears all the time.

SHE

(*Laughing*) Well, it helps me not, I'll tell you that.

HE

(*Laughs too, but remains silent. The flirtation is infernal, the man within the man in flames.*)

SHE

Have you been out today? The whole city is close to tears. Yes, yes, I'm close to tears. It's momentous for me, you can imagine. Can you imagine how we felt last night when—

HE

I was here. I saw it. Did you notice that I was here?

SHE

And you obviously noticed I was here. Something seized you, though, before you met me. It wasn't me. You decided to come see our apartment. Something seized you —what was it? You know, the death threats don't explain to me the extreme thing that you've done with your life. However much you explain by saying I'm a writer who's had these threats made against my life, it is an extreme thing to have done, to go off and live the way you have. I have to keep wondering, What's the real story there? So there were these postcards. So what? The postcards are a pretext. You go away for a year, if it's the postcards, and you have friends and girlfriends, and in time the postcards stop and you come back. But a man who sequesters himself, secludes himself the way you did, does so for a much larger reason. People don't give up on life for a completely circumstantial and external reason like a death threat.

HE

What might that larger reason be?

SHE

Escaping pain.

HE

What pain?

SHE

The pain of being present.

HE

Aren't you describing yourself?

SHE

Perhaps. The pain of being present in the present moment. Yes, that could be said to describe very neatly the extreme thing I'm doing. But for you it wasn't merely the present moment. It was being present at all. It was being present in the presence of *anything*.

HE

Did you ever read a short novel called *The Shadow-Line*?

SHE

By Conrad? No. I remember a boyfriend telling me about it once, but I never read it.

HE

The opening line goes, "Only the young have such moments." These are moments Conrad describes as "rash."

In the first few pages he lays everything out. "Rash moments"—the two words make up the entire sentence. He goes on, "I mean moments when the still young are inclined to commit rash actions, such as getting married suddenly or else throwing up a job for no reason." It goes like that. But these rash moments don't just happen in youth. Coming here last night was a rash moment. Daring to return is another. With age there are rash moments too. My first was leaving, my second is returning.

SHE

Billy thinks that he's indulging a rash moment on my part because if he doesn't, I'll get swamped with depression and fear. But he thinks that it's a rash moment. I never thought of myself as a desperate person. I hate to think that I'd be doing something desperate.

HE

I think you'll like it there. I'll miss you.

SHE

Well, it's your house. You can come up. You can have forgotten something and come up. We can have lunch.

HE

You can have forgotten something and come down.

SHE

Sure.

HE

Okay. You're less curt with me than you were last night.

The fact that I haven't followed Bush's lies shouldn't make me an antagonist.

SHE

Was I nasty?

HE

I didn't feel that you cared for me much. Unless I intimidated you.

SHE

Of course you did. I read all those books in college and all the ones since. You might not be aware of it, locked up alone in the Berkshires, but there are many like me, people my age, and older (*laughing*) and younger, for whom you fill an important need. We admire you.

HE

Well, I haven't seen myself in the public mirror for many years. I don't know that.

SHE

I just told you.

HE

I still don't know it. But it's wonderful to learn of your admiration, because I've quickly come to admire you.

SHE

(*Astonished*) You've come to admire me? Why?

HE

I hate to say this to you, but "someday you'll understand." (*She laughs*)

HE

You postmodernists laugh a lot.

SHE

I laugh because I find things funny.

HE

Are you laughing at me?

SHE

I'm laughing at the situation. You're speaking to me like you're my father. Someday I'll understand. Is the pleasure in the doing of it or only in the having done it? Writing, I mean. I'm changing the subject.

HE

In the doing of it. The pleasure of the having done it lasts a short time. There's pleasure in holding the bundle of pages in your hand, and there's pleasure when the first copy arrives. I pick it up and set it down a hundred times. I eat with it beside me. I've taken it to bed with me.

SHE

I know that. When my story was published, I slept with the copy of *The New Yorker* under my pillow.

HE

You're a very charming young woman.

SHE

Thank you, thank you.

HE

This is why I live in the country.

SHE

I understand.

HE

It's all a little distressing for me to come back to New York, and this is a little distressing too. I think I better go.

SHE

Okay. Perhaps we'll see each other alone and talk again.

HE

That would do it to me, my friend.

SHE

I would like to be your friend.

HE

Why?

SHE

Because I have no one like you.

HE

You don't know me.

SHE

I don't. I have no interactions like this.

HE

Must you use that language? You're a writer—give up "interactions."

SHE

(*Laughing*) I have no conversations like this. I have no situations like this.

HE

I didn't mean to correct you. It's not my business. Excuse me.

SHE

I understand. If you want to get together and talk again, my number is your number. You can always call me.

HE

It's not as if I answered a rental ad. It's as if I answered the personals. "Exceedingly attractive, well-educated WMF occasionally available for intimate conversation . . ." I got more than a new apartment, didn't I?

SHE

Maybe a friend, too.

HE

But this is not a friendship I can have.

SHE

What can you have?

HE

Not much, it seems. Precious things having been taken

away has created a predicament that can't be overcome by hard work, et cetera. Do you follow me?

SHE

I don't quite understand. Do you just mean getting older, or is there something else in particular?

HE

(*Laughing*) I suppose I just mean getting older.

SHE

I understand now.

HE

This is killing me, so I'm going to leave. I'm not going to follow my inclination and try to kiss you.

SHE

Okay.

HE

That wouldn't get us anywhere.

SHE

You're right. I'm glad you came by this afternoon, though. I'm very glad.

HE

Are you a seductress?

SHE

No, no, absolutely not.

You have a husband, you have a lover, and now you want to have me as a friend. Do you collect men? Or do men collect you?

(*Laughing*) I suppose I've collected men and that they've collected me.

You're only thirty. Have you collected many men?

I don't know what's considered many. (*She laughs again*)

I mean since you left college, between commencement day and this afternoon, which has concluded with your collecting me with your seductive power . . . But you're acting childishly now, as though you don't possess such power. Has nobody ever told you about your power?

I've been told. I was laughing because if you include yourself as a collected man, I wouldn't know how to count the men I've collected.

You have collected me.

And yet you will not call me again. And you will not kiss me. We may not even see each other again, except with my husband, when we exchange keys, so I don't see how I've collected you.

HE

Because a meeting like this for a man like me is devastating.

SHE

I certainly don't want to devastate you. I'm sorry if I have.

HE

I'm sorry I couldn't devastate *you.*

SHE

You've given me pleasure.

HE

As I said, this is killing, so I'm going to have to go.

SHE

Thank you for coming by.

On the street, starting back on foot to the hotel, thinking of the scene just enacted—and if he feels himself to be an actor, coming from having rehearsed a scene from an unproduced play, it's because she seemed so like an actress to him, a highly intuitive, intelligent young actress who listens carefully and concentrates totally and responds quietly—he is reminded of the scene in A Doll's House *when the dying, lovesick sophisticate Dr. Rank is summoned to spend a moment with her by Torvald Helmer's beautiful wife, the spoiled tease, flirtatious young Nora. The light fading, the room getting smaller, a cab*

or two going by in the street, the city receding while every-
thing around them becomes close and dark. These two people
taking their time with each other, listening to each other. So
sexual and so sad. Thick with each of their pasts, though nei-
ther knows much of the other's. The pace of it, all that silence
and what might be in there. Each of them desperate for en-
tirely different reasons. For him, however, the last desperate
scene, most certainly with a cunningly gifted actress slyly pass-
ing herself off as a novice writer. A scene constituting the
opening of He and She, *a play of desire and temptation and*
flirtation and agony—agony all the time—an improvisation
best aborted and left to die. Chekhov has a story called "He
and She." Other than the title, he remembers nothing of the
story (perhaps there is no such story), though from words of
advice about such storytelling in a letter Chekhov wrote while
still quite young, he can remember the key sentence even now.
A letter by a greatly admired writer he read in his twenties is
still fresh to him, while the time and place of appointments
he made the day before he now forgets completely. "The cen-
ter of gravity," wrote Chekhov in 1886, "should reside in two:
he and she." It should. It has. It won't ever again.

My bag was where I had left it, half packed on the hotel
dresser when I had rushed off earlier for West 71st Street.
A light flashing on my phone indicated that I had a message. But I still didn't know from whom because once I'd
got back to the room, all I'd done was to sit at the under-
sized desk by the window looking down on the 53rd Street
traffic, and once again, on hotel stationery, set down as

quickly as I could an exchange with Jamie that had not taken place. My chore book recorded what I did do and what I was scheduled to do as an aid to a failing memory; this scene of dialogue unspoken recorded what hadn't been done and was an aid to nothing, alleviated nothing, achieved nothing, and yet, just as on election night, it had seemed terribly necessary to write the instant I came through the door, the conversations she and I don't have more affecting even than the conversations we do have, and the imaginary "She" vividly at the middle of her character as the actual "she" will never be.

But isn't one's pain quotient shocking enough without fictional amplification, without giving things an intensity that is ephemeral in life and sometimes even unseen? Not for some. For some very, very few that amplification, evolving uncertainly out of nothing, constitutes their only assurance, and the unlived, the surmise, fully drawn in print on paper, is the life whose meaning comes to matter most.

3   Amy's Brain

WHEN AT LAST I lifted the phone to take the
message, there was the voice I'd overheard
while leaving the hospital the previous Thursday, the youthful voice of the aged Amy Bellette. "Nathan
Zuckerman," she said, "I learned your whereabouts from
a note left in my mailbox by a colossal pest named Richard Kliman. I don't know if you want to bother to respond
or whether you even remember me. We met in Massachusetts in 1956. In the winter. I'd been E. I. Lonoff's student at Athena College. I was working in Cambridge. You
were a fledgling writer at the Quahsay Colony. We both
stayed as the Lonoffs' guests that night. A snowy evening
in the Berkshires a very long time ago. I'll understand if you

don't care to call back." She left her number and hung up.

Once again, not thinking, not even about Kliman's motive, which was inscrutable to me—what could he possibly expect to get out of putting Amy and me together? But I did not linger on Kliman, nor did I consider what could have prompted this frail woman who was either recovering or dying from brain cancer to contact me once she learned through Kliman that I was nearby. Nor did I stop to wonder why it should be so easy provoking a response in me when I wanted only to undo the error of trying to ameliorate things and return home to resume living as more than my incapacities.

I dialed her number as though it were the code to restoring the fullness that once encompassed us all; I dialed as though spinning a lifetime counterclockwise were an act as natural and ordinary as resetting the timer on the kitchen stove. My heartbeat was discernible again, not because I was anxiously anticipating being within arm's reach of Jamie Logan but from envisioning Amy's black hair and dark eyes and the confident look on her face in 1956—from remembering her fluency and her charm and her quick mind, crammed back then with Lonoff and literature.

While the phone rang I recalled watching at the luncheonette as she removed the faded red rainhat to reveal her disfigured skull and the battering that bad luck had provided. "Too late," I'd thought, and got up and paid for my coffee and left without intruding. "Leave her to her fortitude."

The setting was a standard-issue Hilton hotel room, bland and drained of anything personal, but my determination to reach her had transported me nearly fifty years back, when gazing upon an exotic girl with a foreign accent seemed to an untried boy the answer to everything. I dialed the number now as a divided being no more or less integrated than anyone else, as the fledgling she'd met in 1956 *and* as the improbable onlooker (with the unforeseeable biography) that he had become by 2004. Yet never was I less free of that fledgling and his tangle of innocent idealism, precocious seriousness, excitable curiosity, and wanton desire, still comically ungratified, than while I waited for her to answer. When she did, I didn't know whom to picture at the other end of the line: Amy then or now. The voice conveyed the radiant freshness of a young girl about to break into a dance, but the head carved up by a surgeon's knife remained too grim an image to suppress.

"I saw you at a luncheonette on Madison and Ninety-sixth," Amy said. "I was too shy to speak. You're so important now."

"Am I? Not out where I live. How are you, Amy?" I asked, saying nothing about having been so stunned by the brutality of her transformation that I'd been too shy myself to approach her. "I remember very clearly that night we all met. The snowy night in 1956. I didn't realize he was still married to his wife at the time of his death until I read the obituary. I thought he had married you."

"We never married. He couldn't do it. That was all right.

We were together for four years, mainly in Cambridge. We lived a year in Europe, we came home, he wrote and he wrote, he taught a little, he got sick, and he died."

"He was writing a novel," I said.

"In his late fifties writing a first novel. If the leukemia hadn't killed him, that novel would have."

"Why?"

"The subject. When Primo Levi killed himself everyone said it was because of his having been an inmate at Auschwitz. I thought it was because of his *writing* about Auschwitz, the labor of the last book, contemplating that horror with all that clarity. Getting up every morning to write that book would have killed anyone."

She was speaking of Levi's *The Drowned and the Saved.*

"Manny was that miserable." It was the first time I'd ever called him Manny. In 1956 I was Nathan, she was Amy, and he and Hope were Mr. and Mrs. Lonoff.

"Things combined to make him unhappy."

"So it was a hard time for you then," I said, "having gotten what the two of you wanted."

"It was a hard time because I was young enough to think that it was what he wanted, too. He knew it was nothing more than what he thought he wanted. Once he was rid of her and at last with me, everything changed—he was gloomy, he was remote, he was irascible. He was conscience-stricken, and it was terrible. When we were living in Oslo there were nights when I lay beside him, making no movement, rigid with anger. Sometimes I prayed he would die in his sleep. Then he became ill and it was idyllic again. It was the way it had been when I was his student. Yes," she said, underscoring the fact she wouldn't hide, "that's what happened: in adversity it was strangely rapturous, and when there was no obstacle we were miserable."

"That's imaginable," I said, and I was thinking, Rapture. Yes, I remember rapture. It comes at a very high price.

"Imaginable," she replied, "but startling."

"No. Not at all. Please go on."

"The last few weeks were hideous: he was confused and slept most of the time. He would make noises sometimes and wave his hands in the air, but there was nothing he said that you could understand. A few days before he died he had a gigantic rage. We were in the bathroom. I was kneeling in front of him changing his diaper. 'This is like college hazing,' he said. 'Get out of this bathroom!' and he hit me. He'd never hit anyone in his life. I can't tell you how elated I was. He still had strength enough to strike me like that. He's not going to die! He's not going to die! For days he'd been barely conscious. Or he'd hallucinate. 'I'm on the floor,' he'd cry from bed. 'Pick me up from the floor.' The doctor came and gave him morphine. Then one morning he spoke. He had been unconscious all of the day before. He said, 'The end is so immense, it is its own poetry. It requires little rhetoric. Just state it plainly.' I didn't know if he was quoting somebody, remembering something from all his reading, or if this was the final message. I couldn't ask. It didn't matter. All I did was to hold his head and say it back to him. I couldn't help myself any longer. I cried terribly. But I said it. 'The end is so immense, it is its own poetry. It requires little rhetoric. Just state it plainly.' And Manny nodded as best he could, and I've looked for that quotation ever since, Nathan. I can't find it. Who said that, who wrote that? 'The end is so immense . . .'"

"It sounds like him. His aesthetic in a nutshell."

"And he said more. I had to keep my ear to his mouth to hear him. Barely audibly, he said, 'I want a shave and a haircut. I want to be clean.' I found a barber. It took him more than an hour because Manny couldn't hold his head up. When it was over I showed the barber to the door and gave him twenty dollars. When I got back to the bed Manny was dead. Dead but clean." Here she broke off, though only for an instant, and I had nothing to say anyway. I'd known he died, and now I knew how, and though we'd met but that once, it still came as a shock. "I had it, and I'm glad I did, the four years of it," she told me, "every day and night of it. I'd see his bald head shining under his reading lamp, I'd see him sitting there every evening after dinner, carefully underlining what he was reading and stopping to think and jotting down a sentence in his spiral notebook, and I'd think, There is only one such man."

A woman who's lived fifty years remembering four years—an entire life defined by that. "I have to tell you," I said, "Kliman's pestering me about him too."

"I figured as much when he was the one who led me to you. He wants to write the biography that I'd hoped nobody would. A biography, Nathan. I don't want that. It's a second death. It puts another stop to a life by casting it in concrete for all time. The biography's the patent on the life—and who is this boy to hold that patent? Who is he to be Manny's judge? Who is he to fix him forever in people's minds? Doesn't he seem to you exceedingly shallow?"

"It doesn't matter what he seems or even what he is. That you don't want him is all that matters. What can you do to stop him?"

"Me?" She laughed weakly. "Why, nothing. The manuscripts of all the stories are at Harvard. He can go look at those, anyone can, though when I last checked, not a single person had asked to see them for thirty-two years. Fortunately nobody seems willing to talk to Mr. Kliman, nobody that I know of, anyway. I certainly won't see him, not again. But none of that need necessarily stop him. He can make it all up out of whole cloth, and one has no legal remedy. You can't libel the dead. And if he libels the living, if he manipulates the facts to suit himself, who has resources sufficient to sue him or the publisher he sells his trash to?"

"The Lonoff children. What about them?"

"That's a saga for another time. They never much liked the awestruck young girl who steals the renowned old man. Or the renowned old man who abandons the aging wife for the awestruck young girl. He would never have left if Hope hadn't forced the issue, but the children would have preferred that he remain with their mother till he was properly asphyxiated. His tenacity, his austerity, his achievement—it was as if he'd been selected to climb Mount Everest, then he got to the top and couldn't breathe. The daughter despised me most. A spotlessly virtuous person, dresses in burlap and reads only Thoreau—I could deal with her, but I never learned how not to be affronted by the Lady Sneerwells. They either sneered at me or ignored me. These were the good women of the tolerant, liberal community of Cambridge, Massachusetts, circa 1960, when one of the routine pleasures of faculty wives was moral disapproval. Manny would say, 'You go through too much emotion over something inconsequential.' Manny was the master of the impersonal way of considering everything, but I wasn't able to acquire that skill, even from the man who taught me to read, to write, to think, to know what was worth knowing and what wasn't. 'Stop being so intimidated. These are comical people out of *School for Scandal.*' He's the one who named the wife of our distinguished dean Lady Sneerwell. When we went out to a dinner party in Cambridge, it could be, for me, unendurable. That's why I wanted us to live abroad."

"And for him it wasn't unendurable."

"He was not bothered by such things. In public he could make light of the general prejudice. He had the substance for it. But I was just the pretty girl who'd been his student at Athena. I'd known worse as a child, far worse, of course, but back then I had a family encircling me."

"What became of Hope?" I asked.

"She's in some kind of facility in Boston. She has Alzheimer's disease," Amy said, confirming what I'd been told by Kliman. "She's over a hundred."

"Perhaps I can see you," I said. "May I take you to dinner? Could I possibly take you to dinner tonight?"

Her light, pleasant laugh belied what she was about to say. "Oh, I'm no longer the girl you were mooning over that night in 1956. The next morning, when all the hoopla took place—do you remember the high, hysterical hoopla of Hope pretending to run away from home to leave him to me? That's the morning you told me—do you recall?—that I bore 'some resemblance to Anne Frank.'"

"I recall that."

"I've had brain surgery, Nathan. You won't be dining with an ingénue."

"I'm not as I was either. Though you sound no less beguiling. I never learned where that accent originated. I never found out where you were from. It must have been Oslo. Where you knew worse was as a Jewish child under the Nazis in Oslo. That must have been why you and he went there to live."

"You sound like the biographer now."

"The biographer's enemy. The biographer's obstacle. This boy would get it all so wrong, it'd exceed even Manny's worst fears. I'll help," I said, "however I can," which undoubtedly was what she'd been hoping to hear when she was prompted to contact me in the first place.

So we made a date for that night, without a word spoken about the revelation with which Kliman hoped to launch a literary career.

Yet otherwise, we'd said so much. Two people, I thought, who met only once, and they go straight to the heart of it

156

and are not cautious with each other at all. There was something exciting about that, though what it told me was that she was probably no less steeped in isolation than I. Or maybe there was immediate intimacy between two total strangers just because they had known each other before. Before what? Before it all happened.

I gave myself fifteen minutes to walk from the hotel to the restaurant where I was to meet Amy at seven. Tony was there to welcome me and to accompany me to my table. "After all these years," he said cheerily, pulling back a chair for me.

"You're going to see more of me, Tony. I'm coming down to the city for a while."

"Good for you," he said. "After 9/11 some of our regulars, they took their kids and they moved to Long Island, they moved upstate, they moved to Vermont—they moved all over, they went everywhere. I respect what they did, but it was panic, you know. It died down quick but I gotta be truthful—we lost some wonderful customers after that thing. You alone, Mr. Zuckerman?"

"There'll be two of us," I said.

But she never came. I'd neglected to bring her phone number with me, so I couldn't call to find out if there was anything wrong. I thought perhaps she was too ashamed to let me see up close a debilitated old woman with a head half shaved and a disfiguring scar. Or maybe she had thought better of trying to get me to intervene on her behalf with Kliman and revealing to me, as she would have to, the putative episodes of Lonoff's early life that she, as guardian of the memory of this meticulously private man, dreaded being made public.

I waited for over an hour—holding off ordering anything but a glass of wine on the chance that she might still show up—before it occurred to me that this was not the restaurant where we had agreed to meet. I'd come to Pierluigi's automatically, certain that I'd suggested our eating there, and now I couldn't remember whether I had asked Amy to suggest a restaurant that she might like. If I had, clearly I couldn't recall which restaurant it was. And the thought that she might have been sitting there alone all this time imagining that I had stood her up—because of how she'd described her appearance—made me rush downstairs to the telephone to call my hotel and learn if there were any messages. There was one: "I waited an hour and left. I understand."

Earlier in the day I had stopped at a drugstore to buy the toilet articles that I'd forgotten to bring from home. When I'd paid, I asked the salesclerk, "Could you put these in a box for me?" She looked at me blankly. "We don't have boxes," she said. "I meant a bag," I said, "in a bag, please." A tiny error, but unsettling anyway. I was misspeaking like this almost daily now, and despite the entries I dutifully made in my chore book, despite a persistent attempt to remain concentrated on what I was doing or planning to do, I was forgetting things frequently. While talking on the telephone, I'd begun to notice that well-intentioned people sometimes tried to be obliging by finishing or filling in my thoughts before I'd realized that I'd hesitated or paused in search of the next word, or that they would genially overlook the error when I produced (as I had for my cleaning woman Belinda only the other day) an unintended coinage like "heartbed" for "heartfelt," or when I addressed an acquaintance down in Athena by someone else's name, or when someone's name slipped my mind as I was addressing the person and I had to struggle silently to find it. Nor did vigilance seem much help against what felt less like the erosion of memory than like a slide into senselessness, as though something diabolical residing in my brain but with a mind of its own—the imp of amnesia, the demon of forgetfulness, against whose powers of destruction I could bring no effective counterforce —were prompting me to suffer these lapses solely for the fun of watching me degenerate, the ultimate gleeful goal to turn someone whose acuity as a writer was sustained by memory and verbal precision into a pointless man.

(That is why, uncharacteristically, I'm working here as rapidly as I can while I can, though unable to proceed anywhere near as rapidly as I should because of the very mental impediment that I'm struggling to outflank. Nothing is certain any longer except that this will likely be my last attempt to persist in groping for words to combine into the sentences and paragraphs of a book. Because permanent groping is what it is now, a groping that goes well beyond the anxious groping for fluency that writing is to begin with. During the last year of working on the novel recently sent off to my publisher, I discovered that I had to labor every day against the threat of incoherence. When I had finished—when, after four drafts, that is, I could go no further—I couldn't tell whether it was the reading of the completed manuscript that was itself marred by a disordered mind or whether my reading was accurate and the disordered mind was what was itself mirrored in the writing. As usual, I sent the manuscript to my shrewdest reader, ages ago a fellow student with me at the University of Chicago, whose intuition I trust absolutely. When he gave me his report on the phone, I knew that he had laid aside his customary candor and, out of kindness, was dissembling when he declared that he wasn't this book's best audience and apologized for having nothing useful to say, on the grounds that he found himself so out of touch with a protagonist toward whom I was altogether sympathetic that he'd been unable to sustain the interest to be helpful.

I did not press him, nor was I even puzzled. I understood the tactic that concealed his thoughts, though knowing as well as I do the critical attributes of my friend, and that his observations were never accidental, I would have had to be extremely naive to be untroubled by it. Instead of suggesting that I embark on a fifth draft—because of his having surmised from the fourth that making the substantial changes he'd had in mind was to lay an exorbitant demand on what remained intact of *my* attributes—he thought it best to blame a nonexistent limitation of his own, such as lack of imaginative sympathy, rather than what he had concluded was now missing in me. If I had interpreted his response correctly—if, as I believed, his reading painfully replicated mine—what was I to do with a book that I had worked on for close to three years and considered at once unsatisfactory yet finished? Having never before confronted this predicament—having been able in the past to summon the inventiveness and marshal the energy to battle through to a resolution—I thought of what two American writers of the highest rank had done when they sensed a decline in their powers or a weakness in a piece of work that stubbornly resisted remedying. I could do as Hemingway did—and not just near the end of his life, when the monumental strength and the active existence and the enjoyment of violent conflict were displaced by the bludgeonings of physical pain, alcoholic decay, mental fatigue, and suicidal depression, but in the grand years, when his force was bottomless, his belligerence radiant, and the preeminence of his prose established throughout the world—and put the manuscript aside, either to attempt to rewrite it later or to leave it unpublished for good. Or I could do what Faulkner did and doggedly submit the completed manuscript for publication, permitting the book that he'd labored over unstintingly, and that he could take no further, to reach the public as it was and to yield whatever satisfactions it could.

I needed a strategy by which to endure and go on—as who doesn't?—and, for better or worse, mistakenly or not, the latter was the one I chose, though only vaguely believing that it would have the less damaging effect on my ability to forge ahead, into the twilight of my talent, without an excess of disgrace. And that was before the struggle got as bad as it is now and the deterioration had advanced to the point where even the most uncertain safeguard is nowhere to be found—where it's a matter not just of my no longer being able, after a day or two, to remember the details of the previous chapter but, improbably, of being unable, after only a few minutes, to remember much of the previous page.

By the time I'd decided to seek medical help in New York, the leakage I'd been experiencing wasn't just from my penis, nor was the failure of function restricted to the bladder's sphincter—nor was the crisis waiting to alter me next one that I could continue to hope would isolate the loss in the body alone. This time it was my mind, and this time my foreboding was being given more than a moment's notice, though, for all I knew, not much more.)

I excused myself to Tony and left the restaurant without eating and returned to the hotel. But at the room I couldn't find Amy's number anywhere. I was sure I'd written it on a scrap of notepaper on the night table, but it was neither there nor on the bed itself nor on top of the bureau nor down on the carpet, which I examined with the fingertips of one hand as I slowly traversed it on my knees. I looked under the bed, but it wasn't there either. I checked the pockets of all the clothes I'd brought with me, even those I hadn't worn. Thoroughly I combed the room, searching places where it couldn't possibly be, like the mini-bar, until it occurred to me to take out my wallet, and there was the scrap of paper with the phone number—where it had been all along. I hadn't forgotten to take it with me to Pierluigi's, I'd forgotten that I'd taken it.

My phone light was blinking. Thinking this call might be a second, longer message from Amy, I picked up the phone and listened. It was Billy Davidoff calling from my own house. "Nathan Zuckerman, it's a wonderful place. Small, but suits us perfectly. I've taken photos—I hope you don't mind. Jamie will be delighted by the house, the pond, the swamp across the way—by everything, the whole setting. And Rob Massey is a jewel. Let's complete the formalities as soon as possible. We'll draw up whatever document's required. Rob says he's going to drive your things down when you're installed, but if there's anything you need right away, I can bring it with me tonight. I'll be here another hour if you want to call back. Speak to you later. And thanks. Living here is going to be a great help."

Help to Jamie, he meant. Anything for Jamie. So much devotion, and such pleasure in providing it. What does Billy want? Whatever Jamie wants. What pleases Billy? Whatever pleases Jamie. What absorbs attentive Billy? Jamie! Jamie! Delighting Jamie! Should that worshipful accord unbelievably never lose its power, lucky pair! But should she one day spurn his close attention, withhold her approbation, resist arousal by his passion, miserable, vulnerable, tenderized man! He'll never spend a day without her without thinking of her fifty times. She'll ride roughshod over her successors forever. He'll think about her till he dies. He'll think about her *while* he dies.

163

It was eight-thirty. If Billy was to be there for another hour, he wouldn't be arriving at West 71st Street until around twelve. I could phone her under the pretext of arranging the date for the exchange of residences that I no longer wanted. I could call and tell the truth, say to her, "I want to see you—it's unbearable not to be able to see you." Until midnight this young woman in whose proximity I'd been just three times, and fleetingly, would be sitting at home with her cats—or with the cats and Kliman.

Call off the experiment in self-torture. Get the car and go. Your great exploration is over.

The second message was from Kliman. He asked if I would talk to Amy Bellette for him: she had made promises before having surgery, and now she refused to honor them. He had a copy of the first half of the existing manuscript of Lonoff's novel, and no good was going to be served by his not being allowed to read the rest, as she had assured him he would be only two months earlier. She'd given him Lonoff family photos. She'd given him her *blessing*. "If you can, Mr. Zuckerman, please help. She's not the person she was. It's the surgery. It's all they removed, the damage that's been done. There's a huge mental deficit where there wasn't before. But maybe she'd listen to you."

Kliman? Too implausible. You smell, you smell, old man, and then he calls up and, without even apologizing, asks me for my help? After I've told him I will do everything to destroy him? Is he this audaciously manipulative, or is he just this messy, or is Kliman one of those people who attach themselves to someone they can't let go of?

One of those whom, no matter what you say to rebuff them, you can't drive away. No matter what you do, they will not give up trying to get from you what they want. And whatever they do, no matter what horrifying things they say, the habit of their lives is never to recognize that they have irredeemably crossed the line. Yes, a big, virile, handsome boy with the certitude of his good looks, quite unafraid to give offense and then come back as though nothing happened.

Or was there further contact between us that I've forgotten? But when? "Maybe she'd listen to you." But why does he imagine that Amy Bellette would listen to me when he knows that we met only once? And does he know even that? As far as Kliman is concerned, we never met. Unless I told him. Maybe she told him. She must have—she must have told him that too!

I put Amy's number beside the phone and dialed it. When she answered, I addressed to her words something like those that I'd wanted to address to Jamie Logan. "I want to come to see you. I'd like to come to see you now."

"Where were you?" she asked.

"I went to the wrong restaurant. I'm sorry. Tell me where you live. I want to talk to you."

"I live in a terrible place," she said.

"Tell me where you are, please."

She did, and I left by taxi for her First Avenue address because I had to find out whether what they were saying about Lonoff was true. Don't ask why I had to. I didn't know. And the nonsensical character of my quest didn't stop me. Nothing that was nonsensical was stopping me. An aging man, his battles behind him, who suddenly feels the urge . . . to what? Once around with the passions wasn't enough? Once around with the unknowable wasn't enough? Into the mutability *again?*

It wasn't as bad as I'd been imagining on the way there, though it seemed hardly right for such a woman, the surviving consort of this brilliant writer, to be calling this building her home. There was a spaghetti joint at street level and beside that an Irish bar and no lock on the building's entry door or the inside door leading to the stairwell. Heavily dented metal garbage cans were shoved into a dark alcove beneath the first flight of stairs. When I'd rung her bell, alongside the bank of mailboxes, I saw that one of the boxes was missing its lock and its slotted door hung ajar. I wasn't sure that the bell I pressed worked and was surprised when, from above, I heard Amy's voice calling to me, "Careful. Loose treads on the stairs."

A few naked bulbs screwed into ceiling fixtures lit the stairway well enough, but the hallways leading off it were dark. The odor permeating the interior passages of the building could have been from the urine of cats or rats or from both.

She was waiting on the third landing, her half-shaved head and her single gray braid the first I saw of this old woman, who was now even more pitiful to behold in a long, shapeless lemon-colored dress meant to exude gaiety than in the hospital gown she'd redesigned for her street wear. Yet she looked to be oblivious of her appearance and almost childishly happy to see me. She extended a hand for me to shake, but instead I found myself kissing her on both cheeks, a delight I would have devoted a strenuous effort to winning back in 1956. Everything about kissing her seemed a miracle, the greatest being that, despite the physical evidence to the contrary, she was, alas, herself and no impostor. That she had survived all her ordeals to meet me in these dismal surroundings—that was a grave miracle, almost making it seem as though my seeing her, my completing a meeting, a moment with a young woman who had held such a strong attraction for me almost fifty years ago, was my unknown reason for coming to New York, why I'd come and why I'd impetuously decided to stay. Coming back to someone after that span of time, and after I've had cancer and she's had cancer, our clever young brains both the worse for wear—maybe that's why I was close to trembling and why she had donned a long yellow dress in fashion, if ever, half a century before. Each of us so in need of this figure from the past. Time—the power and the force of time—and that old yellow dress over her defenseless frame overshadowed by death! Suppose I were to turn now and see Lonoff himself walking up the stairs? What would I say to him? "I still admire you"? "I just reread you"? "I'm once again a boy with you"? What he would say—I could hear him saying it— was "Look after her. The prospect of her suffering is unendurable." In death he was more corpulent than in life. He'd put on weight in the grave. "I understand," he continued, quickly adopting a tone of benign sarcasm, "that you are no longer such a great lover. That should make it easier."

"Physical failings," I replied, "make nothing easier. I will do what I can." I had several hundred dollars in my billfold that I could leave for her now, and at the hotel I'd write a check to mail off in the morning, though I'd have to remember, on leaving, to be sure that hers wasn't the mailbox with no lock. If it was, I'd see that she received the funds another way.

"Thank you," said Lonoff as I followed the yellow dress into the apartment, a narrow railroad flat whose two interior rooms—a study and, behind an arched entryway, a kitchen—were windowless. At the front, above the First Avenue traffic and the restaurant, was a small living room with two gated windows, and at the back a still smaller room with but one gated window, the room itself big enough for just a night table and a narrow bed. Three windows. In the Lonoff Berkshire farmhouse there must have been two dozen that you never had to lock.

The bedroom looked out on an air shaft and down to a tiny back alley, where the restaurant's garbage cans were stored. A toilet, I discovered, was in a closet-sized room on the other side of a door beside the kitchen sink. A smallish bathtub raised on claw feet rested on the kitchen floor, fitted with barely inches to spare between the refrigerator and the stove. Since the front of the apartment was noisy because of the buses, trucks, and cars barreling up

First Avenue, and the back of the apartment was noisy because of the incessant racket from the restaurant kitchen, whose rear door remained open for ventilation year round, Amy took us to sit in the relative quiet of her dark study, amid piles of papers and books that crammed the shelves lining the walls and sat stacked around the base of the Formica-topped kitchen table that doubled as a desk. The lamp on the desk furnished the room's only light. It was a wide, tall, semitransparent brownish bottle wired for a bulb and topped by a shade ridged like a fan and shaped like a broad sun hat. I'd last seen it forty-eight years ago. It was Lonoff's homely desk lamp. Off to the side I saw another relic from his study, the large, dull brown horsehair easy chair, molded over the decades to the contour of his substantial torso—and, it seemed to me, to the imprint of his thought and the shape of his stoicism—the same time-worn chair from which he'd first intimidated me with the simplest questions about my youthful pursuits. I thought, "What! Are *you* here?" and then remembered where that very line appears in Eliot's "Little Gidding," at the point where the poet, walking the streets before dawn, meets the "compound ghost," who tells him what pain he will encounter. "For last year's words belong to last year's language / And next year's words await another voice." How does Eliot's ghost begin? Sardonically. "Let me disclose the gifts reserved for age." Reserved for age. Reserved for age. Beyond that I cannot go. A frightful prophecy follows that I don't remember. I'll look it up when I get home.

Silently, I addressed an observation to Lonoff that had only just come to me: "You are no longer my senior by thirty-odd years. I am yours now by ten."

"Did you eat anything?" she asked.

"I'm not hungry," I told her. "I'm too startled by being with you." I was so affected by a visitation so unimaginable that I could say no more. However imprecise or elusive my thinking could become these days, my recollection of Amy, whom I'd met but once long ago, was still sharp and marked by the sense I had in 1956 that she was somebody of unusual importance. Back then, I'd gone so far as to work out an elaborately detailed scenario that endowed her with the horrific data of the European biography of Anne Frank, but an Anne Frank who, for my purposes, had survived Europe and the Second World War to recreate herself, pseudonymously, as an orphaned college girl in New England, a foreign student from Holland, a pupil and then a lover of E. I. Lonoff, to whom one day, in her twenty-second year—after she'd gone off by herself to Manhattan to see the first production of *The Diary of Anne Frank*—she had confided her true identity. Of course I had none of the young man's motives to continue to elaborate that flamboyant fiction. The feelings that had exploited my imagination to that end in my mid-twenties had long since disappeared, along with the moral imperatives pressed upon me then by eminent elders of the Jewish community. Their denunciation of my first published stories as sinister manifestations of "Jewish self-hatred" had not been without its sting despite the galling righteousness of their Jewish self-love, which I opposed with all my loathing—and opposed by transforming Lonoff's Amy into the martyred Anne, whom, with only an ounce of irony, I imagined myself wanting to marry. As the sprightly, youthful Jewish saint, Amy became my fictional fortification against the excoriating indictment.

"Would you like a drink?" she asked. "Would you like a beer?"

I wouldn't have minded something stiffer, but I no longer took more than a glass of wine with dinner because alcohol intensified my mental lapses. "No, I'm fine. Did *you* get something to eat?"

"I don't eat," she said. *I don't.* That had become a great refrain of mine as well.

"Are you all right?" I asked.

"I was. I was fine for months. But they just told me the damn thing's returned. That's what happens—destiny's behind your back and one day pops out and cries 'Boo!' When I had the first tumor, before I even knew I had it, I did things I wouldn't like to repeat. Kicked my neighbor's dog. Little dog, out in the hallway yapping all the time and nipping at your shoes, pain-in-the-ass dog who shouldn't be out there anyway, and I reared back and gave it a good kick. I began writing to *The New York Times*. I had a fit at the public library. I went completely nuts. I went to the library to see an exhibit about E. E. Cummings. I loved his poetry when I first came here as a student: 'i sing of Olaf glad and big.' When I left the Cummings exhibit, I saw that in the corridor, arranged along the walls, there was a much bigger, more dramatic exhibit called Landmarks of Modern Literature. Large portrait photographs hanging above glass cases displaying first editions in their original jackets, and it was all terribly stupid politically correct crap. Ordinarily, I would have kept walking, and on the subway home talked to Manny about it. He was the firebrand of tact—tact, wit, patience. The human folly never surprised him. Even dead, he soothes me so."

"After forty years? Was there no one else in forty years who became important enough to soothe you?"

"Could there have been?"

"Could there not have been?"

"After *him?*"

"You were thirty when he died. To have your entire life defined by one episode . . . You were still a young woman." I stopped myself from saying "Was everything that followed crushed by those few years?" because the answer was obvious by now. Everything, every last thing.

"Inconsequential" was her reply to what I did say.

"So what have you done, then?"

"Done? What a word. Done. I've translated books: from Norwegian into English, from English into Norwegian, from Swedish into English, from English into Swedish. That's what I've done. But mostly what I do is drift. I've just drifted and drifted and now I'm seventy-five. That's how I got to be seventy-five: continually drifting. But you haven't drifted. Your life has been an arrow. You've worked."

"And that's how I got to be seventy-one. This way or

that, arrow or drifter, you still reach the end. Did you never go to that villa in Florence with someone else?"

"How do you know about the villa in Florence?"

"Because he talked about it with me that night. Abstractly, only as something he'd thought about. And then," I confessed, "I overheard the two of you. I took the liberty of overhearing your conversation with him that night."

"How did you manage that?"

"I was sleeping just below you. You wouldn't remember that. He'd made up the day bed in his study for me. I stood on his desk and put my ear to the ceiling. You said, 'Oh, Manny, we could be so happy in Florence.'"

Learning this made her enormously happy. "Oh, my. You were such a bad boy. What else? What else? To have a witness to something so long gone—what a gift! Tell me what you heard, bad boy! Tell me everything!"

Tell me, she was saying to me, tell me, please, about this intimate moment with this irreplaceable person I love who is dead, tell me on the day I've learned of the return of the tumor that is hurtling me toward my own death and in celebration of which I've donned my yellow dress!

"I wish I could," I said. "But I don't remember much more. I remember Florence because he had talked about it too—the villa in Florence and the young woman there with him who would make life beautiful and new."

"'Beautiful and new'—he said that?"

"I think so. Did you ever go to Florence?"

"We two? Never. I went myself. I went there and I stayed there after he died. I cut the flowers for his vase. I wrote in my journal. I took the walks. I rented a car and took the drives. For several years, each June, I'd go to a *pensione* there and take my translation work with me, and perform all the rites."

"And you never dared it with someone else."

"Why would I?"

"How can one live so long in a memory?"

"It's never been that. I speak to him all the time."

"And he to you?"

"Oh, yes. We've circumvented very nicely the predicament of his being extinct. We're so unlike everyone else now and so like each other."

The emotional impact of hearing this made me look at her probingly to see if she had said what she intended to say or was deliberately being immoderate or if her words had been spoken, as it were, accidentally by the brain that was missing a piece. All I saw was someone unprotected by anyone. All I saw was what Kliman saw.

"What would he think of your living like this?" I asked her. "Wouldn't he have wanted you to find someone? What would he have thought of your living alone all these years?" Then I added, "What does he tell you about it?"

"He never mentions it."

"What does he think of your living here, now, in this place?"

"Oh, we don't bother about that."

"What then?"

"Books I read. We talk about books."

"Nothing else?"

"Things that happen. I told him about the library."

"What did he say?"

"He said what he always said. He laughed. He said, 'You take such matters too seriously.'"

"What does he say about the brain tumor?"

"I mustn't be frightened. It's not good, but I mustn't be frightened."

"You believe what he tells you?"

"When we talk, there's no more pain for a while."

"Just the love."

"Yes. Absolutely."

"So what did you tell him about the library? Tell me the rest about the library."

"Oh, I stormed up and down that corridor, fuming at the photographs of these writers who'd written the great landmarks of modern literature. I lost my temper. I began to shout. Two guards rushed up, and in no time I was out on the library steps. They must have thought I was a madwoman who'd strayed in off the street. I thought so too. A mad, evil woman with her evil thoughts. That's when I was beginning to talk a mile a minute. I still do. I do it even when I'm by myself. I didn't know yet about the tumor, you see. I said that already. But it was already there at the back of my head, turning me inside out. All my life, whenever I couldn't find my way, I've always been able to ask myself, What would Manny do? What would Manny do with this ridiculous state of affairs? All my life he's been here to guide me. I was in love with a great man. That lasts. But then came the tumor, and I couldn't hear him, not above the incessant roar."

"There are noises?"

"No. I should have said 'a cloud.' It's a cloud. In your head you have a thundercloud."

"What was the terribly stupid politically correct crap?"

She laughed, the face, finely wrinkled and without a vestige of the beauty once inscribed there—the face laughed, but because of the half-shaved skull with the new-grown fuzz and that demonic scar, the laugh itself was shot through with all the wrong meanings. "You can guess. They had Gertrude Stein in the exhibit but not Ernest Hemingway. They had Edna St. Vincent Millay but not William Carlos Williams or Wallace Stevens or Robert Lowell. Just nonsense. It started in the colleges and now it's everywhere. Richard Wright, Ralph Ellison, and Toni Morrison, but not Faulkner."

"What did you shout?" I asked.

"I shouted, 'Where is E. I. Lonoff? How dare you leave out E. I. Lonoff!' I'd intended to say, 'How dare you leave out William Faulkner!' but Manny's was the name that came out. I drew quite a crowd."

"And how did you discover the tumor was there?"

"I was getting headaches. Headaches so terrible they made me vomit. You'll help me get rid of this Kliman, won't you?"

"I will try."

"The thing's come back. Did I tell you that?"

"Yes," I said.

"Somebody has to protect Manny from this man. Any biography he writes will be the resentment of an inferior person writ large. The Nietzschean prophecy come true: art killed by resentment. Before I knew I had the tumor, he paid me a visit. It was just after the library fiasco. I was already talking a mile a minute. I served him tea and he was so proper and he seemed, to my tumor, to speak so brilliantly about Manny's stories—to my tumor, he seemed a purely literary being, an earnest, Harvard-educated young man who wanted nothing more than to restore Manny's reputation. My tumor found Kliman *winning.*"

"Well, you should have found the dog winning and kicked Kliman. How did you get a diagnosis?" I asked.

"I passed out. I was putting the kettle on the stove one day, and I switched on the gas, and the next thing I knew there were two policemen standing over me in the emergency room of Lenox Hill Hospital. The super smelled the gas, and he found me there"—she pointed behind us to the kitchen with the bathtub in it—"on the floor, and they thought I'd tried to kill myself. *That* made me angry. *Everything* made me angry. I was once a nice, sweet girl, was I not?"

"You seemed well behaved to me."

"Well, I really gave it to those cops."

It occurred to me for the first time since I'd been waiting for her at Pierluigi's that it wasn't I who had gone to the wrong restaurant; it was Amy. The tumor that had come back was turning her inside out again—the tumor that had come back that had induced a state of mind that did not seem to allow for her to be terrified by its return. Twice she had told me it was back, and not as though she had come to this evening off of this momentous day, but each time as though she were talking about little more than a check that had not cleared because she'd overdrawn her account.

Out of the silence we'd been sitting through for several minutes, she said, "I have his shoes."

"I don't follow you."

"Eventually I got rid of all his clothes, but I couldn't part with his shoes."

"Where are they?"

"In my bedroom closet."

"May I see them?" I asked only because it seemed that she wanted me to ask.

"Would you like to?"

"Sure."

The bedroom was tiny and the door to the closet opened only partway before bumping into one side of the bed. A string with a frayed end hung down inside the closet, and when she pulled it a low-wattage bulb went on. The first thing I noticed hanging amid the dozen or so garments there was the dress she'd made of a hospital gown. Then, lined up on the floor, I saw Lonoff's shoes. Four pairs, all pointed forward, all black, all well worn. Four pairs of a dead man's shoes.

"They're just as he left them," she told me.

"You see them every day," I said.

"Every morning. Every night. Sometimes more."

"Is it ever eerie to see them there?"

"To the contrary, no. What could be more comforting than his shoes?"

"He had no brown shoes?" I asked.

"He never wore brown shoes."

"Do you ever put them on?" I asked. "Do you ever stand in them?"

"How did you know?"

"It's only human. That's human life."

"They are my treasures," she said.

"I would treasure them too."

"Would you like a pair, Nathan?"

"You've had them a long time. You shouldn't give them up."

"I wouldn't be giving them up. I'd be passing them on. If I should die of this tumor, I don't want everything to be lost."

"I think you should keep them. You never know how things are going to turn out. You may have them here to look at for years to come."

"I will probably die, Nathan, this time round."

"You keep all the shoes, Amy. Keep them for him right where they are."

She pulled the string that turned off the light and closed the closet door, and we passed through the kitchen and returned to her study. I felt the fatigue of one who'd just run ten miles at top speed.

"Do you remember what you talked about with Kliman?" I asked her, now that I had seen the shoes. "Do you remember what you told him, the time you met?"

"I don't think I told him anything."

"Nothing about Manny, nothing about you?"

"I don't know. I don't positively know."

"Did you give him anything?"

"Why? Does he say I did?"

"He says he has a photocopy of half the manuscript of Manny's novel. He says you promised him the rest."

"I never would have done that. I couldn't have."

"Might the tumor have done it?"

"Oh, dear. Oh, God. Oh, no."

There were some loose pages atop the table, and in her agitation she began to fiddle with them. "Are those from the novel?" I asked.

"No."

"Is the novel here?"

"I have the original in a safe-deposit box in Boston. I have a copy here, yes."

"He couldn't write it because of the subject."

She looked alarmed. "How do you know that?"

"You said so."

"Did I? I don't know what I'm doing. I don't know what's going on. I wish everyone would let me be about that book." Then she looked at the pages in her hand and, laughing brightly, she said, "This is a brilliant letter to the *Times*. It's so brilliant they never printed it. Oh, I don't care."

"When did you write it?" I asked.

"A few days ago. A week ago. They had an article about Hemingway. Maybe it was a year ago. Maybe five years ago. I don't know. The article is around somewhere. I clipped it out, and the other night I found it, and it got me so worked up I sat down and wrote the letter. A reporter went to Michigan to try to hunt down the real-life models for Hemingway's Upper Peninsula stories. So I wrote and told them what I thought about that."

"Looks long for a letter to a paper."

"I've got them even longer."

"May I read it?" I asked her.

"Oh, it's just a nutty old woman rambling on. The excrescence of the excrescence." Abruptly she went into the kitchen to turn on the kettle and make something for us to eat, leaving me alone with the letter. It was written with a ballpoint pen. At first I thought it must have been composed not in one night but bit by bit over a period of days, weeks, or months because the color of the ink changed a couple of times at least on every page. Then I thought she *had* written it in a single sitting—a response to an article perhaps five years old—and the various colors of ink attested only to the pervasiveness of her confusion. Yet the sentences themselves were coherent, and the way of thinking was anything but the excrescence of her brain's excrescence.

To the Editor:

There was a time when intelligent people used literature to think. That time is coming to an end. During the decades of the Cold War, in the Soviet Union and its Eastern European satellites, it was the serious writers who were expelled from literature; now, in America, it is literature that has been expelled as a serious influence on how life is perceived. The predominant uses to which literature is now put in the culture pages of the enlightened newspapers and in university English departments are so destructively at odds with the aims of imaginative writing, as well as with the rewards that literature affords an open-minded reader, that it would be better if literature were no longer put to any public use.

Your paper's cultural journalism—the more of it there is, the worse it gets. As soon as one enters into the ideological simplifications and biographical reductivism of cultural journalism, the essence of the artifact is lost. Your cultural journalism is tabloid gossip disguised as an interest in "the arts," and everything that it touches is contracted into what it is not. Who is the celebrity, what is the price, what is the scandal? What transgression has the writer committed, and not against the exigencies of literary aesthetics but against his or her daughter, son, mother, father, spouse, lover, friend, publisher, or pet? Without the least idea of what is innately transgressive about the literary imagination, cultural journalism is ever mindful of phony ethical issues: "Does the writer have the right to blah-blah-blah?" It is hypersensitive to the invasion of privacy perpetrated by literature over the millennia, while maniacally dedicated to exposing in print, unfictionalized, whose privacy has been invaded and how. One is struck by the regard cultural journalists have for the barriers of privacy when it comes to the novel.

Hemingway's early stories are set in Michigan's Upper Peninsula, so your cultural journalist goes to the Upper Peninsula and finds out the names of the locals who are said to have been models for the characters in the early stories. Surprise of surprises, they or their descendants feel badly served by Ernest Hemingway. These feelings, unwarranted or childish or downright imaginary as they may be, are taken more seriously than the fiction because they're easier for your cultural journalist to talk about than the fiction. The integrity of the journalist's informant is never questioned—only the integrity of the writer. The writer works alone for years on end, stakes his or her everything on the writing, pores over every sentence sixty-two times, and yet is without any sort of overriding literary consciousness, understanding, or goal. Everything the writer builds, meticulously, phrase by phrase and detail by detail, is a ruse and a lie. The writer is without literary motive. Any interest in depicting reality is nil. The writer's guiding motives are always personal and generally low.

And this knowledge comes as a comfort, for it turns out that not only are these writers not superior to the rest of us, as they pretend to be—they are worse than the rest of us. Those terrible geniuses!

The way in which serious fiction eludes paraphrase and description—hence requiring *thought*—is a nuisance to your cultural journalist. Only its imagined sources are to be taken seriously, only *that* fiction, the lazy journalist's fiction. The original nature of the imagination in those early Hemingway stories (an imagination that in a handful of pages transformed the short story and American prose) is incomprehensible to your cultural journalist, whose own writing turns our honest English words into nonsense. If you told a cultural journalist, "Look inward at the story only," he wouldn't have a thing to say. Imagination? There is no imagination. Literature? There is no literature. All the exquisite parts— even the not so exquisite parts—disappear, and there are only these people whose feelings are hurt because of what Hemingway did to them. Did Hemingway have the right . . . ? Does any author have the right . . . ? Sensationalist cultural vandalism masquerading as a responsible newspaper's devotion to "the arts."

If I had something like Stalin's power, I would not squander it on silencing the imaginative writers. I would silence those who write about the imaginative writers. I'd forbid all public discussion of literature in newspapers, magazines, and scholarly periodicals. I'd forbid all instruction in literature in every grade school, high school, college, and university in the country. I'd outlaw reading groups and Internet book chatter, and police the bookstores to be certain that no clerk ever spoke to a customer about a book and that the customers did not dare to speak to one another. I'd leave the readers alone with the books, to make of them what they would on their own. I'd do this for as many centuries as are required to detoxify the society of your poisonous nonsense.

Amy Bellette

Had I read these pages without knowing Amy, I would have taken the argument at face value and received the outburst not without some sympathy, though my putting myself out of range of what Amy called "cultural journalism" relieved me of ever having to think about it or to speak of it as she did, which was no small boon. Under the circumstances, however, the key to the letter's intention and its interest for me seemed to lie in a couple of sentences in the second paragraph, which I reread while Amy continued in the kitchen to prepare our snack of toast and jam and tea. "What transgression has the writer committed, and not against the exigencies of literary aesthetics but against his or her daughter, son, mother, father, spouse, lover, friend, publisher, or pet?" Could it be that "half-sister" didn't appear in the list of those transgressed against because she was not fully aware of what was driving her indignation, or was it because she knew very well and monitored her own composition, line by line, to be certain "half-sister" wasn't furtively smuggled in by the tumor?

It seemed to me that the letter to the Times had mainly to do with Richard Kliman.

When she came out of the kitchen, carrying our food on a tray, I said, "And what grade did Manny give you for sentences so cogent and biting?"

"He didn't give me a grade."

"Why not?"

"Because I didn't write it."

"Who did?"

"He did."

"Did he? You told me before these were the words of a nutty old woman rambling on."

"That wasn't entirely true."

"How so?"

"He dictated it. They're his words. He said, 'Reading/ writing people, we are finished, we are ghosts witnessing the end of the literary era—take this down.' I did as he told me."

I was there listening to her until well after midnight. I said hardly anything, heard a lot, and tended to believe most of it and to be able to make sense of it. There was never a deliberate attempt to mislead, as far as I could tell. Rather the rapid divulging of a massive backlog of information caused the particulars of her many stories to become so intertwined that at times it appeared that she was wholly at the mercy of the tumor. Or that the tumor simply overturned the obstacles ordinarily established by inhibition and convention. Or that she was just a desperately ill and lonely woman drinking in a man's interest after all the years of doing without, a woman who, five decades earlier, had lived for four precious years with a brilliant loved one whose integrity, which to her was the key to his majesty as both a writer and a man, was now threatened with demolition by the inexplicable "resentment of an inferior person" who'd anointed himself the loved one's biographer. Maybe the flood of words revealed nothing more than how old and deep her suffering was and how long she'd been without him.

It was curious to watch a mind being compressed and distended all at once. And sometimes alarmingly misfiring, as when, after several hours of holding forth, she looked at me wearily and, perhaps with more wit than I could discern, asked, "Was I ever married to you?"

I laughed and said, "I don't think so. I thought about it, however."

"Our being married?"

"Yes, when I was a boy, when we first met at the Lonoffs'. I thought it would be marvelous to be married to you. You were something to behold."

"I was, was I?"

"Yes, you looked tamed and well behaved, but obviously you were unusual."

"I had no idea what I was doing."

"Then?"

"Then, now, always. I had no idea of the risk I was taking with this man so much older than me. But he was irresistible. *He* was something. I was so proud of myself for inspiring his love. How had I done it? I was so proud of not being afraid of him. And all the while I was terrified: terrified of Hope and what she'd do, and terrified of what I was doing to her. And I hadn't any idea of the wound that I was marking *him* with. I *should* have married you. But Hope undid the marriage, and I ran off with E. I. Lonoff. Too naive to understand anything, thinking I was taking a great, bold womanly risk, I returned to my childhood, Nathan. The truth is, I've never left it. I'll die a child."

A child because she was with someone who was so

much older? Because she stayed in his shadow, always looking up adoringly at him? Why was this harrowing union that must have destroyed many of her illusions a force that kept her in her childhood? "Which isn't to say that you were childish," I said.

"It isn't, no."

"I don't understand, then, about your being a child."

"Then tell you I must, mustn't I?"

And here the legendary biography with which I had invested her in 1956 was replaced by the genuine biography, which, if less inflated with the moral significance my own invention held for me back then, was factually contiguous with what I'd come up with. It had to be, for everything had happened on the same doomed continent to a member of the same doomed generation of the same doomed enemy of the master race. Transforming herself out of what I'd transformed her into did not permit erasing the fate by which her family had been no less besieged than the Franks. That was a disaster whose dimensions no mind could rewrite and no imagination undo and whose memory even the tumor wouldn't displace, until it had killed her.

This was how I learned Amy was not from the Netherlands, where I had hidden her in the sealed-off attic above a warehouse on an Amsterdam canal that would later become a martyr's shrine, but from Norway—from Norway, from Sweden, from New England, from New York—which is to say, by now from nowhere, like any number of other Jewish children of her era born in Europe instead of in America, who'd miraculously escaped death during World War Two, though their youths had coincided with Hitler's maturity. This was how I learned of the circumstances of that suffering whose reality never ceases to arouse, along with rage, incredulity. In the listener. In the narrator there was no heat. And certainly no disbelief. The deeper into her misfortune she proceeded, the more deceptively matter-of-fact she became. As if all this loss could ever lose its hold.

"My grandmother came from Lithuania. On my father's side they came from Poland."

"What got them to Oslo, of all places?"

"My grandparents were on their way to America from Lithuania. When they came to Oslo they were stopped, and my grandfather was forced to stay there. American officials stopped him, and he didn't get the papers. My mother and my uncle were born in Oslo. My father had been in America, almost as a youthful adventure. He was on his way back to Poland when the First World War broke out. He was in England at that time, and he didn't want to go back and go into the army. So he stopped in Norway. 1915. And he met my mother. Jews hadn't been allowed in Norway. But there was a well-known Norwegian writer, and he campaigned for the Jews, and in 1905 Jews began to be admitted. My parents married in 1915. We were five, four brothers and me."

"And everybody was saved," I asked, making the hopeful assumption, "mother, father, your four brothers?"

"Not my mother and not my father and not my oldest brother."

And so I asked, "What happened?"

"In 1940, when the Germans came, they didn't do anything. Everything was normal-seeming. But in October 1942 they arrested all the Jewish men eighteen and up."

"The Germans or the Norwegians?"

"The Germans gave the orders, but it was Norwegian Nazis, the Quislings. Five o'clock in the morning they appeared at the door. My mother said, 'Oh, I thought you were the ambulance coming. I just called the doctor. My husband had a heart attack. He's in bed. You can't touch him.' And we younger children were crying."

"She made this story up?" I asked.

"Yes. My mother was very smart. She begged them and she begged them, and so they said okay, we'll be back at ten and see if he's gone. So she called the doctor, and my father was taken to the hospital. In the hospital he planned his escape to Sweden. But he was afraid that when they found out he'd escaped, they would come and take us. So he waited almost a month, and one morning the hospital called us and said the Gestapo was there. There was shouting that you could hear even over the phone. We didn't live far from the hospital, so my mother and my brothers and I ran to the hospital. I was thirteen. My father was lying on a stretcher. We begged them not to take him."

"Was he ill?"

"No, he wasn't ill. It wouldn't have mattered anyway.

They took him away. We went home, and it was November, and we got warm clothes for him and went back to Nazi headquarters. We tried to talk to people and we cried, we told them he was sick, he had nothing to wear but his hospital gown, but nothing helped. We said we would go home and would come back again tomorrow, but they told us, 'You can't go home, you're arrested.' My mother said no. My mother was strong and said, 'We are Norwegians like everyone else, and we are not going to be arrested.' There was a great argument but after a while they let us go home. Outside it was dark. Everything was black. My mother said we could not go home—she was sure that if we went home they would come for us in the morning.

"So there we were, out in the dark street, and just then there was an air raid. In the confusion of the air raid one of my older brothers disappeared, and my oldest brother, who had just got married, went into hiding with his wife's family. That left my mother, two younger brothers, and me. When the air raid was over, I said to my mother, 'The lady in the flower store is nice to me. I know she's not a Nazi sympathizer.' My mother said to call her. So we found a phone and I called her, and I said, 'Can we come up and have a party?' She understood, and she said yes. 'Try to be careful when you come,' she said. And so we went there and she let us stay. But we couldn't walk on the floors—we all had to sit squeezed together on the couch. She was friendly with her neighbors across the hall, and the next morning she went to see them. They had a con-

nection with the Resistance. They were non-Jewish Norwegians, he was a taxi driver, and he told us that they were
rounding up all the Jews and taking them away. That
night he came back with two other men, and they took
my two younger brothers, twelve and eleven. They said
the rest of us would have to wait. They would come back
for us. That was my mother and me. But when they came
back, they said they could take only one of us at a time. I
said to my mother, 'If I go, will you come?' 'Absolutely,'
she said. 'I would never let you down.' I learned afterward
that later that evening, she was picked up in a taxi, men
with guns, Resistance fighters who, on the way out of
Oslo, picked up another woman and a boy, a mother with
her son, whom my mother knew by name. Oslo was a
small community. Most Jews knew one another. Anyway,
they drove out of Oslo and were never seen again. Meanwhile, they had taken me and put me on a train. There
was a Nazi officer on the train with a swastika armband. I
was told that when he got off, he would give me a wink,
and I should follow him. I was sure that I was falling into
a trap. He got off close to the border with Sweden, and
I got off, and then another man took over and we began
to walk. Through the woods. We walked and we walked.
The one who takes you knows the markings on the trees.
It's a long walk, five, six miles. We walked to Sweden.
Through the woods to the farmlands. And my brother
who got lost the night of the air raid—he was the one who
met me. He thought he had lost his whole family. Then
my two younger brothers turned up, and after them, me.

But that was all. We waited for my mother and my married brother, but they never came."

When she finished, I said, "Now I understand."

"Tell me, please. You understand what?"

"For most people, to say I've stayed in my childhood my whole life would mean I've stayed innocent and it's all been pretty. For you to say I stayed in my childhood my whole life means I stayed in this terrible story—life remained a terrible story. It means that I had so much pain in my youth that, one way or another, I stayed in it forever."

"More or less," she replied.

Late as it was when I got back to the hotel, I immediately set to work to record all I could manage to remember Amy's having told me about her escape from occupied Norway to neutral Sweden and about the years with Lonoff and about the novel he'd failed to finish while they lived together in Cambridge, then Oslo, then back in Cambridge, where he died. Three or four years back, I could still have carried the bulk of her monologue in my head for days on end—my memory had been a strong resource since earliest childhood and gave ballast to one who, for professional reasons, always had to write everything down. But now, less than an hour after leaving Amy, I had to wait patiently on my recollections in order to piece together as best I could what she'd confided in me. It was a struggle at first, and I often felt helpless and wondered why I persisted in attempting what I clearly could no longer do. Yet I was too stimulated by her and her predicament not to, and too habituated to free myself from the task, too dependent on the force that guided my mind and made my mind mine. By three A.M. I had filled fifteen pages of hotel stationery, front and back, with all I could manage to recall of Amy's ordeal, wondering, as I wrote, which of these stories she had told to Kliman and how, full of his own intentions, he would transform them, garble them, distort them, misinterpret and misunderstand them, wondering what could be done to deliver her from him before he made use of her to turn everything into a sham and a shambles. I wondered which of these stories she had herself transformed, garbled, distorted, misinterpreted, and misunderstood.

"He began to write totally unlike himself," she had told me. "Before, he'd tried to see how much he could leave out. Now it was how much he could put in. He saw his laconic style as a barrier, and yet he hated what he was doing instead. He said, 'It's boring. It's endless. It has no shape. No design.' I said, 'None that you can impose. It will impose its own design.' 'When? When I'm dead?' He became so bitter and cutting—the man and the writer both, so completely changed. But he had to give some meaning to the upheaval in his life, and so he wrote his novel and got stuck for weeks, and he said, 'I can't ever publish this. Nobody needs this from me. My children hate me enough without this.' And always I was sure he regretted going off with me. Hope had shown him the door because of me. His children had turned on him because of me. I should never have stayed. Yet how could I go when this was what I'd wanted for so long? He even told me to go. But I couldn't. He could never have survived alone. And then he didn't anyway."

The evening's climax came with the plea Amy made to me when I was at the door, ready to leave. Earlier, I had asked her for an envelope, a mailing envelope, and into it I had put all my cash, except for what I'd need for a taxi to the hotel. I thought it would be easier for her to accept the money that way. I handed her the envelope and said, "Take this. In a few days I'll send you a check. I want you to cash it." I had written my Berkshires address and phone number on the face of the envelope. "I don't know what I can do about Kliman, but I am able to help you financially, and I want to. Manny Lonoff treated me like a man when I was nothing but a boy with a couple of published short stories. That invitation to his house was worth a thousand times what's in this envelope."

She did not offer the resistance I was prepared for but simply reached out and accepted the envelope, and then, for the first time, began to cry. "Nathan," she said, "won't *you* be Manny's biographer?"

"Oh, Amy, I wouldn't know where to begin. I'm not a biographer. I'm a novelist."

"But is that terrible Kliman a biographer? He's an impostor. He'll blemish everything and everyone, and pass it off as the truth. It's Manny's integrity he wants to destroy —and he doesn't even want that. It's just the way it's done

195

now—to expose the writer to censure. To compose the definitive reckoning of every last misdoing. Destroying reputations is how these little nobodies make their little mark. People's values and obligations and virtues and rules are nothing but a cover, camouflage only to hide the disgusting slime underneath. Is it because of their powers that everyone's so fascinated by their faults? Is it some sort of hypocrisy on their part that they're made of flesh and blood? Oh, Nathan, I had that damn tumor, and I made mistakes in judgment. I made mistakes with him that were unforgivable even *with* the tumor. And now I can't get rid of him. *Manny* can't get rid of him. It won't be that there was once a free and unique imagination loosed upon the world that went by the name of E. I. Lonoff—everything will be seen through the lens of the incest. With that he'll dispose of Manny's every book, of every wonderful word he wrote, and no one will ever have the faintest idea of all this man was and how hard he worked and with what precise workmanship he worked and what he worked for and why. Instead he will turn a man who was upright and dutiful and self-supervising to a fault, who wanted only to produce strong works of enduring fiction, into nothing more than a pariah. That will be the sum of Manny's achievement on earth—the sole fragment of him to be remembered! To be *reviled!* Everything will be crushed beneath *that!*"

"That" being incest.

"Shall I stay a while longer?" I asked. "May I come back in?" And we returned to her study, where she sat back down at her desk and stunned me by saying right off—and now without a single tear being shed—"Manny had an incestuous affair with his sister."

"Lasting how long?"

"Three years."

"How did they conceal it for three years?"

"I don't know. With the cunning that lovers have. With luck. They concealed it with the same excitement that they pulled it off. It was not accompanied by any torment. I fell in love with him—why shouldn't she? I was his student, less than half his age—he let that happen. Well, he let this happen too."

So there was the subject of the novel he couldn't write and the reason he couldn't write it and why he said he could never publish it. So long as he was married to Hope, Amy told me, he never mentioned to anyone having had a sister, let alone written a word about their illicit adolescent lust. After they were discovered together by a family friend and the scandal was revealed to their Roxbury neighbors, Frieda was spirited away by their parents to begin life anew with them in the morally pure atmosphere of pioneering Zionist Palestine. Manny was judged the guilty party, denounced as a demon, the corrupter of his older sister and author of the family's disgrace, and purged —left behind in Boston to fend for himself at seventeen. Had he stayed in his marriage to Hope, he would have kept writing his brilliant, elliptical short stories and never have had to come anywhere near exposing the hidden shame. "But when he became an outcast to his family again by living with a younger woman," Amy explained, "when chaos struck Manny's discipline for the second time, everything came undone. When he was abandoned by his family in Boston he was only seventeen, penniless and an anathema. Yet cruel as that expulsion was, he was strong and he survived and he made himself into everything that *wasn't* an anathema. But the second time, when it was he who abandoned his family, he was over fifty and he never recovered."

"Now this is what he wrote about his being seventeen," I said to her, "but this is not what he told you about his life at seventeen."

My assertion flustered her. "Why would I lie to you?"

"I only wonder if you're confused. You're telling me that he told you this about himself and that you knew about it before he began writing the book."

"I only knew about it when the book began to drive him crazy. No, I never knew about it before. No one in his adult life knew."

"I don't understand, then, why he told you, why he didn't just say to you, 'It's driving me crazy because it's something I cannot fathom. It's driving me crazy because I have set myself to imagining what I cannot imagine.' He tried to be equal to a task he could not perform. He was imagining not what he did do but what he could never do. He wasn't the first."

"I know what he said to me, Nathan."

"Do you? Describe to me the circumstances in which Manny told you that the book he was writing, unlike anything he had ever written before, was drawn wholly from his personal history. Remember for me the time and the place. Remember the words that were spoken."

"This was all a hundred years ago. How can I possibly remember those things?"

"But if this was his biggest secret, and if it had preyed on his mind for so long—or even if it had been repressed for so long—then the articulation of it would have been like Raskolnikov's making his confession to Sonia. After all those years of his muffling the family explosion, his confession would have been unforgettable. Tell me, then. Tell me what his confession was like."

"Why do you attack me like this?"

"Amy, you're not under attack, certainly not by me. Listen, please," and this time when I sat, I chose deliberately to settle into Lonoff's easy chair ("What! Are *you* here?") and speak to her from it. "The source for Manny's tale of incest wasn't his life. It couldn't have been. The source was the life of Nathaniel Hawthorne."

"What?" she said loudly, as though I'd startled her from sleep. "Have I missed something? Who's talking about Hawthorne?"

"I am. With good reason."

"You're confusing me hopelessly."

"I don't mean to. Listen to me. You won't be confused. I mean to make everything clear to you."

"Oh, would my tumor love that."

"Listen, please," I said. "I cannot write Manny's biography, but I can write the biography of that book. So can you. And that's what we're going to do. You know the fluctuations of a novelist's mind. He puts everything in motion. He makes everything shift and slide. It couldn't be clearer how this book came about. Manny was deeply read in the lives of writers, of the New England writers, particularly, on whose terrain he'd lived with Hope for over thirty years. Had he been born and reared in the Berkshires a hundred years earlier, Hawthorne and Melville would have been his neighbors. He was a student of their work. He read their correspondence so often, he knew portions by heart. Of course he knew what Melville had said of his friend Hawthorne. That Hawthorne had lived with a 'great secret.' And he knew what renegade scholars had drawn from that remark, and from others made by family and friends, about Hawthorne's reticence. Manny knew the cunning, scholarly, unprovable conjectures about Hawthorne and his sister Elizabeth, and so in searching for a story to encapsulate his own improbabilities—to examine all the surprising new emotions that had transformed him, as you say, into a man so utterly unlike himself—he laid claim to these conjectures about Hawthorne and his beautiful, enchanting older sister. For this wholly unautobiographical writer, blessed with his genius for complete transformation, the choice was almost inevitable. It's what opened his predicament out for him and enabled him to leave the personal behind. Fiction for him was never representation. It was rumination in narrative form. He thought, I'll make this my reality." While, in fact, I was thinking in much the same vein: I'll make this reality mine, Amy's, Kliman's, everyone's. And for the next hour I proceeded to, effulgently arguing its logic until I had come to believe it myself.

4　My Brain

Why would a woman like you marry anyone at twenty-five or twenty-four? In my era, it went without saying that you would have had a child by twenty-four or twenty-five—or twenty-two. But now . . . tell me . . . I don't know anything you know. I haven't been around.

Well, besides the obvious of having met someone I fell in love with, and who fell crazily in love with me, and some-one who . . . anyway, besides all that obvious stuff, if any-thing for exactly the opposite reason—because nobody would do such a thing in my era. If everyone did it when you were my age, I was the only person I knew from my college class, the only person among my friends who moved to New York after Harvard who (*laughing*)—who got married when she was twenty-five. It seemed kind of a wild adventure we'd go on together.

HE

(*Not quite believing her*) Is this true?

SHE

It is true. (*Laughing again*) Why would I lie about it?

HE

What did your friends make of it when you did it?

SHE

People were . . . no one was shocked. People were happy. But I was the first to do it. Daring to settle in. I like being a first.

HE

Yet you haven't any children.

SHE

No, not yet. Not now, anyway. I think we both want to establish ourselves a bit more before that happens.

HE

As writers.

SHE

Yes. Yes. That's part of the idea of going up there. We'll just work and work.

HE

As opposed to?

SHE

As opposed to working and being here and being confined in a city apartment, and running up against each other all the time, and seeing our friends all the time. I've been so nervous recently, I can't sit still. I can't work. I can't do anything. So I think if we can deal with that, I'll have a better shot at getting something done.

HE

But why did you choose this young man to marry? Is he the most exciting person you could find? You say you wanted an adventure. I've met him. I like him, he's been extremely considerate toward me in just these last twenty-four hours, but I would have thought Kliman would be more of an adventure. He was your lover in college—correct?

SHE

It would be impossible being married to Richard Kliman. He's a live wire. He's better in other capacities. Why Billy? He's smart, he was interesting, we could talk for hours, he didn't bore me. He's nice, and there seems to be an idea that a nice person can't be interesting. Of course I know all that he's not: he's not intense, he's not a fireball. But who wants a fireball? He can be gentle, he can be charming, and he adores me. He absolutely adores me.

HE

Do you adore him?

SHE

I love him very much. But he adores me in another way. He's moving to Massachusetts for a year because I want to. He doesn't want to. I probably wouldn't do that for him.

HE

But you have the money. Of course he does it for you. You two are living on your money, aren't you?

SHE

(*She looks startled by his bluntness.*) What makes you think that?

HE

Well, you've published one story in *The New Yorker*, and as yet he's published nothing in a commercial magazine. Who's paying the rent? Your family is.

SHE

Well, it's my money now. It comes from my family but it's my money now.

HE

So he's living off your money.

SHE

You're saying that's why he's going off with me to Massachusetts?

HE

No, no. I'm saying that in an important way he is beholden to you.

SHE

I suppose.

HE

Don't you feel a certain advantage because you have the money and he doesn't?

SHE

I suppose, yes. A lot of men would be very uncomfortable with that.

HE

And a lot of them would be very comfortable with it.

SHE

Yes, a lot of them would love it. (*Laughing*) And he's not either of those.

HE

Is there a lot of money?

SHE

Money's not a problem.

HE

Lucky girl.

SHE

(*Almost with wonderment, as though she is amazed whenever she remembers*) Yes. Very.

HE

Is this oil money?

SHE

Yes.

HE

Is your father a friend of George Bush's father?

SHE

Not friends. The elder Bush is somewhat older. There's business to be done. (*Emphatically*) They're not friends.

HE

They voted for them.

SHE

(*Laughing*) If Bush's friends were the only ones who voted for him, we'd be much better off. Wouldn't we? It's that world. It's the same world. My father—and (*she confesses*) I suppose I—have the same financial interests as Bush and his father. But they're not friends—I wouldn't say that.

HE

They don't socialize?

SHE

There are parties both go to.

HE

The country club?

SHE

Yeah. Houston Country Club.

HE

Is that the club for the bluebloods?

SHE

Yes. For the nineteenth-century bluebloods. The older Houstonians. A lot of debutante balls take place there.

They're put on parade. There's a swirl of white. And the rest is dancing and drinking and puking.

HE

Did you go swimming at that country club when you were a girl?

SHE

I spent every day of the summer there swimming and playing tennis, except on Mondays, when it was closed. My friend and I helped the Australian pro pick up balls when he was giving a lesson. I was fourteen. My friend was two years older and far sassier, and she slept with him. The assistant pro was the cute son of one of the club members. He was captain of the tennis team at Tulane. I didn't sleep with him, but we did all the other stuff. A cold fish. I didn't enjoy it. Adolescent sex is awful. You don't understand it, and mostly you're trying to see if you can even do it, and it's not enjoyable at all. Once I threw up, fortunately all over him, when he kept thrusting himself too far down my throat.

HE

And you were still only a girl.

SHE

Girls weren't like this in the 1940s?

HE

Nothing like this. Louisa May Alcott would have been at home in my high school. Did you come out? Were you a debutante?

SHE

Oh, you're getting into my dirty secrets. (*Laughing heartily*) Yes, yes, yes. I did. It was awful. I hated every second of it. My mom was so bent on it. We fought through the entire thing. We fought through high school. But I did it for her. (*Laughs more gently now—the range of her laughter is considerable, yet another indication of how at ease she is in her skin.*) And she appreciated it. She did. It was probably the right thing. When I went off to college the first year, my Savannah-born mother told me, "Be nice to the eastern girls, Jamie Hallie."

HE

And did you fall in with the other debutantes at Harvard?

SHE

People hide their debutante luster at Harvard.

HE

Yes?

SHE

Yes. One doesn't talk about that. You keep your sordid secret to yourself. (*Both laugh*)

HE

So you fell in with the other rich girls at Harvard.

SHE

Some of them.

HE

And? What was that like?

SHE

What do you want to know?

HE

I don't know anything. I went to another school in another era.

SHE

Honestly, I don't know what to say. They were my friends.

HE

Were they like Billy—interesting and never boring?

SHE

No. They were pretty, very well dressed, very superior. So they—we—thought.

HE

Superior to whom?

SHE

To the stringy-haired, not terribly well-dressed girls from Wisconsin who were great at science. (*Laughs*)

HE

What were you great at? Where did you get the idea that you wanted to be a writer?

SHE

Early. I think I knew that back in high school. Plugged away at it.

HE

Are you any good?

I hope so. I always thought I was. I haven't had all that much luck.

The *New Yorker* story.

That was great. I thought I'd jumped on, and then—(*trajectory gesture with one hand*) phooo . . .

How long ago was that?

That was five years ago. A time of delight. I got married. I got my first story published in *The New Yorker*. But I've lost confidence, and I can't concentrate anymore. As you know, concentration is everything, or a large part of it. And that has made me feel desperate, which makes me less able to concentrate and gives me less confidence. I feel I've moved away from being a person who could do something.

That's why you're talking to me.

How do you put the two together?

Maybe you haven't lost as much confidence as you think. You don't appear to be without confidence.

I'm not without confidence with men. I'm not without confidence with people in general. I have less and less confidence with my computer.

HE

And when you're in my house, across from the swamp, with only the tall reeds and the heron for company out the window . . .

SHE

That's part of the idea. Then I won't have men, I won't have people, I won't have parties, I won't be able to gather what I need from any of those sources, and I won't be so worked up, hopefully, and I won't be so frayed, hopefully, and I won't be in such a state, hopefully, and I figure—

HE

You misuse "hopefully."

SHE

(*She laughs. Shyly—to his surprise—she asks*) Am I? Do I?

HE

"I hope" would do. You could try "with any luck." In the old days, before well-brought-up adolescent girls had their faces fucked forcefully, you never heard "hopefully" misused like that. The vulgate "in hopes of" was sometimes substituted for "in the hope of," but that was as bad as things got when I was your age and wanted to be a writer.

SHE

Don't do that. You did it yesterday. Don't do it again.

HE

I was only correcting a little English usage.

SHE

I know. Don't do that. If you want to talk, we should talk. If I ever were to give you something that I wrote, that I would want you to read, then please correct my English. But if we're speaking—it's not an exam. If I start to think it's an exam, then I won't speak as freely. So please don't do that. (*Pause*) But yes, the thought is that if I can't draw my confidence from my social life, then I'll return the effort to my work, and hopefully the confidence will follow that. Stop laughing at me.

HE

I'm laughing because you, who were so superior to the stringy-haired girls from Wisconsin, haven't corrected yourself. Won't correct yourself.

SHE

Because I got interested in my thought and wasn't thinking about whether you'd approve of me or whether you'd approve of my wording or not.

HE

Why am I doing this to you, do you think?

SHE

To assert *your* superiority?

HE

With "hopefully"? How stupid of me.

SHE

Yes, (*laughs*) how stupid of you.

HE

I guess I'm afraid of you.

SHE

(*Long pause*) I'm a little afraid of you.

HE

Did it ever occur to you that I might be afraid of you?

SHE

No, I didn't think you'd be afraid of me. It occurred to me that you might enjoy me, that you might like to be in my presence, but it didn't occur to me that you might be afraid of me.

HE

I am.

SHE

Why?

HE

Why do you think? You're the writer. Hopefully.

SHE

(*Laughs*) So are you. (*Pause*) The only thing I can think is that I'm young and I'm female and I'm good-looking. But I won't be young forever, and then the female part won't matter so much, and the good looks—what does that have to do with anything? But maybe there are other reasons that I don't know about. Why do you think?

HE

I haven't had a chance to figure it out.

SHE

If you think of any other reasons, I'd love to know them. If you come up with just those three, you don't need to tell me. But if you think of anything else, you might help me out a lot by telling me, so please do.

HE

You exude confidence. The way you sit with your arms crossed over your head like that and holding your hair up with your hands like that so that I can see that you're no less beautiful that way too. All of you is in that pose. You exude confidence when you smile. You exude confidence with your shape, with your body. That must give you confidence.

SHE

It does. But it won't give me confidence with the swamp and the heron. Then I'll have to find my confidence here. (*She tilts her head.*)

HE

In your brain rather than in your breasts.

SHE

Yes.

HE

Do your breasts give you confidence?

SHE

Yes.

HE

Tell me about that.

SHE

About my breasts giving me confidence? I know I have something people will like, people will be jealous of, people will want. To have the confidence that you will be wanted—that's what confidence is. Confidence that you will be approved of, thought well of, desired. If you know that, then you're confident. I know that anything that has to do with these—

HE

Your breasts.

SHE

My breasts. I can do well.

HE

You're an original, Jamie. There aren't a million copies of you.

SHE

You figure out what people want, you figure out what will impress people, and you give them what will impress them, and you get what you want.

HE

So, what will impress me? What will I want? Or do you not care to impress me?

SHE

Oh, I'd like very much to impress you. I look up to you. You're a great mystery, you know. You're a source of great fascination.

HE

Why of fascination?

SHE

Because except for that heron out your window, nobody knows anything about you. Anyone who's famous, everyone knows everything about them—so they think. But with you, you've written these things that make you famous among a certain group of people. You're no Tom Cruise. (*Laughs*)

HE

Who's Tom Cruise?

SHE

He's somebody so famous that you don't even know who he is. That's who Tom Cruise is. If you read all the star magazine stuff about someone day in and day out, of course you don't know anything about them, but you can imagine that you do. But no one can imagine they know anything about you.

HE

They think they know everything each time I publish a book.

SHE

Those are the idiots. You're a mystery.

HE

You want to impress a mystery.

SHE

Yes. Yes, I want to impress you. So what will impress you?

HE

Your breasts impress me.

SHE

Tell me something I don't know.

HE

All of you impresses me.

SHE

What else?

HE

Your brain. I know I'm supposed to say that under the rules of 2004, but I don't live by those rules.

SHE

So is it or isn't it true that my brain impresses you?

HE

So far so good.

SHE

Anything else?

HE

Your beauty. Your charm. Your gracefulness. Your candor.

SHE

Well, there you have it.

HE

Billy has it.

SHE

He does.

HE

What do you mean when you say Billy adores you? What's the adoration like?

SHE

When we go to Texas he wants to see where I played as a child. He wants to sit on the swing where my nanny would swing me and the seesaw where she sat on one end and I on the other when I was four. He has me take him out to my school, Kinkaid, so he can see the third-grade classroom where we churned butter and the fourth-grade classroom where we did a science experiment with a petri dish. I took him to the library because I'd belonged to the Library Club, a special club for the best students, and at the window, he gazed out at the lush grounds of the school like the romantic poet beholding his rainbow. He had to see the big playing field where I was in the stilt race on

Field Day in the fourth grade, and it was so like a medieval pageant, with purple and gold flags fluttering everywhere, that I got so excited I fell, fell on my face ten feet from the starting line, though I was the speedy one slated to win. We had to drive from our house in River Oaks and follow exactly my route to school so he could see the lawns and the trees and the shrubs and the houses that the chauffeur had to drive by to get me the five miles out to Kinkaid. In Houston he'll only jog along the path I used when I was fifteen. It's unending with Billy. My me-ness is his magnetic pole. When I have dreams that I'm having sex, the sort of dreams that everyone has, male or female, he's jealous of my dreams. When I go to the bathroom, he's jealous of the bathroom. He's jealous of my toothbrush. He's jealous of my barrette. He's jealous of my underwear. Pieces of my underwear are in all of his pants pockets. I find them when I take his clothes to the cleaner. More, or will that suffice?

HE

So adoration means he's in love not merely with you—he's in love with your life.

SHE

Yes, my biography's a wonder to him. Rhapsodic words of love are all I hear. When I dress or I undress it's like being just behind a window that his face is pressed against.

HE

The curves no less hypnotic than the seesaw.

His praise for my silhouette is unstinting when I'm back-lit in the bedroom. When I'm in my underpants in the kitchen making the morning coffee and he comes up behind me to hold my breasts and lick my ears, he recites Keats: "There's a sigh for yes, and a sigh for no, / And a sigh for I can't bear it! / O what can be done, shall we stay or run? / O cut the sweet apple and share it!"

HE

Well, quoting from memory a love poem by Keats makes Billy a rare member of his generation.

SHE

It does. He is. He quotes me reams of Keats.

HE

Does he quote the letters? Has he quoted from Keats's last letter? He wrote it when he was five years younger than you and gravely ill. Only months later he was dead. "I have an habitual feeling of my real life having past," he said, "and that I am leading a posthumous existence."

SHE

No, I don't know his letters. As for a posthumous existence, it's not come up.

HE

Tell me, how does the object of such uxorious worship find the strength to endure it?

SHE

Oh, (*tenderly laughing*) I know how to behave.

HE

You have all this sexual attention. Yet you're restless and desperate.

SHE

We have plenty of sex. But sex is not always the source of tremendous excitement for one partner that it is for the other. It often is at the beginning.

HE

I remember that.

SHE

When was the last time you had an affair with a woman?

HE

When you were a debutante.

SHE

Has it been hard not to have an affair with a woman for that long? Have you not had sex for that long?

HE

I haven't.

SHE

Has that been hard?

HE

Everything is hard at a certain point.

SHE

But particularly hard. (*Their voices are faint now, barely able to be heard when a car passes beneath the window.*)

HE

It's among the things that are particularly hard.

SHE

Why? I know you live in the country, in the middle of nowhere, but there must be . . . well, you say there's a college nearby. I know your age, but there must be girls there that read your books and would be quite impressed. Why? Why did you decide to give that up, too, along with the city?

HE

It decided to give me up.

SHE

What do you mean?

HE

Just that.

SHE

I don't understand.

HE

And you won't.

SHE

Not if you won't tell me, I won't. Would you ever change your mind about giving that up too?

HE

I'm changing it. That's why I'm still here.

SHE

Well . . . I'm flattered. If it's true that it's been years and years, I'm extremely flattered.

HE

Jamie. Jamie Logan. Jamie Hallie Logan. Do you speak any languages, Jamie?

SHE

Not well.

HE

You speak English well. I like your Texas accent.

SHE

(*Laughs*) I worked hard to get rid of my Texas accent when I got to college.

HE

Is that right?

SHE

I did, yes.

HE

I would have thought you'd have exploited it.

SHE

It was one and the same as not telling anyone about the debutante. As not telling anyone that I went to the same country club as both George Bushes.

HE

But it's still there.

SHE

Well, I try not to have one. Except for ironic purposes. I did go off to Harvard with my "y'all" intact but I dropped it quickly enough.

HE

Too bad.

SHE

Oh, I didn't know anyone, I was just eighteen, and I turned up at Wigglesworth and everyone looked at me and I said, "Hi, y'all." They thought I was the biggest hick. I never said it again. I was quite naive compared to a lot of the freshmen there. Compared to the kids who'd gone to prep schools in Manhattan, I *was* a hick. They were terrifying. If I have it today it's because I'm unhinged today. Perhaps it's there a bit more than usual. When I get unhinged, it comes out.

HE

You don't miss a trick. You have a reason for everything.

SHE

Well, I know myself. Quite well. I think.

HE

That's three things. I know myself. Quite well. I think.

SHE

You know who does that? Conrad.

Triplets.

Yeah. Conrad's triplets. Have you noticed? (*She shows him the paperback book that's been lying out of sight beneath a magazine on the glass-topped coffee table.*) I got *The Shadow-Line*. You mentioned it, so I went to Barnes and Noble and got it. The passage you recited for me you got exactly right. You have a good memory.

For books, for books. You move quickly.

Listen to this. The triplets, the drama of the triplets. Page 35, he's just gotten his first command, and he's ecstatic. "I floated down the staircase. I floated out of the official and imposing portal. I went on floating along." Page 47, still in the grip of the ecstasy. "I thought of my unknown ship. It was amusement enough, torment enough, occupation enough." Page 53, describing the sea. "An immensity that receives no impress, preserves no memories, and keeps no reckoning of lives." He does it all the time, and near the end especially. Page 131. "'But I'll tell you, Captain Giles, how I feel. I feel old. And I must be." Page 130. "He looked like a frightful and elaborate scarecrow, set up on the poop of a death-stricken ship, to keep the seabirds from the corpses." Page 129. "Life was a boon to him—this precarious hard life—and he was thoroughly alarmed about himself." Page 125. "Mr. Burns wrung his hands, and cried out suddenly." Then one: "'How will the ship get into harbour, sir, without men to handle her?'" Next paragraph, two: "And I couldn't tell him." Next paragraph, three: "Well—it did get done about forty hours afterwards." Then all over again. Still page 125. "I shall never forget the last night, dark, windy, and starry. I steered." The paragraph goes on. Then the next paragraph begins, "And I steered . . ."

HE

(*Everything is a flirtation, including quoting Conrad.*) Read the whole thing to me.

SHE

"And I steered, too tired for anxiety, too tired for connected thought. I had moments of grim exultation and then my heart would sink awfully at the thought of that forecastle at the other end of the dark deck, full of fever-stricken men—some of them dying. By my fault. But never mind. Remorse must wait. I had to steer." I could read more. (*Sets the book down*) I enjoy reading to you. Billy doesn't like to be read to.

HE

Steer. I had to steer. Have you read any other Conrad?

SHE

I used to. Quite a bit.

HE

What did you like best?

SHE

Have you ever read a story called "Youth"? Quite wonderful.

HE

"Typhoon"?

SHE

Great.

HE

When you were down there in Texas, and you were at the pool of the country club in your bikini with all the other oil millionaires' daughters, did you read?

SHE

Funny you should mention that.

HE

Were you the only one who read?

SHE

Yes. It's true. You know, when I was younger, when I was really young, at a certain point it got ridiculous. One day I was caught, and it was so embarrassing that I stopped. I used to take my books and fold them inside *Seventeen* magazine so no one could see what I was reading. But I got over that. The embarrassment, if caught, was so much greater than if I just read the book, so I stopped doing that.

HE

Which books would you hide inside *Seventeen*?

SHE

The time I was caught I was thirteen and I was reading *Lady Chatterley's Lover* inside *Seventeen*. They made fun of me, but if they'd started to read it, they would have realized it was much juicier than *Seventeen*.

HE

Did you like *Lady Chatterley's Lover*?

SHE

I like Lawrence a lot. *Lady Chatterley's Lover* wasn't my favorite. I hate to disappoint you, but I didn't quite get it at that age. I read *Anna Karenina* when I was fifteen. Luckily I reread that later. I was always reading books I wasn't ready for. (*Laughing*) But it did me no harm. Yes, it's a good question, what did I read when I was fourteen. Hardy. I read Hardy.

HE

Which books?

SHE

I remember *Tess of the D'Urbervilles*. I remember . . . what's the other one? It's funny. Not *Jude the Obscure*. What's the other one?

HE

You mean the one with the reddler in it? Not *Far from the Madding Crowd*.

SHE

Yeah. *Far from the Madding Crowd*.

There's also the one with the reddler in it, the reddleman. What's that book called? And the heroine, the tragic heroine. Oh, my memory. (*But she does not hear his three-word lament. She is too busy remembering her fourteenth year. And with such ease.*)

SHE

Wuthering Heights. I loved *Wuthering Heights.* I was a little younger, maybe twelve or thirteen. Got there through *Jane Eyre.*

HE

Now men.

SHE

(*Yawning a little, quite familiar now*) Are you interviewing me for a job?

HE

Yes, I'm interviewing you for a job.

SHE

What job?

HE

The job of leaving the husband who adores you and coming to live instead with a man you can read aloud to.

SHE

Well—you must be crazy.

HE

I am, but so what? I'm crazy to be here. I'm crazy to be in

New York. The reason I came to New York was crazy. Sitting here and talking to you is crazy. Sitting here and being unable to leave you is crazy. I can't leave you today, I couldn't leave you yesterday, and so I'm interviewing you for the job of your leaving your young husband and coming to live a posthumous existence with a seventy-one-year-old. Let's continue. Let's continue with the interview. Tell me about men.

SHE

(*Softly now, almost as if in a trance*) What do you want to know?

HE

(*Just as softly*) I want to die of jealousy. Tell me about all the men you've had. I've heard about the boy from the Tulane tennis team who thrust his cock so far down your throat in the summer of your fourteenth year that you threw up all over him. But though that was sufficiently difficult to take, I seem to want to hear more. Yes, tell me more. Tell me everything.

SHE

Well, there was the first. The first lover. He was my teacher. In high school. It was my senior year of high school. He was twenty-four. And he was—he seduced me.

HE

How old were you then?

SHE

It was three years later. I was seventeen.

HE

Nothing to report between fourteen and seventeen?

SHE

Yes, there were further adolescent mishaps.

HE

All of them mishaps? None were exciting?

SHE

Some were exciting. It was exciting when a grown man pulled up my T-shirt at the staid old Houston Country Club and sucked on my nipples. I was dumbstruck. I didn't tell anyone. I waited for him to come back and do it again. But he must have frightened himself because when I saw him next he acted as though nothing had ever happened between us. He was a friend of my older sister's. In his early thirties. He had just gotten engaged to my sister's most beautiful friend. I cried and cried. I believed he didn't come back because there was something wrong with me.

HE

How old were you?

SHE

That was earlier. I was thirteen.

HE

Go on. Your teacher.

SHE

He was completely his own person. He wasn't trying to

impress anyone. (*Laughing*) But then, he wasn't a high school senior. He was older. That was impressive enough.

HE

To *you* much older, I would think. Tell me, does twenty-four seem older to a seventeen-year-old girl than seventy-one seems to a thirty-year-old woman? Does thirty seem older to a thirteen-year-old girl than seventy-one seems to a thirty-year-old woman? We must get to those questions sooner or later.

SHE

(*Long pause*) Yes, the teacher seemed much, much older. He was from Maine. Maine seemed exotic to me. It seemed wonderfully exotic. He wasn't from Texas and he had no money. Which was why he was doing this job. He was committed to teaching. He'd done Teach for America for two years after college. Where you make no money.

HE

What's Teach for America?

SHE

Oh dear, you *are* out of it. It's a program where college graduates volunteer two years of their time in the most deprived schools in America, in what they call "under-privileged"—

HE

"Underprivileged" bothers you.

SHE

(*Laughing heartily*) I don't like that word.

HE

Why?

SHE

Well, what does it mean? Under privileged. Either you do have privilege or you don't have privilege. If you are underprivileged, you just don't have privilege. Privilege in and of itself is something above the mean. I hate that word.

HE

You were yourself so privileged. One might even say overprivileged.

SHE

Okay. Is that to punish me for not being Louisa May Alcott? Is that for sucking off my young tennis player when I was fourteen or for the man who excited me by sucking my nipples when I was thirteen?

HE

I was only asking if that's what makes the word unnerving.

SHE

I just think it's bad usage. Bad English usage. Like "hopefully."

HE

You're charming this man to death. Torturing him and charming him both.

SHE

By telling you about my first love? You want to be charmed to death?

HE

Yes.

SHE

A good way to go. In any case, that's what Teach for America is—a domestic equivalent of the Peace Corps. So he'd done that, this young idealist, but he needed to pay off some school loans, and he didn't want to stop teaching and go off and be a banker, so he went to teach at a rich school in Houston, where you got paid a decent salary. That's all he was doing there—he had nothing to do with that social world. He was unimpressed by it. In fact, he was quite disgusted by it. In the parking lot, there were the BMWs that the students drove to school, and then there were the faculty cars, the Hondas and such, and then there was his—a twelve-year-old rusting something-or-other that had Maine plates and a rope to shut the back door because the handle was missing. Completely his own person—like no one I'd ever met before. He didn't give a damn about the Kinkaid caste system. He was my history teacher. Ours was the only section in the school that had a unit that did work in current events.

HE

How did it start?

SHE

How it started? I would just go for my weekly meeting to his office. He opened up a world of thought that I had no idea existed. I'd go and we would talk and we would talk and we would talk, and I had such feeling for him, and despite the early experiences that so perplex you—and whether you know it or not, that are by now all but universal—I was still a girl, only a girl, and I had no idea it was sexual feeling. (*Smiles*) But he knew. It was wonderful. So that was the first.

HE

How long did it go on?

SHE

Through the whole year. When I left for college, we had a plan to stay together. And I was heartbroken when we didn't. I cried through much of my first semester of college. But I wasn't thirteen anymore. This time I got myself *up* and *out*. I met these girls and I met their guys and I got myself back together. I had fun. Yeah, I got to college, and he stopped returning my calls, and I had fun.

HE

The young idealist must have had another seventeen-year-old.

SHE

You don't like him any more than you like the tennis player.

236

That shouldn't be hard to figure out for a girl who went to Kinkaid from kindergarten through grade twelve.

He wrote me a letter a year later, when I'd finally gotten over it. Said he'd done it because he thought that's what was best for me, and he had been so confused . . . But you're probably right.

I don't think I can take more of this.

Why not? (*A light laugh*) I've only told you about one.

You've only told me about three. But I get the idea. You were appealing very early.

Does that surprise you?

No, it just kills me.

Why?

Oh, Jamie.

You don't want to say it?

HE

Say what?

SHE

Say why it kills you.

HE

Because I'm crazy about you.

SHE

Well . . . I just wanted to hear it.

HE

(*Long pause, pain more on his side than hers; curiosity reigns on hers*) So. That concludes our interview for the job of she-who-leaves-her-husband-for-the-much-much-older-man. I'll call you.

SHE

You'll call me?

HE

I'll call you and let you know how you did.

SHE

Okay.

HE

Are you free for the job?

SHE

If the job gets offered to me, I'll have to figure out whether or not I can arrange my life so that I can do the job well. Then *I'll* get back to *you*.

This isn't fair. I've lost my authority.

How does it feel?

I came here with so much authority. I'm leaving with none.

Does it feel good?

A man disoriented by everything that once he knew so very well is now a lost man to boot. I'm going.

It never gets better for you alone with me.

It can't.

The better it gets, the worse it gets.

That's the situation. Yes.

(He gets up and he leaves. Outside, on the steps of her apartment building and looking across to the church, he remembers something: The Return of the Native, *the title of the Hardy novel with the reddleman in it. He has a good memory for books? No, not even for books. Only now does he re-*

call the tragic heroine's name that had always beguiled him: *Eustacia Vye*. He does not move for the street, yet works strongly to suppress the desire to turn back and lift his hand to ring the bell and tell her, "The Return of the Native, Eustacia Vye," and in that way get back upstairs alone with her. They never kiss, he never touches her, nothing: this is his last love scene. His memory failed him only that once. During all that conversation, only once. Twice: when she asked how long he'd been alone. Or had she asked that question the day before? Or hadn't she asked that question at all? Well, she needn't know any more of the forgetfulness than what she'd seen so far. So they never kiss and he never touches her—so what? He takes that hard? So what? His last love scene? Let it be. Never mind. Remorse must wait.)

5 Rash Moments

I WAS AWAKENED by the phone ringing. I had fallen asleep on the bed, clothed and with my underlined copy of *The Shadow-Line* beside me. I thought, "Amy, Jamie, Billy, Rob," but failed to include Kliman in the list of those who might find reason to call me at the hotel. Having spent until almost five A.M. at the desk writing, I felt like a man after a night of too much drinking. And I'd had a dream, I now remembered, a very small dream airy with childish hopefulness. I am on the phone to my mother. "Ma, can you do me a favor?" She laughs at my naiveté. "Sweetheart, there's nothing I wouldn't do for you. What is it, darling?" she asks. "Can we have incest?" "Oh, Nathan," she says, laughing again, "I'm a rotting old corpse. I'm in the grave." "Still, I'd like to commit incest with you. You're my mother. My only mother." "Whatever you want, darling." Then she is in front of me, and she is not a corpse in a grave. Her presence thrills me. She's the slender, pretty, vivacious twenty-three-year-old brunette my father married, she has the lightness of a young girl and that soft voice that is never severe, while I am the age I am now—and *I* am the one in the ground forever. She takes my hand as though I'm still a little boy with the most innocent aims and goals, we leave the cemetery for my bedroom, and the dream ends with my desire gaining strength and the room of large bare windows flooded with light. The last triumphant words she says are "My dear one, my dear one—birth! birth! birth!" Was there ever a mother more tender and kind?

"Hi," Kliman said. "Shall I wait down here?" "For what?" "Lunch." "What are you talking about?" "Today. At noon. You said I could take you to lunch today at noon." "I said no such thing." "You certainly did, Mr. Zuckerman. You wanted me to tell you about George Plimpton's memorial service." "George Plimpton is dead?" "Yes. We talked about this." "George died? When did he die?" "Just over a year ago." "He was how old?" "He was seventy-six. He had a fatal heart attack in his sleep." "And you told me this when?" "On the phone," Kliman said.

No need to report that I remembered no such phone call. Yet to have forgotten it seemed impossible—as impossible as George's dying. I'd met George Plimpton in the late 1950s when, after my discharge from the army, I first came to New York to live, for seventy bucks a month, in a two-room subterranean apartment and began publishing in his new literary quarterly the stories that I'd been writing at night while I was in the service; till then they'd been turned down everywhere I'd submitted them. I was twenty-four when George invited me to lunch to meet the *The Paris Review*'s other editors, young men in their late twenties and early thirties, for the most part, like him mainly from wealthy, old-line families who'd sent their sons to exclusive preparatory schools and then on to Harvard, which, in those early postwar years, as in prior decades, was mainly a bastion for educating the offspring of the socially elite. There they'd all got to know one another, if they hadn't met previously during the summer on the tennis courts or at the yacht clubs of Newport or Southampton or Edgartown. My familiarity with their world or the world of their immediate forebears was limited to the fiction I'd read by Henry James and Edith Wharton as a student at the University of Chicago, books I'd been taught to admire but that had for me as little bearing on American life as *Pilgrim's Progress* or *Paradise Lost*. Before meeting George and his colleagues I'd no idea what such people looked like or sounded like other than from hearing FDR over the radio and in the newsreels as a child—and to such a child, the son of a Jewish podiatrist educated in night school, FDR was not a representative of either class or caste but rather a politician and statesman unique unto himself, a democratic hero perceived by the preponderance of America's Jews, including my large extended family, as a blessing and a gift. George's unlikely manner of speaking might have seemed to me a comical exaggeration of a swell's, one perhaps even outright preposterous if encountered in a less forthright, gifted, intelligent, and graceful young man, steeped as it was in the Anglified enunciation and cadences of the monied Protestant hierarchy that had reigned over Boston and New York society while my own poor ancestors were being ruled by rabbis in the ghettos of Eastern Europe. George afforded my first glimpse of privilege and its vast rewards—he seemingly had nothing to escape, no flaw to hide or injustice to defy or defect to compensate for or weakness to overcome or obstacle to circumvent, appearing instead to have learned everything and to be open to everything altogether effortlessly. I'd never imagined getting anywhere without the unstinting persistence in which my hardworking family had diligently schooled me; George would have known from the outset all he was automatically destined for.

At parties at his comfortable East 72nd Street apartment, I met virtually every other young writer in New York and some of the famous established ones, and gazed longingly at the limbs of the glamorous young women who flocked around him, American debutantes, European models, and princesses whose families had been exiled in Paris since the Treaty of Versailles. In the early days I saw more of a few lesser associates of the magazine, whose writing worries and love struggles disclosed an undercurrent of hardship I could better understand, those like me for whom Difficulty had the status of a god. Yet I was there at Stillman's seedy Eighth Avenue gym to marvel at his courage on that afternoon he dared to go the three short, vigorous rounds with boxing's then light-heavyweight champion of the world, Archie Moore, a bout that left him with a broken, bloodied nose and the material for an account in *Sports Illustrated*. And I was a guest at a friend's apartment on Central Park South where George married for the first time, in the 1960s, and for several summers I sat with a hundred or so others on the dark, wide beach at Water Mill, Long Island, when George presided over his lavish annual Fourth of July fireworks display, thereby remaining a daredevil of a boy even as he pursued the interests of a playful, debonair, deeply inquisitive man of the world, a journalist, editor, and occasional film and television performer. It was little more than a year earlier (and, I now realized, only weeks before he died) that George had phoned me and, speaking nearly as formally to me as to someone he'd never met, and yet, as was his nature, as warmly as if we'd had dinner together only the night before—and by then we hadn't seen each other for a decade at least—asked if I'd come down to New York to make some introductory remarks at a fundraising gala for *The Paris Review*. I could remember that phone conversation perfectly, not only because of the good feeling exchanged but because it launched me into spending my evenings over the next couple of weeks rereading his famous works of "participatory journalism"—the books in which he assaults the mystery of his charmed life by recording his mishaps and failures as a bumbling amateur athlete up against the mighty pros—

and the several collections of shorter pieces, in which he wrote as himself, as the urbane, witty gentleman of easy intelligence and aristocratic bearing that made him anything but a bumbler to anyone who knew him.

There, his charm (as in the accounts of taking his nine-year-old daughter to a Harvard-Yale game or the poet Marianne Moore to Yankee Stadium), his lyricism (as in the evocative hymn to fireworks), his filial gravity (as in the eulogy to his father) attest to the skills of an elegant essayist able to write rings around the disadvantaged George Plimpton he concocted for the sports books, where, repeatedly cast by his ineptness in the role of the virginal victim, he goes to the most extreme lengths to acquire the semblance of humiliation and is able fleetingly to relish the masochistic ignominy of being out of his league. In his parody of Truman Capote writing of his face-lift in the style of Ernest Hemingway he was the equal of Mark Twain in his lambasting satire of James Fenimore Cooper; indeed, watching others perform foolishly rather than purportedly watching himself perform foolishly, he was at his subtle best. Yes, I remembered the good feeling permeating our call that night a year before and the pleasure I'd had rereading his books afterward, but I could not remember any call from Kliman about having lunch to discuss George's death.

Nor could I believe in George's death. The idea was excessive in every way that George wasn't, and incongruent with his curiosity's robust engagement with the "great variety of life"—a phrase he used when he was happily imagining himself as an African riverbird eyeing everything with wings and paws and hooves and feathers and scales and hide that was drawn to the rushing waters. Kliman must have meant to say something else about George Plimpton, because if I had been asked, "Who among your contemporaries will be the last to die? Who among your contemporaries is least likely to die? Who among your contemporaries will not only elude death but write with wit, precision, and modesty of his amused bafflement at successfully pulling off eternal life?" the only answer possible would have been "George Plimpton." Like the ninety-four-year-old count in *A Farewell to Arms* with whom Frederic Henry plays a game of billiards—to whom Frederic Henry, on parting, says, "I hope you live forever," and who replies, "I have"—George Plimpton was on his way to living forever from the time he was born. George had no more intention of dying than, say, Tom Sawyer; his not-dying was an assumption inseparable from his competitive encounters with the greatest of athletes. I am pitching against the New York Yankees, I am running plays for the Detroit Lions, I am in the ring with Archie Moore in order to report with authority what it is to survive everything that is superior to you and lined up to crush you.

There was more underlying those books, of course, and George was never more graciously attentive than the evening many years ago when I speculated over dinner with him on his hidden motives. It was the issue of social class that seemed to me the deepest inspiration for his writing so singularly about sports, cagily venturing into situations where he plays at being bereft of his class advantages (except for the upper-crust manners, which, in a world wholly alien, if not hostile, to good breeding, he knowingly employs for the comic effect of their unsuitability). "Me" is his self-mocking double—the working journalist —unburdened of the privileged George that he inescapably was, that he masterfully was and so enjoyed being. To be sure, his advantages—as embodied in what he modestly called his "Eastern Seaboard cosmopolitan accent" but which was more the accent of the Eastern Seaboard's disappearing ruling class—made him the butt of the jokes of the professional athletes with whom he competed as an amateur. Yet he did not attempt in *Paper Lion* or in *Out of My League* anything like what the modern era's first astonishingly percipient "participatory journalist"—the other George with a gentleman's accent, who missed not a one of the social differences, gross or minute, that he saw everywhere he went—painstakingly describes himself doing in *Down and Out in Paris and London*. Like Orwell, Plimpton tried to look straight at the thing and describe plainly what he saw and how it worked and so grasp hold of it for the reader. He did not, however, take on the lowliest jobs in the dirty, overheated restaurant kitchens of Paris, to be reduced in those turbulent pigsties to the status of a brutalized slave and to learn an object lesson in poverty, nor did he attempt, as Orwell subsequently did when he went on the road as a tramp in England, to see what it was to touch bottom. Instead, he entered a world no less glamorous than his own, the world of the ruling class of America's transcendent popular culture, the world of professional sports. *Down and Out in the Major Leagues. Down and Out in the NFL. Down and Out in the NBA.* Courting embarrassment and losing his dignity and flaunting his inadequacies with the pros, George in fact succeeded in maximizing his glamour rather than repudiating it, a ploy for which I admired him and that was at the heart of my enjoyment of the books. Books advertised as pitting the ungainly amateur against the impregnable professional were in actuality about a well-coordinated, excellently equipped athlete born into America's oldest elite playing at being a bumbler of an athlete with the majestically equipped athletes of America's newest elite, the superstars of sports. In *Out of My League* the easygoing master of self-possession goes so far as to envy the poise of the Yankee batboy; in *Paper Lion* he pretends that he hardly knew how to hold a football when he was quarterbacking the Detroit Lions, though I clearly remember touch football games on the Westchester lawn of one of his closest friends, in which George threw spirals as accurate as any a pass receiver could hope for in *any* league. Hemingway had it wrong when he described George's adventures with professional athletes as "the dark side of the moon of Walter Mitty." It was the bright side of being born George Plimpton, who uniquely managed to make a tremendously enjoyable vocation of leaving his old world of glamorous privilege to partake vicariously of the new world of glamorous privilege, the only American world that could possibly equal his own in the prestige his once had. Therein lay George's true brilliance, his ability to move across the class line of scrimmage, making himself, as he put it, "a laughingstock," without becoming, like George Orwell barely surviving among "the dregs" as an abject Paris dishwasher and a hungry, penniless London tramp, punishingly and horribly—and in deadly earnest—a déclassé. George escaped his glamour without losing his glamour, only further enhancing it in autobiographical books seemingly driven by self-deprecation. Climbing into the ring with Archie Moore he was simply practicing noblesse oblige in its most exquisite form—a form, moreover, that he had invented. When people say to themselves "I want to be happy," they could as well be saying "I want to be George Plimpton": one achieves, one is productive, and there's pleasure and ease in all of it.

Nobody on such casual good terms with the mighty and the accomplished and the renowned, nobody so in love with the excitement of deeds and words, for whom the suffering that is mortality seemed so remote, nobody with as many admirers as George had, with as many attributes as George had, nobody who could speak to anyone and everyone as easily as George did . . . On I went, thinking that the closest George would ever come to dying would be to simulate it in an article for *Sports Illustrated*.

*   *   *

I got up from the bed and, on the desk where I'd been writing for most of the night, found my chore book and began to leaf backward through the pages, looking for a notation about an appointment with Kliman and meanwhile telling him, "I can't go to lunch with you."

"But I have it. I brought it with me. You're welcome to see it."

"See what?"

"The first half of the novel. Lonoff's manuscript."

"I'm not interested."

"But you're the one who told me to bring it with me."

"I did no such thing. Goodbye."

The hotel stationery covered on both sides with recollections of my evening with Amy and the pages of repartee from *He and She*—all that writing I'd done between getting back from Amy's and falling asleep fully clothed and dreaming about my mother—was still there on the desk. In the five minutes before Kliman called again, I was able to review my notes to find out what I'd said to Amy about Kliman and the biography. I'd promised her I'd stop him from writing it. I'd impressed upon her that Lonoff's inspiration for his novel had been taken not from his own life but from highly dubious scholarly speculation about the life of Nathaniel Hawthorne. I'd given her some money . . . I read over what I'd said and done but was not immediately clear about my overall intention, if I'd even had one.

When Kliman rang from the lobby, I wondered if it could have been he who'd sent those death threats to me and to the reviewer eleven years back. His doing that then was wholly unlikely—and yet what if it were so? What if the malicious prank of a college freshman with a craving for mischief had launched me into how and where I've lived during the past decade? Ridiculous if true, and for the moment I couldn't help but be convinced it *was* true, because of its absurdity. The ludicrousness of that decision to go out to the country and never return—as ludicrous as my belief that Richard Kliman was the one who'd pushed me to make it.

"I'll be down in a few minutes," I told him, "and we'll go to lunch." And I'll frustrate your every ambition. I'll ruin you.

I thought this because I had to. I couldn't just talk about it, I couldn't just write about it—before I left Manhattan for home, I had to master Kliman, if nothing else. Mastering him was my last obligation to literature.

How could George be dead? I kept coming back to that. George's having died a year ago made everything absurd. How could that happen to *him?* And how did what happened happen to me for these past eleven years? Never to see George again—never to see anyone again! I did this because of that? I did that because of this? I defined my life around that accident or that person or that ridiculously minor event? How outlandish I seemed, and all because, without my knowing it, George Plimpton had died. Suddenly my way of being had no justification, and George was my—what is the word I'm looking for? The antonym of doppelgänger. Suddenly George Plimpton stood for all that I had squandered by removing myself as forcefully as I had and retreating onto Lonoff's mountain, to seek asylum there from the great variety of life. "It's our time," George said to me, his singular voice ringing with its spirited confidence. "It's our humanity. We have to be a part of it too."

Kliman took me to a coffee shop just down the street on Sixth Avenue, and no sooner had we ordered than he began telling me about George's memorial service. Used to systematically regulating my day's routine and apportioning every hour as I saw fit, I now found myself—in clothes I hadn't removed for almost thirty hours and, I realized, wearing a pad inside my plastic briefs that I hadn't changed since the night before—seated at lunch across from an unpredictable force bent on dominating me. Wasn't that why I was getting the full brunt before I'd even gotten my orange juice—to have demonstrated to me that, contrary to my warning and threats, I was not his equal, let alone his superior, and that he was beyond my control and attached to no restraints? I thought, The Jews can't stop making these. Eddie Cantor. Jerry Lewis. Abbie Hoffman. Lenny Bruce. The Jew at his most buoyant, capable of a calm relationship with nothing and no one. I would have supposed the type had all but disappeared from his generation and that mild, reasonable Billy Davidoff was closer to the current norm—and for all I knew, Kliman *was* the last of the agitators and affronters. I had been out of contact with anyone like him for a long time. I had been out of contact with a lot of things for a long time, and not just with the resistance of vital beings but with having either to endlessly enact the role of myself or to parry fantasies of the author extrapolated from fiction by the most naive readers—a stale labor from whose tedium I had also disengaged. For I had been something of an affronter once too. It was the affronter whom George Plimpton had first published when no one else would. But nothing like that now, I thought. No, it's not watching George in the ring at Stillman's Gym with Archie Moore in 1959, but me in the ring of an unknown Manhattan with this club-fisted kid in 2004.

"It was just about a year ago, last November," Kliman said. "At Saint John the Divine. Huge place and it's jammed —every seat taken. Two thousand people. Maybe more. Begins with a gospel group. George had seen them somewhere and loved them, and so there they were. Leader very tall, good-looking black guy, groovin' on the pomp and circumstance, and as soon as they start in singing, he starts his shouting. 'It's a celebration! It's a celebration!' and I thought, Oh Christ, here we go, somebody dies and it's a celebration. 'It's a celebration! Everybody say it's a celebration. Tell your neighbor it's a celebration!' So all the white folk begin to nod their heads out of time with the music, and, I tell you, it doesn't look too good for George. Then the minister gives the minister speech, and the speakers step up one by one. First George's sister talks about the museum he made of his room in the house on Long Island, where he kept all his animal skins and dead birds, and how passionate a boy he was about all these things, and the delivery is stunning. Totally affectless she is, has that strange absolute absence of strangeness that only the purest-bred old-fashioned Wasp can pull off. Then a guy from Texas named Victor Emanuel, probably in his fifties, maybe a little older, an authority on birds, he and George fast friends through their powerful interest in birds. Knew all the birds. This guy talks very plainly, about birding with George and the birding trips they took together, and all of it being uttered in the house of the Lord— though the only ones who care to mention the Lord are the minister and the gospel singers. On that subject everybody else is mum, man, like it has nothing to do with *them*. They just happen to *be* there. Then Norman Mailer. Overwhelming. I'd never seen Norman Mailer off the screen before. Guy's eighty now, both knees shot, walks with two canes, can't take a stride of more than six inches alone, but he refuses help going up to the pulpit, won't even use one of the canes. Climbs this tall pulpit all by himself. Everybody pulling for him step by step. The conquistador is here and the high drama begins. The Twilight of the Gods. He surveys the assemblage. Looks down the length of the nave and out to Amsterdam Avenue and across the U.S. to the Pacific. Reminds me of Father Mapple in *Moby-Dick*. I expected him to begin "Shipmates!" and preach upon the lesson Jonah teaches. But no, he too speaks very simply about George. This is no longer the Mailer in quest of a quarrel, yet his thumbprint is on every word. He speaks about a friendship with George that flourished only in recent years—tells us how the two of them and their wives had traveled together to wherever they were performing in a play they'd written together, and of how close the two couples had become, and I'm thinking, Well, it's been a long time coming, America, but there on the pulpit is Norman Mailer speaking as a husband in praise of coupledom. Fundamentalist creeps, you have met your match."

There was no stopping him. What had happened between us so far he had set out to obliterate with a big performance designed to quell me, and it was doing its job: I felt myself—despite myself—growing progressively smaller the more flamboyant the display of Kliman's self-delight. Mailer is no longer in quest of a quarrel and can barely walk. Amy is no longer beautiful or in possession of all of her brain. I no longer have the totality of my mental functions or my virility or my continence. George Plimpton is no longer alive. E. I. Lonoff no longer has his great secret, if such a secret there ever was. All of us are now "no-longers" while the excited mind of Richard Kliman believes that his heart, his knees, his cerebrum, his prostate, his bladder sphincter, his *everything* is indestructible and that he, and he alone, is not in the hands of his cells. Believing this is no soaring achievement for those who are twenty-eight, certainly not if they know themselves to be beckoned by greatness. They are not "no-longers," losing faculties, losing control, shamefully dispossessed from themselves, marked by deprivation and experiencing the organic rebellion staged by the body against the elderly; they are "not-yets," with no idea how quickly things turn out another way.

He had a battered briefcase at his feet that I believed contained the half of Lonoff's manuscript. Maybe it contained as well the photographs that Amy had given him while under the influence of the tumor. No, extricating Amy wasn't going to be simple. Any effort at persuasion wasn't going to discourage Kliman; it would only further validate his significance to himself. I tried to figure out if a lawyer might help or if money might help or a combination of both—threatening him with legal action and then paying him off. Maybe he could be blackmailed. Maybe, it occurred to me, Jamie wasn't fleeing bin Laden —maybe she was fleeing him.

SHE

Richard, I'm married.

HE

I know that. Billy's the guy to marry and I'm the guy to fuck. You tell me why all the time. "It's so thick. The base is so thick. The head is so beautiful. This is just the kind I like."

SHE

Leave me alone. You have to leave me alone. This has to be over.

HE

You don't want to come anymore? You don't want the intense sensations anymore? You don't want that ever again?

SHE

We're not going to have this discussion. We don't talk to each other like this anymore.

HE

You want to come now, right now?

SHE

No. You stop it. It's over. If you ever talk to me like this again, we won't talk ever again.

HE

I'm talking to you now. I want you to suck the beautiful head.

SHE

Get the fuck away from me. Get out of my apartment.

HE

The brutal lover makes you come and the obedient lover does not.

SHE

That's not what we're talking about. I'm married to Billy. I'm not with you. Billy's my husband. You and I are over. What you're saying doesn't matter.

HE

Yield.

SHE

No. You yield. Leave.

HE

That's not the way it works between us.

SHE

That's the way it works now.

HE

You love to yield.

SHE

Shut the fuck up. Stop it. Just stop it.

HE

I thought you were so articulate. You are when we play our games. You say all kinds of devilish things when we play call girl and client. You make all sorts of delicious sounds when we play at Jamie being taken by force. Is this all you can say now—"Shut the fuck up" and "Stop it"?

SHE

I'm telling you this is over, and it's over. Leave my house.

HE

I'm not leaving.

SHE

Then I'm leaving.

HE

Where are you going?

Away.

Come on, sweetie. You've got the prettiest cunt in the world. Let's play the strange games. Say the devilish things.

Get away from me. Get out of here right now. Billy's coming home. Get out. Get out of my house or I'll call the police.

Wait'll the police see you in just that top and those shorts. They won't leave either. You've got the prettiest cunt and the basest instincts.

Whatever I say you're just going to talk about my cunt? You try to say something to someone and they don't hear you.

This makes me hot.

This makes me angry. I'm leaving this house right now.

Here. Look.

No!
(*But he doesn't stop, and so she flees.*)

People in the coffee shop might easily have thought Kliman was my son from the way I let him go on in his self-delighted and domineering way, and also because, at strategic moments, he reached out to touch me—my arm, my hand, my shoulder—in order to drive home his point.

"Nobody let you down that day," he told me. "Most interesting of all was a journalist named McDonell. He said something like, 'I'm dedicated to being lighthearted, because it's the only way I can keep myself together up here.' Told many illustrative stories about George. Spoke out of real love. I don't mean the others didn't speak with love. But you felt from McDonell an intense male love. And admiration. And the understanding of what George was. I think he was the one who told the story about George and his T-shirt, though maybe it was the bird guy. Anyway, they went to look for some bird in Arizona. They went out into the desert around dusk. That's when this bird is supposed to be around. They couldn't find it. Suddenly George pulled off his T-shirt and threw it high in the air. And bats swooped in and swarmed the T-shirt and followed it all the way down to the ground. So George began to toss it up in the air, over and over, as high as he could. And more and more bats swarmed around it, and George cried, 'They think it's a giant moth!' It reminded me of *Henderson the Rain King*, at the end, where Henderson gets off the plane in Labrador or Newfoundland, I forget which, and he begins to dance around on this ice cap with all his African rain king exuberance, with that rare strain of privileged, wealthy, Wasp exuberance that you see in one out of ten thousand of them. And that was George's triumph. It's what George *was*. The Exuberant Wasp. I wish I could remember more of what this wonderful guy said, because he was the one who carried the message. But then that damn singing started up again. 'Oh magnify the Lord! Magnify the Lord!' and every time I heard 'magnify the Lord,' under my breath I said, 'He's not here, and everyone knows he's not here except you. Here is the *last* place he'd be.' Every size and shape of black woman was in that singing group. The ones with the enormous cans, and the little balding gnarled ones looking a hundred years old, and the thinnish, longish, elegant, pretty girls, shy girls some of them, the ones who, when you see them, you know what terror there was in the fields when the master came around looking for his fun. And the big ones who are confident and the big ones who are angry, and about half a dozen sleek black guys singing along too, and I kept thinking of slavery, Mr. Zuckerman. I don't think I've ever thought of slavery so much when I've been with blacks before. Because it was so white an assemblage they were entertaining, it seemed like minstrelsy to me. I saw the last faint remnants of slavery there in that Christianity. Back of them at the head of the apse there was a gold cross huge enough to crucify King Kong. And I have to tell you—two things I hate most about America are slavery and the cross, especially the way they were intertwined and the slave owners justified owning their Negroes by what God told them in their holy book. But that's extraneous, my hating that shit. The speakers started up again. Nine in all."

Lunch had arrived, and he took a moment to drink half his coffee but I remained silent, determined to ask no questions and just wait to see what he came up with next to steamroll me into believing he was a twenty-eight-year-old titan of literature and I should get out of his way.

"You're wondering how I met George," he said. "I met him when he came up to Harvard for a party at the *Lampoon*. He danced on a table with my girlfriend. She was the sexiest, so he picked her out. He was great. Gave a great speech. George Plimpton was a great man. People said that even dying he managed gracefully. Bullshit to that. He just didn't have a chance to put up a fight. He was a competitor. If it had happened to him during the day, he'd have had a shot at beating it. But at night, asleep? Blindsided."

I remembered then that in one of his books George had set himself to interviewing his literary friends about what he called their "death fantasies." When I got back home to my library I discovered that the book was *Shadow Box,* which opens with his description of his adventure in the ring with Archie Moore in 1959 and ends in 1974 in Zaire, where George had gone to cover the heavyweight championship fight between Muhammad Ali and George Foreman for *Sports Illustrated.* Plimpton was fifty when *Shadow Box* was published, in 1977, and probably somewhere in his late forties when he was researching and writing it, and so it must have seemed a lark of an assignment to ask other writers to tell him how they imagined themselves meeting death—scenarios that, as he recounts them, were invariably comical or dramatic or bizarre. The columnist Art Buchwald told him that he "fancied himself dropping dead on the center court at Wimbledon during the men's final—at the age of ninety-three." In the bar of Kinshasa's Intercontinental Hotel a young Englishwoman who described herself as a "free-lance poet" informed George that "it would be terrific to be electrocuted while playing a bass guitar in a rock group." Mailer was also in Kinshasa to write about the championship fight, and he seemed fondest of the idea of being killed by an animal—if on land, a lion; if at sea, a whale. As for George, he saw himself dying at Yankee Stadium, "sometimes as a batter beaned by a villainous man with a beard, occasionally as an outfielder running into the monuments that once stood in deep center field."

Humorously and unusually—that's how George and his friends imagined themselves dying back before they believed they would, back when dying was just another idea to have fun with. "Oh, there's death too!" But the death of George Plimpton was neither humorous nor unusual. It was no fantasy either. He died not in pinstripes at Yankee Stadium but in pajamas in his sleep. He died as we all do: as a rank amateur.

I couldn't bear him. I couldn't bear his outsized boy's energy and smug self-certainty and the pride he took in being an enthusiast and a raconteur. The crushing immediacy of him—surely George couldn't have borne it either. But if I intended to do whatever could be done to prevent Kliman from becoming Lonoff's biographer, I would have to suppress that ebbing and flowing inclination to get my car and go back to the Berkshires. I would have to wait to see what he came up with next that he imagined would advance his interests. Having, in recent years, all but forgotten how to negotiate antagonism head-on, I instructed myself not to underestimate an opponent's shrewdness because he masquerades as a garrulous geyser.

When he'd finished a second cup of coffee, he said abruptly, "Lonoff and his sister changes things, does it not?"

So Jamie had told him she'd told me. Yet another unsettling facet of Jamie. What, if anything, should I make of her serving as the conduit between Kliman and me? "It's nonsense," I said.

He reached down to slap the side of the briefcase.

"A novel is not evidence," I said, "a novel's a novel," and resumed eating.

Smiling, he reached down again, and this time he opened the briefcase, removed a thin manila envelope, unclasped it, and poured its contents out onto our table, in the midst of our dishes. We were sitting in the window of the luncheonette and could see people walking by on the street. At the moment I looked up, every one of them was talking on a cell phone. Why did those phones seem like the embodiment of everything I had to escape? They were an inevitable technological development, and yet, in their abundance, I saw the measure of how far I had fallen away from the community of contemporary souls. I don't belong here anymore, I thought. My membership has lapsed. Go.

I picked up the photos. There were four faded pictures of a tall, skinny Lonoff and a tall, skinny girl who Kliman would have me believe was his half-sister, Frieda. In one they were standing on the sidewalk in front of a nondescript wooden house on a street that looked to be baking in the sun. Frieda wore a thin white dress and her hair was in long, heavy braids. Lonoff leaned on her shoulder, feigning heat exhaustion, and Frieda was smiling broadly, a big-jawed girl showing the large teeth that gave her a sturdy livestock look. He was a handsome boy with a dark pompadour and a cast to his lean face that might have enabled him to pass for a young desert dweller, half Muslim, half Jew. In another picture the two were gazing up from a picnic blanket laughing at something indistinguishable that Lonoff was pointing to on one of the plates. In a third they were several years older. Lonoff was holding one arm high in the air, and Frieda, who had grown stouter, was pretending to be a dog, begging with her paws. Lonoff looked stern, giving her his command. In the fourth she must have been twenty and no longer the willing handmaid to her half-brother's whimsy but a tall, heavyset, unsmiling young woman; by contrast, at seventeen, Lonoff looked ethereal and beyond the lure of temptation by anything other than the harmless muse of juvenilia. A case could be made that the photographs revealed noth-

266

ing unusual other than to a mind as eager to be inflamed as Kliman's, and that the most one could reasonably conclude was that half-sister and half-brother enjoyed each other, were devoted to each other, appeared to understand each other, and, in the first quarter of the twentieth century, were sometimes photographed together by a parent or a neighbor or a friend.

"These pictures," I said. "There's nothing in these pictures."

"In the novel," he said, "Lonoff makes Frieda the instigator."

"There is no Lonoff and no Frieda in a novel."

"Spare me the lecture about the impenetrable line dividing fiction from reality. This is something Lonoff lived through. This is a tormented confession disguised as a novel."

"Unless it's a novel disguised as a tormented confession."

"Then why did it shatter him to write it?"

"Because writers can be shattered by writing. The primacy of the imaginative life can do that, and more."

"I've shown you the photographs," he said, as though what I'd seen were a set of filthy pictures, "and now I'll show you the manuscript, and then you dare to tell me that writing about a possibility that *wasn't* a reality was the force that drove this book."

"Look, you're coming off badly, Kliman. This news can't register wholly as a surprise on a *littérateur* like yourself."

Here he extracted the manuscript from his briefcase and placed it on the table, atop the photographs—between two and three hundred pages held together by a thick elastic band.

What a disaster. This reckless, hard-driving, shameless, opportunistic young man, whose way of absorbing a work of fiction was absolutely antithetical to Lonoff's, in possession of the first part of a novel that Lonoff never finished, felt he'd bungled, and might well never have published had he lived to complete it.

"Did Amy Bellette give this to you? Or did you take it from her?" I asked. "Did you steal it from under the poor woman's nose?"

His answer was just to push it toward me. "It's a photocopy. I had it run off especially for you."

He remained intent on gathering me in. I could be useful to him. Just to say he'd given me a copy could perhaps be useful to him. I wondered how feeble he thought I was, then wondered how feeble I had become up in my cabin on my own. Why was I even here at this table? None of what he told me had taken place between the two of us had really taken place—not the phone call, not the date for lunch, not the request to hear about Plimpton's memorial service, not the request to see the Lonoff manuscript. I remembered now precisely what *had* happened. *You smell bad, old man, you smell like death.* And I smelled again, the odor rising from my lap, very like the odor I'd encountered in the interior passages of Amy's building—

and all the while he who had shouted those insults at me continued calmly finishing off his sandwich only a few feet from where I ate mine. That I had allowed this meeting to occur left me feeling without any more protection than Amy, porous, diluted, weaker mentally than I could ever have imagined becoming.

And Kliman knew that. Kliman had fostered that. Kliman had gauged my condition right off: Who would have thought that Nathan Zuckerman couldn't take it? Yet he can't, he's kaput, a tiny isolated little being, an exhausted escapee now from the coarse-grained world, eviscerated by impotence and in the worst state of his life. Just keep him confused, don't temper the battering, and down the doddering old fucker will go. Reread *The Master Builder*, Zuckerman: make way for the young!

I watched him, up on his pinnacle, move in on me for the kill. And suddenly I saw him not as a person but as a door. I see a heavy wooden door where Kliman is sitting. Meaning what? A door to what? A door between what? Clarity and confusion? That could be. I never know whether he is telling the truth or I have forgotten something or he is making things up. A door between clarity and confusion, a door between Amy and Jamie, a door to George Plimpton's death, a door swinging open and shut just inches from my face. Is there more to him than that? All I know is the door.

"With your imprimatur," he told me, "I could do a lot for Lonoff."

I laughed at him. "You've callously preyed on a grievously ill woman with brain cancer. You've stolen these pages from her, by one means or another."

"I did no such thing."

"Of course you did. She wouldn't have given you just the first half. If she wanted you to have the book, she would have given you the whole thing. You stole what you were able to lay your hands on. The other half was out of sight or somewhere in the apartment where you couldn't grab it. Of course you stole it—who gives somebody half of a novel? And now," I said, before he could answer, "now you want to impose on a specimen like me?"

Unfazed, he said, "You can take care of yourself. You've written lots of books. You've had your share of adventures. And you can be ruthless too."

"I can," I said, hoping that was still true.

"George always spoke of you with great admiration, Mr. Zuckerman. He admired the fortitude that fired the talent. I share that admiration."

Simply as I could, I said, "Good. Then don't go anywhere near her, and don't try in any way to contact me." I laid some cash on the table to cover the cost of the meal and headed for the door.

It took seconds for Kliman to pack his things and come racing after me. "This is censorship. You, yourself a writer, are trying to block the publication of another writer's work."

"Not assisting you with this spurious book is not

blocking you in any way. If anything, by crawling into my hole to die, I'm getting out of your way."

"But it's not spurious. Amy Bellette herself recognizes the incest. It's she who first *told* me about it."

"Amy Bellette has had half of her brain removed."

"But she hadn't when I spoke to her. This is *before* the surgery. She hadn't been operated on then. She hadn't even been diagnosed with the tumor."

"But the tumor was there, was it not? She had a head full of cancer, did she not? Undiagnosed, to be sure, but she had that tumor invading her brain. Her *brain,* Kliman. She was passing out and she was vomiting and she was blinded by headaches and she was blinded by fear and the woman didn't know what she was saying to *anyone.* At that point she was *truly* out of her mind."

"But it's *obvious* that this is what happened."

"Obvious to no one but you."

"I cannot believe this!" he cried, walking beside me and showing me the baffled face of his fury. He was no longer in a mood to enjoy my contempt, and so down came the defenses against my judgment, and the rancorous beggar beneath the presumptuous bully at last made his entrance —unless that too was an act of guile and, from beginning to end, I was there only to play his old fool. "You of all people! The man had a penis, Mr. Zuckerman. His penis made them criminals in their world for over three years. Then came the scandal, and he hid from it for the next forty years. Then at the end he wrote this book. This book that is his masterpiece! Art arising from the tormented conscience! The aesthetic triumph over shame! *He* didn't know it—he was too frightened and miserable to know it. And Amy was too frightened by his misery to know it. But how can *you* be frightened? You who know what makes people insatiable! You who know the howling hunger for more! Here is a great writer's reckoning with the crime that intimidated him every day of his life. Lonoff's final struggle with his impurity. His long-delayed effort to let in the repellent. You know all about that. Let the repellent in! That's your achievement, Mr. Zuckerman. Well, this is his. His effort to lift this burden is too heroic for you to turn your back on now. The portrait of himself is not a flattering one, believe me. The young boy rising from a forty-year sleep! It's extraordinary. This is Lonoff's *Scarlet Letter*. It's *Lolita* without Quilty and the stupid jokes. It's what Thomas Mann would have written if he'd been someone other than Thomas Mann. Hear me out! *Help* me out! At some point you must take seriously the incest! Your hiding from it makes no sense and does you no credit! Antagonism to me is blinding you to the truth, sir! Which is simply this: that it took his giving up the home with Hope and going through his hell with Amy for him to release from captivity the sorrows of young Lonoff. I beseech you: read the amazing result!"

He was now in front of me, walking rapidly backward, thrusting the photocopy of the manuscript into my chest. I stopped where I was, hands at my sides and my mouth shut. I should have greeted him with silence from the start. I should—thought I for the hundredth time—never have left home in the first place. The years I'd been gone, the fort I'd constructed against the intruders drawn to my work, the armored layers of suspicion—and yet here I was, looking into those beautiful eyes aglitter with their rabid gray sheen. A literary lunatic. Another one. Like me, like Lonoff, like all whose most violent passion is for a book. Why couldn't it have been gentle Billy Davidoff wanting to write the Lonoff biography? Why couldn't deeply disrespectful, ardent Kliman be gentle Billy, and gentle Billy be deeply disrespectful, ardent Kliman, and why couldn't Jamie Logan, instead of being theirs, be mine? Why did I have to get cancer of the prostate? Why did I have to get those death threats? Why must strength's abatement be so quick and cruel? Oh, to wish what is into what is not, other than on the page!

Suddenly, his exasperation reached its crescendo, but rather than hurling the manuscript at my head—as I fully expected, instinctively raising my arms to protect my face —he dropped it onto the pavement, onto the New York sidewalk only inches in front of my feet, and fled into the traffic, darting between the streaming cars that I could only hope to see shatter the rampaging would-be biographer to bits.

At the hotel, after discarding my urine-soaked underclothes and washing myself at the sink, I phoned Amy. I wanted to know where Kliman's manuscript had come from. I had it in the room with me. I had picked it up and taken it with me. I had waited till Kliman was out of sight and then snatched it off the pavement and carried it back to the hotel. What else could I do? I had no interest in reading it. I could participate no further in this frenzy. I'd survived frenzy enough back when I was younger and clearheaded and a lot more wily and resilient than I was now. I didn't want to know what Lonoff had made of himself and his sister and their great misadventure, or to continue to argue what I still believed—that no such misadventure had ever occurred. However much the man had fascinated me when I was first starting out—and even though just the other day I had gone off to buy all his books, copies of books that I'd owned for decades—I wanted to be rid of the manuscript and completely free of Richard Kliman and everything about him that I could not assess and that was alien to everything I took seriously. Even if the forceful exertions all somehow looked like an act, like the reckless, loathsome, boyish stunt of someone superficial pretending to have a mind and a reverence for letters, he seemed to me no less my nemesis than Lonoff's. I foresaw only defeat should I persist in colliding with this impostor's aims and the vitality and ambition and tenacity and anger that fueled them. After I spoke with Amy and arranged to get those pages back into her hands, I'd phone Jamie and Billy and tell them the deal was off. And I'd leave New York without returning to the urologist. I hadn't that fortitude Kliman so admired, at least not for any further interventions. The urologist could change nothing, as I could change nothing. I may have accumulated over four decades the prestige of writing book after book, but I had reached the end of my effectiveness nonetheless. I had reached the end of my protectiveness as well, and had known as much when I ceased being able to protect myself other than by disappearing. I couldn't stop that kid, even by taking Amy back to the Berkshires or posting a guard at her door.

Nor could I stop him, when he was finished with Lonoff, from turning his blazing attention on me. Once I was dead, who could protect the story of my life from Richard Kliman? Wasn't Lonoff his literary steppingstone to me? And what would my "incest" be? How will I have failed to be the model human being? *My* great, unseemly secret. Surely there was one. Surely there was more than one. An astonishing thing it is, too, that one's prowess and achievement, such as they have been, should find their consummation in the retribution of biographical inquisition. The man in control of the words, the man making up the stories all his life, winds up, after death, remembered, if at all, for a story made up about him, his covert brand of baseness discovered and described with uncompromising candor, clarity, self-certainty, with grave concern for the most delicate issues of morality, and with no small measure of delight.

So I was next. Why had it taken till now to realize the obvious? Unless I had realized it all along.

* * *

There was no answer at Amy's apartment. I phoned Jamie and Billy. The machine picked up after only one ring. I said, "This is Nathan Zuckerman. I'm calling from my hotel. The number—"

Here Jamie herself answered. I should have hung up. I shouldn't have phoned. I should do this and I shouldn't have done that and now I should do the other thing! But I had no control over my thoughts once I was accosted by the stimulus of her voice. Instead of proceeding to extricate myself from the disaster of believing I could alter my condition—the condition of having been unalterably altered—I did the opposite, my thoughts rooted not in what I was but in what I was not: the thoughts of one still capable of making an onslaught on life.

"I'd like to talk to you," I said.

"Yes."

"I'd like to talk to you here."

During the pause that followed, I dealt as best I could with the ridiculous words the past was pressing me to speak.

"I don't think I can do that," she said.

"I was hoping that you could," I said.

"It's an interesting idea, Mr. Zuckerman, but no."

What could I, an exhausted "no-longer" with neither the confidence for the seduction nor the capacity for the performance, say to make her waver? All I had left were the instincts: to want, to crave, to have. And the stupid strengthening of my determination to act. At last, to act!

"Come to my hotel," I said.

"I'm quite thrown," she said. "I never expected this call."

"I didn't either."

"Why did you make it?" she asked.

"Something has got into me since we were together at your place."

"But it's something that I can't satisfy, I'm afraid."

"Please come."

"Please stop. It doesn't take much to make me go off the rails. You think I'm combative? Bristling Jamie? Aggressive Jamie? I'm a combative bundle of nerves. You think Richard Kliman is my lover? You think that still? That I would have nothing to do with him sexually should be abundantly clear to you by now. You've imagined a woman who isn't me. Can't you realize what a relief it was when I met Billy and someone wasn't screaming all the time when I didn't accede to his wishes?"

What could I say to draw her on? What could I possibly say that she would be susceptible to?

"Are you alone?" I asked.

"No."

"Who is there?"

"Richard. He's in the other room. He's been telling me what happened with you. That's all we're doing here. He's talking. I'm listening. That's it. The rest is your illusion. What a wounded person you are to imagine otherwise."

"Please, Jamie, come." Out of all the resources of language, those words were the richest I could light upon to repeat.

"I'm foolish," she said, "so please stop."

I saw myself, heard myself, was appropriately sardonic about myself and disgusted with myself and revolted by the degree of my desperation, but years ago the sexual union with women had been broken so abruptly by the prostate surgery that now, with Jamie, I could not prevent myself from pretending otherwise and acting in behalf of an ego I no longer possessed.

"I phoned you," I said, "to say something else entirely. I did not call with this in mind. I thought I had freed myself of all this."

"Is that possible?" She sounded as if she were asking not about me but about herself.

"Come, Jamie. I feel you can teach me something that it's too late for me to learn."

"That's a hallucination. It all is. No, I can't come, Mr. Zuckerman." And then, to be kind, or merely to get herself off the hook, or even perhaps because a part of her meant it, she added, "Another time," as though I had all the days that she did to hang around and wait.

And so I fled the forces that once had sustained my own force and challenged my strength and aroused my enthusiasms and my passions and my power of resistance and my need to take everything, big or small, to heart and to make everything of significance. I did not stay and fight as of old but fled Lonoff's manuscript and all the emotion it had stirred up, and all the emotion it *would* stir up when

I came upon Kliman's notes in the margin and found there the deadly literal-mindedness and vulgarity that attributes everything to its source in a wholly stupid way. I could not meet contention's demands, wanted no part of its perplexities, and—as if this were work by a writer I had been indifferent to all my life—I dumped the manuscript unread into the hotel room wastebasket, got the car, and was home just after dark. In flight you hurriedly make a choice of what you take with you, and I chose to leave behind not only the manuscript but the six Lonoff books I'd got at the Strand. The set I had at home, bought fifty years earlier, was sufficient to see me through the rest of my life.

The upheaval of New York had taken little more than a week. There is no more worldly in-the-world place than New York, full of all those people on their cell phones going to restaurants, having affairs, getting jobs, reading the news, being consumed with political emotion, and I'd thought to come back in from where I'd been, to resume residence there reembodied, to take on all the things I'd decided to relinquish—love, desire, quarrels, professional conflict, the whole messy legacy of the past—and instead, as in a speeded-up old movie, I passed through for the briefest moment, only to pull out to come back here. All that happened is that things almost happened, yet I returned as though from some massive happening. I attempted nothing really, for a few days just stood there, replete with frustration, buffeted by the merciless encounter between the no-longers and the not-yets. That was humbling enough.

Now I was back where I needed never be in collision with anyone or be coveting anything or go about being someone, convincing people of this or that and seeking a role in the drama of my times. Kliman would pursue Lonoff's secret with all his crude intensity, and Amy Bellette would be as powerless to stop him as she'd been as a girl to prevent the murder of her mother, her father, and her brother, or to stop the tumor from killing her now. I would send her a check that very day and another on the first of every month, but she would be dead within the year anyhow. Kliman would persist and perhaps make himself of literary importance for a few months by writing the superfluous exposé revealing Lonoff's alleged wrongdoing as the key to everything. He might even steal Jamie away from Billy, if she was sufficiently troubled or deluded or bored to seek her escape in his obnoxious swagger. And along the way, like Amy, like Lonoff, like Plimpton, like everyone in the cemetery who had braved the feat and the task, I would die too, though not before I sat down at the desk by the window, looking out through the gray light of a November morning, across a snow-dusted road onto the silent, wind-flurried waters of the swamp, already icing up at the edge of the foundering stalks of the skeletal bed of plumeless reeds, and, from that safe haven, with all of them in New York having vanished from sight—and before my ebbing memory receded completely —wrote the final scene of *He and She*.

HE

Billy's still probably two hours away. Why don't you come to my hotel? I'm at the Hilton. Room 1418.

SHE

(*Lightly laughing*) When you left her, you said it was killing you and you didn't want to see her again.

HE

Now I do want to see her.

SHE

What changed?

HE

The degree of desperation changed. I'm more desperate. Are you?

SHE

I . . . I . . . I'm feeling less. Why are you more desperate?

HE

Go ask desperation why it's more desperate.

SHE

I have to come clean with you. I think I know why you're more desperate. And I don't think that my coming to your hotel room is going to help. I have Richard here. He came over and told me about your meeting earlier. I have to tell you that I think you're making a big mistake. Richard's only trying to do his work as you do your work. He's extremely upset. You're obviously extremely upset. You're calling and inviting something into your life you don't want to invite—

HE

I'm inviting you to my room. To come to me here in my hotel room. Kliman is your lover.

SHE

No.

HE

He is.

SHE

(*Emphatically*) No.

HE

You said as much the other day.

SHE

I didn't. You either misunderstood or heard incorrectly. You've got it all wrong.

HE

So you can lie too. Well, good. I'm glad you can lie.

SHE

What makes you think I'm lying? You're saying because I was his lover in college, I must be his lover now?

HE

I said I was jealous of your lover. I took him for your lover. You're telling me he's not your lover.

SHE

No, he's not.

HE

So someone else is your lover. I don't know whether that's worse or better.

SHE

I'd prefer not to discuss my lover. You want to be my lover—is that what you're saying to me?

HE

Yes.

SHE

You want me to come over now, six o'clock. I'd be there by six thirty. I can come home with some groceries as late as nine and say I was out shopping. I'd have to pick up some groceries or you can go grocery shopping for me now—we can have a few more minutes together.

HE

What time are you coming?

SHE

I'm just working it out. You could go grocery shopping now. I could get Richard out of here. Get in a cab. I could be at your place by six thirty. I'd have to leave by eight thirty. We'd have two hours together. Does that sound like a good idea to you?

HE

Yes.

SHE

And then what?

HE

We'd have had two hours together.

SHE

I'm insane today, you know. (*Laughing*) You're taking advantage of an insane woman.

HE

I'm reaping the harvest of the election.

SHE

(*Laughing*) Yes, you are.

HE

They stole Ohio—I'm going to steal you.

SHE

I could use a little strong medicine today.

HE

Once upon a time, I sold strong medicine door-to-door.

SHE

This all makes me think of the bayous.

HE

What are you saying?

SHE

The bayous in Houston. We'd get to them by cutting through somebody's property and we'd find a rope swing and jump in. Swimming in that mysterious chocolate-milk-colored water filled with dead old trees, where you couldn't see your hand in the water it was so opaque, moss hanging from the trees and the water this muddy color—I don't know how I did it, except that it was one of the things my parents wouldn't have wanted me to be doing. My older sister took me along with her my first time. She was the daredevil, not me. She was the one driven totally crazy by my mother's staggering concern for appearances. She was the one not even my admonishing father could control, let alone my mom. I married Billy. The worst he was was Jewish.

HE

That's the worst I am, too.

SHE

Is it?

HE

Come, Jamie. Come to me.

SHE

(*Lightly, quickly*) Okay. Where are you again?

HE

The Hilton. Room 1418.

SHE

Where's the Hilton? I don't know New York hotels.

HE

The Hilton is on Sixth Avenue, between 53rd and 54th. Across from the CBS building. Diagonally across from the Warwick Hotel.

It's that huge hotel that's not very beautiful.

That's it. I thought I was going to be here only a few days. I came down to see my friend who's ill.

I know about your friend who's ill. We won't discuss any of that.

What did Kliman tell you about her? Do you know what he's doing to a woman who's dying of brain cancer?

He's trying to get her story. Not even her story. The story of a person she loved whose work has been lost, whose reputation has vanished. Look, Richard, unfortunately, is his own bad press. But you oughtn't to be misled by that. Here is an energetic, compulsive, dedicated, interested person who has fastened onto this now very obscure writer who nobody reads anymore. He's compelled by him, he's excited by him, he thinks he's got some secret about him that could be instructive and interesting rather than simply scandalous. Yes, he has the insane rapaciousness of the biographical drive. Yes, he has the ruthless desire to get what he wants. Yes, he'll do anything. But if he's serious, why should he not? He's trying to restore this person to his true place in American literature, and he wants her help—to tell a story that hurts no one. No one. The people it involves have been dead for years and years.

HE

He has three living children. What about them? How would you like to find this out about your father?

SHE

When he was seventeen he had an affair with his half-sister—he was younger, he was fourteen when it began. If anything, he was the innocent, he was the younger child. There's no shame in that.

HE

You're so generous. Do you think your father and mother will be so generous when they read about Lonoff's youth?

SHE

My father and mother voted for George Bush on Tuesday. So the answer is no. (*Laughing*) If you worked for their approval, you'd never publish anything that my father and mother would look kindly on. None of your books would have been published, my friend.

HE

What about you? Would you look kindly on your father if you found this out about him?

SHE

It wouldn't be easy.

HE

Do you have an aunt?

I don't have an aunt. But I have a brother. I don't have children. But if I did, it's not something I would want my children to know about if that happened between my brother and me. But I think there are some things that are more important than—

Please. Not art.

What have you given up your life for, then?

I didn't know I was giving it up. I did what I did, and I didn't know. Do you understand what the papers will do with this? Do you understand what the reviewers will do with this? This has nothing to do with art and less with truth or even with comprehending transgression. It has to do with titillation. Lonoff, if he were around, would be sorry he ever wrote a word.

He's dead. He won't be sorry.

He'll just be maligned. For no good reason, maliciously maligned by the moralist prigs, by the feminist scolds, by the sickening superiority of the lice of literature. A lot of the reviewers who are nice people will consider his a great sexual crime. What are you laughing at now?

SHE

The condescension. You think if it hadn't been for the "feminist scolds" I'd even be considering coming to your hotel room in twenty minutes? Do you think a girl brought up like me would begin to have the guts to do such a thing? So you're reaping the benefits of the election *and* the feminists. George Bush *and* Betty Friedan. (*Speaking tough, suddenly, like a moll in a movie*) Listen, do you want me to come over—is that what you want? Or do you want to talk about Richard Kliman on the phone?

HE

I don't believe you. I don't believe you about Kliman. That's all I'm saying.

SHE

Fine. Fine. Does that matter for our two hours together? You can believe me or not believe me, and if you don't believe me and you don't want me to come over, that's fine. If you don't believe me and you do want me to come over, that's fine. If you believe me and you want me to come over, that's fine too. You tell me what you want.

HE

Are you all so extremely self-possessed these days, all you thirty-year-old young women, or is there only so long that the performance can be maintained?

SHE

Neither.

HE

So is it just the thirty-year-old women with literary aspirations?

SHE

No.

HE

Is it the thirty-year-old women who grew up in oil-rich Houston families? Is it the superprivileged young women?

SHE

No, it's *me*. You're talking to *me*.

HE

I adore you.

SHE

You don't know me.

HE

I adore you.

SHE

You're madly attracted to me.

HE

I adore you.

SHE

You don't adore me. You can't. It's impossible. The words are meaningless. You strike me as a person who was spoiling for adventure but didn't know it. You, who spurned all experience for eleven years, who closed himself off to everything other than writing and thinking—you who'd held his existence so very close to his vest, you had no idea. Only when he finds himself back in the big city does he discover that he wants to be back in life and that the only way to get there is through his unreasoned, unconsidered . . . well, himself at the mercy of a completely unreasonable drive. I'm talking to a virtually inhumanly disciplined, rational person who has lost all sense of proportion and entered into a desperate story of unreasonable wishes. Yet that is what it is to be in life, isn't it? What it is to *forge* a life. You know your reason can reassert itself at any time—and if it does, there goes life and the instability that *is* life. Everyone's lot: instability. The only other possible motive you could have to think you adore me is that at the moment you're a writer without a book. Start another book and get into it and we'll see how much you adore Jamie Logan. Anyway, I'll be right over.

HE

Your agreeing to come to my hotel suggests to me that you're in big trouble yourself. Rash moments. This is yours.

SHE

Rash moments that lead to rash encounters. Rash moments that lead to perilous choices. You might not want to remind me of that too forcefully.

HE

I think I can rely on you to remind yourself all the way here in the taxicab.

SHE

Well, I've told you you're taking advantage of the election returns. So yes, you're right.

HE

You're crossing Conrad's shadow-line, first from childhood into maturity, then from maturity into something else.

SHE

Into insanity. I'll be there shortly.

HE

Good. Hurry. Into insanity. Off with your clothes and into the bayous. (*He hangs up.*) Into the chocolate-milk-colored water filled with dead old trees.

(*Thus, with only a moment's more insanity on his part—a moment of insane excitement—he throws everything into his bag—except the unread manuscript and the used Lonoff books—and gets out as fast as he can. How can he not [as he likes to say]? He disintegrates. She's on her way and he leaves. Gone for good.*)

www.vintage-books.co.uk